The
WOLF'S
EYE

The WOLF'S EYE

a novel

LUANNE G. SMITH

AUTHOR OF *THE RAVEN SPELL*

47N**O**RTH

Published by 47North, Seattle

www.apub.com

Amazon, the Amazon logo, and 47North are trademarks of Amazon.com, Inc., or its affiliates.

ISBN-13: 9781662510175 (paperback)
ISBN-13: 9781662510182 (digital)

Cover design by Kimberly Glyder
Cover image: © Joanna Czogala / ArcAngel; © Shan 16899, © thunder-st,
© Photo Win1, © pixssa / Shutterstock; © alexei_tm / Getty

Printed in the United States of America

The WOLF'S EYE

CHAPTER ONE

Petra stared up at the collection of bones in the candlelight. Femurs dangled like calcified fringe along the ceiling of the infamous old chapel. The bones, polished white by time, had long relinquished their relation to skin and muscle. So curious the way the skulls and tibias had been alternated like beads on a cord, as though some ancient giant had strung them together in front of the fire to pass a winter's eve. The elaborate Gothic design boggled the mind, and yet she supposed the display served as a prominent reminder that all must die. *Memento mori.* The motto etched itself in her mind as she gazed up, contemplating the distance one walked from the cradle to the grave only to have one's bones hung up as a decoration. And while she understood both the church's artistic effort and the practical application of what to do with so many plague bones, the macabre dedication to the tens of thousands of dead unsettled Petra while she was forced to listen to the sound of a blade scraping against bone and the whimpering of a grown man.

They'd landed at the bone church after having flown through the night aboard their enchanted wagon, courtesy of the benevolent King Wahaj of the western jinn. Viktor Veselý, the moon-mad glassmaker who'd been recruited alongside Petra a week earlier to battle the growing upíri threat on the eastern front, had guided the wagon as they retreated from the mountain pass. While he'd held the reins of the horseless wagon, his love-light glowing in the sky above him, she'd sat with Yanis and Josef, letting thoughts of what the future held for her within the Order of the

Seven Stars tumble through her head. She'd surprised herself during the last few days, finding the strength both physically and magically to defend against the undead creatures who'd infected the army's ranks. Forced to react, she'd rediscovered her long-suppressed magic, finding a purpose and a place among her fellow recruits. She was part of the Great War, a defender on the front lines, but her newfound purpose had come at a cost, learning her husband's fate through the lens of her camera.

After the tsar's men had overtaken the pass, forcing her team to retreat, they'd made the hasty decision to flee west and head for home to heal up for a few days and await their next assignment. But as they approached the familiar fields and streams of their homeland and saw the red tile roofs of the outlying towns, the more they worried about their unconventional travel being discovered. After all, where does one land a horseless wagon in the middle of a bustling city full of mortals? Roads and rooftops were too risky, and the king's bridge in the heart of the Old Town district was obviously out of the question, so they'd thought it best to touch down somewhere south, where they could catch a train the rest of the way come morning.

They'd landed sometime before dawn in a muddy field beside the medieval church that housed the odd collection of bones, where Petra now found herself half mesmerized and half repelled by the skeletal sculptures' ghoulish beauty. That, and the apparent medical application they afforded an injured sorcerer who knew what to do with a little bone dust.

"Nearly ready." Yanis sat with his back against a pillar aside a tower of skulls with his false leg stretched out beneath his robes, sucking in a breath to ride out the pain. The sorcerer, a warrior-priest with the Order of the Seven Stars, the organization tasked with monitoring supernatural irregularities whose authority they worked under, had asked if he might take advantage of the millions of bones housed in the chapel's basement to repair his broken ribs. Sacrilegious yet pragmatic. The man had been in excruciating pain ever since being injured when the truck he was riding in got flipped by a powerful zduhać who'd brought a whirlwind down on him. He'd sucked in sharp breaths most of the night. The slightest change in air current had him gasping, but it had been the landing outside the church that made Yanis scream like a fox with its foot caught in a steel trap. No one in the wagon objected when the sorcerer suggested, rather breathlessly, that he might need to take a few moments to sort out a remedy.

Viktor pushed his glasses on top of his head, then dragged the edge of his knife along the flat plane of an ancient femur. He collected the shavings of powdered calcium on a black cloth until Yanis motioned with his hand that it was enough. The sorcerer opened his satchel, wincing from the movement.

"Is there anything I can do to help?" Petra asked. She wasn't proficient at most spells involving incantations, but she was a witch with some skill.

Yanis shook his head at her offer. The bags under his worry-worn eyes seemed to sag even heavier from the ordeal. "The preparation of the herbs is part of the ritual of healing," he said and took out a pinch of brown turmeric and the dried head of a dandelion before it had gone to seed and added the herbs to the cloth, crushing them slightly between his fingers first.

"However, I will need a cup," Yanis said. "A little wine, too, if there's any left to be found."

"I'll get it," Petra said. She took her eyes away from the grotesque chandelier above her head and searched behind the altar. A flagon of ceremonial wine sat on a tray, but there was no cup other than a silver chalice, which she didn't think would mix well with the sorcerer's bone magic. Improvising, she found a votive candle and fashioned it into a small stemless goblet by cupping it in her hands. The wax lost its soft, dull quality, sharpening into cut glass as the matter molded into the shape she'd envisioned.

Petra had dimmed her talent for ten years to avoid detection when she'd still believed herself a murderess on the run. Hers was a different sort of magic from other witches'. For reasons she didn't fully understand, she could change any object into something else, and not just with an illusion but by manipulating the matter itself so that it became the thing she imagined in her mind. Books, mugs, shoes, clothing, even the bones dangling above her head might be altered if she touched them. If the material was inanimate, she could change its form. But mostly she was infamous for being the girl who could turn objects into gold, which made her worth her weight in the stuff. At least to some.

"I found these." Petra set the goblet and flagon of wine beside Yanis. The sorcerer cringed in pain with every movement, but he weakly thanked her.

"Fill the cup about a third of the way," he said, sweeping a sweaty lock of graying hair out of his eyes.

Petra did as Yanis asked while keeping one eye on the door. They'd sneaked into the chapel in the predawn light and worried they'd be discovered before they could be on their way. No one wished to explain the need to desecrate human bones in order to heal a foreign sorcerer's broken ribs, so Josef had gone outside to watch for the lights coming on in the abbey next door. As team leader, he'd been quick to volunteer, but Petra suspected Josef had simply needed to get away from this witch business with the bones and to scan the perimeter for upíri who may have escaped undetected with the army, as that was still the crux of their mission.

Josef Svoboda had occupied more of Petra's thoughts than she cared to admit as a new widow. It was he who'd found her and recruited her for the assignment in the mountains, where one emperor's army fought against another, each side employing witches to further wound the mortal soldiers. The men already fought to stay alive against the barrage of bullets and artillery fire, not to mention the unforgiving winter conditions, but now they had to contend with curses and hexes too. Josef had been one of the earliest wounded. Afflicted with a strain of the vlkodlak curse, he'd been fortunate to be placed in the care of a healer working in camp who'd known how to create an elixir to slow the worst effects of the wolf curse. He was regrettably out of that remedy at the moment, something that made him both tragic and dangerous the farther they traveled from the front.

"Pour the powder and herbs into the cup," Yanis instructed. He adjusted his weight so his back leaned straighter against the pillar. His breath caught in his chest as he gritted his teeth to hold back the howl that might have escaped otherwise. After the wave of pain subsided, he asked Petra to set a candle down beside the cup. He closed his eyes as though to calm his mind before drawing a series of sigils on a piece of paper: circles, stars, hexagrams, and some ancient lettering from his desert home she did not recognize. His hand shook while he held the paper over the candle flame, a sort of smoky offering of magic symbols to the power he called to.

Yanis drank the wine, holding his breath while the liquid traveled down his throat, past his ribs, and into his stomach. At first it seemed nothing was happening, but then the sorcerer raised his eyebrows and doubled over, clutching his middle as though he might be sick. The moment soon passed, and he exhaled as Petra helped him sit up straight without screeching like an injured animal for the first time in hours.

The door to the church upstairs opened, letting in a wave of moist winter air. Josef took a final look outside the door before closing it quietly behind him. His *ushanka* was dusted with droplets of mist, and his boots were speckled in mud to his shins. His gaze landed on Petra for a moment before he spoke, and while she might have replied to his look with a smile under different circumstances, she merely watched to see what news he brought.

"It's still quiet up there," he whispered, a finger held over his mouth. "The abbey remains dark, but we mustn't linger much longer." His expression soured as he glanced at a fat cherub sitting atop a rack of skulls. "The sun is rising, and I don't wish to explain our circumstances to anyone connected with this place."

Petra blew out one of the candles and inhaled the waxy smoke while she gathered up any evidence of their presence. Viktor helped, though he kept an eye on the sorcerer, seemingly as amazed as she was at what a little bone dust could do given the right spell.

Josef knelt beside Yanis and nodded as though pleased by the magic's quick work. "Your color is back," he said to the sorcerer. "Are you able to walk?"

"Help me up and we'll see." Yanis steadied himself on his false leg as Josef and Viktor pulled him up. He grimaced briefly but nodded he was able to move on his own.

With the sorcerer on his feet, they put both the flagon of wine and the scraped femur back where they found them, then slipped out the little chapel's door. As the sun came up, their wagon, which had carried them over all manner of terrain throughout the night, reverted into the dilapidated cart with a missing wheel they'd first been shown. The jinni king's magic had reached the limit of its generosity, sinking the wagon in the mud beside the churchyard as though it had always been there.

Josef urged them to move quickly toward the train station, walking ahead with his quick stride. Few other people were out, aside from a few shop and café owners getting ready to open for the day. And still, as the team neared the station, walking along a stacked-stone wall that lined the road, a gentleman in a black suit approached from the opposite direction on the sidewalk with no intention of stepping aside as he neared. The man bumped into Yanis, hitting him shoulder to shoulder as they passed. The jarring contact made the sorcerer wince slightly and hug his ribs to check for damage. Petra swung around to see if the gentleman would apologize or at least give a tip of his hat to signal he was in the wrong, but there was no one there. Not on either side of the street. The man had vanished.

Ahead of them, Josef noticed they'd stopped walking and turned around. "What's wrong?"

"That man," Petra said. "He bumped into Yanis and then just . . . disappeared."

Josef took a few steps in the direction they'd come, lifting his nose in the air, while Viktor scanned the top of the wall, east to west. As members of a group tasked with ridding undead creatures from the battlefields on the eastern front, their suspicions were rightfully aroused.

"What man?" Josef asked with a shake of his head. "What did he look like?"

Petra was about to describe the gentleman until she found she couldn't conjure an image of him in her mind no matter how hard she concentrated. "I can't remember, but he was there." She looked at Yanis, wondering what magical mischief was at play to instantly erase the memory of a man, when the sorcerer patted his chest.

Yanis held up his hand as though to calm them from any further wild thoughts. "I have been delivered a message," he said and produced an envelope from inside his robes, one that had presumably not been there a minute earlier. "It's from the Order," he said, splitting open the seal. "They often use young jinn to deliver urgent instructions to priests in the field. They are not always as subtle as they should be."

Josef, Viktor, and Petra gathered closer, making a wall of their bodies around the letter.

"What does it say?" Josef asked.

"We are to return to the mountains." Yanis scanned ahead on the page in silence, then slowly folded the letter without reading the rest out loud. "The Order is aware the emperor's witch has been killed. Now we are tasked with destroying the controversial work of Ava König."

"What does that mean?" Petra glanced uncomfortably at Josef—at the thick stubble covering his chin, the brown eyes that never missed the slightest movement, and his fur ushanka the color of winter wolves.

Yanis ran his fingers over the crease on the paper, his mind cast adrift on faraway thoughts. "Specifically, we are to get rid of any evidence of the strain of the wolf curse she brought into existence before it is able to spread beyond the boundaries of battle." He tucked the letter away before briefly meeting Josef's unblinking stare.

"Rid all evidence how?" Viktor scratched the back of his head. "She cursed men to turn into vlkodlak. How are we supposed to fix that?"

"He means we're to hunt down the victims of her curse and kill them all," Josef said. "I can only assume the instructions include getting rid of controversial half-cursed men like me as well."

Though Yanis initially brushed aside Josef's conclusion, Petra suspected there was no such thing as "half-cursed" in the eyes of the Order by the way he avoided showing the letter to the rest of the team.

CHAPTER TWO

Yanis had put the letter away before the others had a chance to read it over his shoulder. The gesture triggered mild suspicion in Petra. She trusted the sorcerer implicitly, though she wasn't in possession of enough experience to say the same about the organization he worked for. Or, rather, the group they all worked for now.

"They're ordering us to destroy her wolves?" Petra asked. The predatory glint in Josef's eye, so common when his instinct to attack was primed, gleamed like cut obsidian.

Yanis's mood soured. The relief he'd expressed at easing the pain of his cracked ribs had transformed into a posture that hunched his shoulders. "That appears to be the mission, yes."

Petra thought of the shackles and straitjacket she'd seen in the attic above the makeshift hospital in camp. Before the army withdrew, an enemy prisoner had been treated there for the same vlkodlak curse Josef suffered from. She wondered now what had happened to the man after the tsar's army had swooped in. Had there been enough time to complete his treatment? And what had happened to Hana and Valentina, the women helping the soldier manage the sickness the way they had with Josef? The healer women had called both men lucky when the wolf creatures they'd each been bitten by had been caught. The blood recovered from the infected vlkodlaci, when stirred in Hana's elixir, was said to tame the worst aspects of the curse—the urge to rip and kill.

"They can't mean *all* of them," Petra argued. "Clearly Josef's curse is no longer a threat to anyone. Or that other man in the attic who was being treated for the curse."

"But they can't be certain the danger we present is contained." Josef slid his ushanka off his head and dabbed at the sweat around his forehead with his coat sleeve. "It's easier and safer to destroy than to trust and watch an innocent person be killed."

"It isn't right." Petra stared down the street, where the scent of cardamom and clove hung in the air after the jinni's disappearance. "There's a permanent cure," she said. "Not just a remedy for the side effects. König said there was a way to rid Josef of the curse. We shouldn't give up on the idea."

Yanis reluctantly nodded. "Yes, but she was the only one who knew what the cure was, and now she's dead. What remains is her legacy of several possible fanged killers on the loose."

"So are we expected to restrain Josef, even though we all know he's no threat?" Petra reached for the wooden stake attached to her belt and held it out to Yanis, feeling her temper catch fire. "Will you be the one to drive the stake through his heart? Isn't that how we kill the undead? Even our friends?"

Yanis angrily swiped the stake away from her. "You know that's not what I want." He spared a glance at Josef. "It's not what any of us want."

Petra stood mortified, frozen in place by her own idiocy. She'd gone too far, knowing what Josef had been forced to do to their comrade Karl, the shy wood-carver with the enchanted knife, after he'd been bitten by an upír and the shadow of the undead curse darted behind his eyes. "I'm sorry," she said to Josef. "That was a careless thing for me to say. You did what the rest of us couldn't do. We all knew you had no choice."

Josef lowered his head and ran a hand through his hair. The air went out of him as he leaned against the wall. His eyes had gone glossy and red when he looked up again. "This business of curses always seems to end in death," he said.

With the team lost for what to say, viscous tension filled the silent space between them. Exhaustion and emotion had colored Josef's voice so that he didn't sound himself. She knew him as a fighter, always the first to rush into action, but now he looked defeated as he slumped against the wall. Petra suspected König's death had convinced him he'd never be rid of his curse. But there was still a way. There must be. They just had to find it. He deserved that much. He was one of them, not a cursed unfortunate without redemption.

"We should keep heading toward home," Viktor said, breaking the silence. "That's the logical place to look for König's notes on transformative curses. That's where we'll possibly find her original grimoire notes."

Yanis balked. "Who said we're looking for König's grimoire?"

"She did." Viktor pointed at Petra. "She said there was a cure and that we shouldn't give up looking for it. I agree."

Josef straightened and put his ushanka back on. "König was the emperor's witch. Wouldn't her work be held in the capital under his authority?"

"We're not going to the capital either!" Yanis walked down the sidewalk in the direction of the train station, where an eastbound locomotive engine puffed out great plumes of white steam. "It's out of the question."

"Hold on, there's something I need to explain first." Viktor stood in place, refusing to follow Yanis, while he sheepishly scratched his beard and stared at his boots. Petra and Josef remained with him, forcing the sorcerer to stop walking or leave without them. After a sigh, Yanis—dragging his false leg more dramatically than was necessary—returned to hear what Viktor had to say.

"Ava König is well known in the city back home," Viktor said. "She worked there years ago on all kinds of projects when she was first making a name for herself."

Yanis raised a skeptical brow. "And how do you know this?"

"Because she used to work with the people I work for now."

Petra shook her head. "I thought you were a glassmaker?"

"I am," Viktor said. "But I don't make decorative goblets in any factory."

Josef scowled at the revelation, perhaps thinking he'd thoroughly vetted the glassmaker before taking him on as part of his team. "Then where do you work?" he asked.

"I blow glass for a group that does research on the origins of magic." Viktor paused while he waited for a woman carrying shopping bags to pass by. "They go through a lot of bottles doing their experiments. It's why they prefer to have the materials made in-house, so they don't raise any alarms by having truckloads of beakers showing up at the back door every month. Anyway, I know I've seen references to König's notebooks there before. Direct quotes. They're still doing research based on some of her early studies. At least one of their leading researchers worked with her years ago. She may be able to help point us in the right direction. If anyone knows, it would be her."

"Would she let us see König's notes?" Petra asked.

"We are not going to the city," Yanis said, looking to the sky as though searching for divine help.

"Why not?"

"We have our instructions," he said. "We must follow them or they will know we've veered off track."

Petra looked around. "Who will know?"

"The Order."

"Augustus and Martina ought to let us use the research library," Viktor said, still thinking about his employers, though he looked away as though he had to give it a second thought. "At least I think they will."

"We have to try for Josef's sake," Petra said to Yanis. "I understand why the Order wants us to go after König's cursed men, but what if there is a cure that can reverse their condition?"

"Impossible." Yanis signaled the matter settled with the sweep of his hand.

"Is it?" Petra squared her shoulders in front of Yanis. "Hana knew how to help Josef so he wouldn't transform into the full vlkodlak. He's never succumbed to the urge to kill as the wolf. Maybe she was already halfway there to figuring out the solution. Maybe we can find the rest. Besides, how do we even locate these creatures of König's? They walk around as men until the moon grows full again, right? That's nearly a full month away, so we have some time."

"She's just entered the first night of her waning phase," Viktor confirmed.

Josef appeared to be only half listening to Petra's argument on his behalf when he spoke up. "What was that part about the Order knowing if we went in the wrong direction or not?" he asked. "How would they even know our position? How did they get a message to us here? And how do they already know Ava König is dead? It hasn't even been twenty-four hours."

It was the sorcerer's turn to stare awkwardly at his feet. "The train will be departing any minute. Perhaps we should get to the station and buy our tickets."

"Yanis, how does the Order know?" Josef asked again. "How do they know where to find us on a random street in a small town outside of the city?"

The others crowded closer, ready to revolt if they didn't get some answers. The sorcerer let out an exasperated breath before relenting. "I'll explain, but only if we keep moving toward the station and stop attracting attention on the public sidewalk."

The group agreed and began walking. They were all eager to catch the next train. The question was which one.

Ahead, a handful of passengers gathered on the platform waiting to go to the city. Men on their way to work buried their noses in their morning newspapers while women stood with their scarves tied snug on their heads and handbags hung in the crooks of their elbows. Yanis paused a few meters away as the eastbound train hissed and spewed a plume of hot, white steam. "You must understand such enigmas are to be expected in our work." The sorcerer scraped the back of his hand meditatively against the stubble growing beneath his chin. "I used to question the logic of the Order's instructions, as you do now. Most of the time we are only able to see one step in front of us at a time on a mission, and we have to learn to take that leap of faith." He removed a coin purse from his robes and fished out enough for their train fare. "But understand there are others who study the tumbling of the stars with great insight, who calculate the path of the twisting universe and how it affects, well, everything. They peer into the distance, make determinations, and guide us toward our quest."

"That's all well and good," Petra said, "but it still doesn't explain how they knew where to find us."

Yanis bit his lip and closed his eyes briefly, as though he'd made up his mind about something he knew he'd regret. A moment later he put his coin purse away and took out a small brass instrument from his satchel. It had a series of gear-like wheels that overlapped, with arrows pointing to different astrological markings. "It's my astrolabe," he said. Petra and Josef leaned forward as he made a minor adjustment to one of the wheels, turning it one notch to the right. "It's enchanted to let the Order keep track of my whereabouts based on longitude and latitude. Others carry scrying stones that work much the same way, only their locations are visible through crystal orbs that project their appearance to their handlers."

"We're being tracked?"

"It's a safety precaution," Yanis insisted, making a slight adjustment to another wheel. "And, too, it saves time communicating. A handful of witches still use doves or pigeons to relay messages; others rely solely on the telephone now, though the device has its obvious weaknesses. But the Order prefers to keep track of its agents in real time. They don't want to wait hours for a bird to tell them where someone is."

"Why is it so important for the Order to know where you are at every moment?" Viktor asked. "Don't you file regular reports?"

"The danger to its members from the creatures they—*we*—make contact with has ramifications beyond the immediate confrontation," he said, lowering his voice. "Knowing where and how often those creatures occupy an area that puts others in harm's way is of immense value to understanding how to keep them segregated from the mortal world. And I think we can all agree that's an outcome we should all aspire to."

"You mean keeping creatures like me safely locked up from the public until I can be dealt with properly?" Josef stood with his hands in his coat pockets as the westbound train to the city eased into the station on the other side of the platform.

Yanis looked away, but the lines in his face suggested he'd learned long ago the answer to Josef's question was yes. Always yes, if the circumstances called for it.

The eastbound engine let off steam below its wheels, preparing to leave. The last of the passengers climbed the steps to the coach cars with their small leather and cloth valises in hand. Soon the conductor would announce the last call to board. Still, none of them went to the ticket booth. Not even Yanis after the crew swung the standpipe away from the boiler and the stoker fed the last shovelful of coal into the engine's belly.

"Not sure that my employers will like having their location advertised," Viktor said. "They're very protective of the work they do there."

"We aren't going to the city," Yanis insisted.

Petra eyed the eastbound train, huffing like a beast on the tracks ready to break free. "Yes, we are," she said. "We have to try. Josef is one of us. He isn't an animal to be hunted and killed because of a curse he had no way of preventing." Not waiting for another argument, she snatched the astrolabe out of Yanis's hands and marched up to the departing train.

Yanis, eyes widening in disbelief, limped after her. "What are you doing?"

"Buying us some time," she said. With Josef and Viktor flanking her, she tossed the instrument into the open door on the baggage car just as the train pulled away. "Now the Order will be satisfied that we've gone east like they want." She brushed her hands together. "But we are going to the city just like we planned, and we're going to hunt for a cure with the month we have before the next moon."

Seeing he'd been outmaneuvered, Yanis closed his eyes briefly before pulling out his coins again. "Then we have a new mission," he conceded, walking up to the ticket agent. "And I sincerely hope it isn't one we come to regret."

CHAPTER THREE

God, but Josef was grateful for Petra and her rashness as they stepped onto the street outside the city's main train station. He was half healed already just seeing the streetcars shuttling up and down the road, the people bundled in their black shawls and overcoats, and the spires in the distance rising against the clouds. It was a far cry from the frozen mountains and ravenous undead they'd left behind. It was home.

Viktor, on the other hand, was a sly one, Josef decided as they walked north through the busy neighborhood, where horses, bicycles, automobiles, and trams all competed for the same stretch of road. His strange obsession with the moon made him appear touched in the head, going on and on about his *bella luna*, yet the man had proven himself time and again in their battles against the upír. And he'd shown more backbone in defying Yanis than Josef had come to expect from the bespectacled witch with eyes like a Siamese cat who preferred to sit and read in his downtime. Josef easily admitted he'd underestimated the man. After all, the glassmaker had managed to stay alive through their ordeal in the mountains. Not all his recruits had—a thing that weighed like a stone tied around his heart now that they were home.

"This way," Viktor said. He made a quick left turn down a side street before heading north again.

Given the urgency of the matter, they'd decided to go straight to the center of the Old Town district first. The glassmaker walked with his shoulders hunched like a man battling a headwind as he led them to his secretive place of employment. But the sun was out, and considering the conditions where they'd come from, the moderate winter temperature felt almost balmy. No, Josef decided, the man wasn't bracing himself against any chill in the air. He was nervous about where they were going, and that made him nervous.

Though Josef was thankful to be on familiar ground again, the people around him on the sidewalks moved as though they were pigeons pecking the ground for tossed seeds, agitating an instinct recently planted deep inside him. His legs constantly yearned to sprint, to lope, to run. The urge revved beneath his skin. It throbbed behind his eyes. He was always watching for the clear path, the break in the underbrush, and the open field where he could dash into a full run. Hana, the witch who'd helped him recover, had given him a second chance at life, but some days he suspected she'd just traded one curse for another when he was forced to pace himself.

Josef's affliction wasn't ruled by the moon or bloodlust like others who'd been bitten, yet his need to change was just as strong. He sometimes wondered if he might even suffer more, since the yearning in the blood was never sated under the killing moon. Over the two agonizing months he'd spent chained to a wall in an attic, when his body craved the bone-buckling change under the full moon, Hana had taught him how to focus through the pain of the curse to locate his center of gravity. She'd conditioned him to find himself in the chaos when others had been lost to the wolf's hunger. She'd done it by slowly feeding him spoonfuls of soup mixed with blood from the vlkodlak that had bitten him. He assumed his attacker, too, had been a normal man at one time. A soldier, most likely. But the men on patrol with Josef that night had caught and killed the beast, leaving behind a wrecked carcass of fur and bone. By mixing the vlkodlak's tainted blood in with Josef's nourishment, Hana had slowly weaned him off the worst parts of the curse. He likened it to using diseased cow's blood as an inoculation against smallpox.

Hana's treatment allowed him to control when and how often he changed—but change he must, once a month, or else burst out of his skin. He preferred to change before the full moon shot her dart of madness into most men's eyes. Any touch of moonlight while at her apogee could still deliver him into peril if he wasn't careful. And while admitting the transformation ultimately brought him relief and a sense of freedom like none he'd experienced before, it also inflicted a physical illness that rendered him as weak as a calf newly slipped loose from the womb once he returned to his human form.

The constant fight not to give in to the lust of the vlkodlak was what drained him. But Hana, with her books and herbs, had created an elixir he could swallow upon returning to his human form. One that alleviated the heavy burden of resistance. The potion also helped calm his mind so he could still think as a man when his body next took on the form of the wolf. In the end, he knew he owed the witch for his life, albeit one that was left to battle in constant tension with itself. But Hana was gone, and so was the last of his supply of elixir. Without it, he didn't know how he would survive the transformation he must make before the next full moon.

He'd briefly believed his nightmare might be permanently over when Petra had found the witch responsible for his curse. Ava König had promised there was a cure. They had been mere moments away from freedom on that cursed mountainside when the emperor's witch was struck down by the same ungodly force of nature that had broken Yanis's ribs. In that single crack of lightning, all hope had been incinerated. At least until Petra insisted they return to the city.

Josef slowed his stride. As frustrating as it was physically to walk among his fellow citizens, mentally he knew there was nothing to be done about the pace, so he lifted his nose to take in the scents of the city and was met with a pleasant surprise. His parents' bakery was two streets away, and the smell of fresh *rohlíky* carried on the air between buildings. His father was putting the second batch in the oven while his mother certainly shaped the dough for the third. It had been the same every day since his earliest memories. The morning's first rolls would have already been sold to the most eager customers, and now the latecomers waited for the second tray to come out of the oven. He smiled at the clarity the scent brought him despite his wary mood.

Petra responded to the change in his expression by smiling too. "You must be glad to be back home," she said.

"It's always good to be in familiar territory," he answered truthfully, but there was no way to explain the growing sense of anxiety he also felt. How could he describe the fear breeding inside him at the thought of endangering everyone and everything he loved simply because he did not possess a vial of herbs mixed with the right oil and spellwork? Still, he supposed if anyone understood his dilemma, it would be Petra.

In another time, in another life, his heart would be racing with possibility to have a woman like Petra at his side. He would invite her to a concert at the new Municipal House to listen to the incredible music of clarinetist Benjamin Laska, who had a way of manipulating the listener's emotions with his brilliant compositions. Later he would take her hand as they walked home and kiss her under the arch of the old city gate. The next day he would carry the buoyant optimism of new love in his chest, letting it rise to make him smile whenever his mind drifted from his work at the bakery.

But that was what the old Josef would have done in the time before the war. Before Laska was missing and presumed dead. And long before he was fluent in this new language of curses and spells and the shadow of the undead that hung just out of eyeshot.

Josef lowered his head, hoping not to be seen by anyone he knew from his neighborhood. "How much farther?" he asked.

"Just up there," Viktor said, pointing to a run-down house on the edge of where the dilapidated ghetto had stood only a few years earlier. Rebuilt now, new shops and apartments lined the streets around the old synagogue with its ancient graveyard tucked under the trees. Some of the headstones were so worn down by time and weather as to be unreadable, but people still left small rocks atop them to remember. A part of him loved the stubborn survival of the three-hundred-year-old cemetery in the face of so much modern life trying to swallow it whole.

The house they approached was a familiar yet eerie mystery to Josef. He'd passed the building dozens of times while making deliveries for the bakery, but the only time he'd ever given any proper thought to the derelict property was to wonder how it had escaped demolition when everything around it, except for the old synagogue, had been torn down. "This is where you work?" he asked.

Viktor spun around and held up his hand, stopping them all on the pavement just before they approached the front door. "It is, yes, but wait just a minute."

"Something wrong?" Yanis asked.

The glassmaker's unease had become palpable. The scent of his sweat grew so strong Josef could taste it on his tongue when he inhaled. He glanced up at the four-story building. The stonework was crumbling, the shutters were rotting off their hinges, and the roof tiles had begun to slip loose. Whatever situation Viktor was leading them into was going to come with consequences. A tremor of foreboding crept up the base of Josef's neck, where his hair never quite lay flat anymore, no matter how many times he brushed it.

Viktor shrugged the strap of his satchel higher on his shoulder. "Listen, it's just . . . I should probably go in first. Alone. Make sure they're in."

"Or maybe . . ." Josef paused to inspect the brass plate fixed to the wall that read: THE LIBUŠE SOCIETY, DEDICATED TO THE PURSUIT OF ENLIGHTENMENT AND KNOWLEDGE. He peeked in the front window, hoping for a clue to what they were about to walk into, but saw only shadows in a small parlor room. After Viktor's deception about where he worked, Josef was in no mood to let himself be fooled again. "We should all go in together as planned."

Viktor scratched the patch of beard beneath his lip, thinking. "It's not that you won't be welcome, only they don't know we're coming.

They can be touchy about unplanned visitors. You have to understand. It's the nature of the work they do."

Josef ignored him and rang the bell. It might not be a convenient time for those inside, but it was even less so for the witch, the foreign sorcerer, and the cursed man who might give in to the call of the wild at any moment who waited on their doorstep. The last thing Josef needed was to attract attention from anyone in the neighborhood. If things didn't work out, if there was no cure, no vial to revive him, then he preferred to be anonymous while they were in the city. He would rather preserve whatever memories his friends and family had of the old Josef they once knew—the baker's son, the moving-picture enthusiast, the music lover. Because if there was no cure, then he was as good as dead to them already.

"You see, I'm just the glassblower." Viktor shook his head as though apologizing. "I make the beakers and bottles in the old glassworks on the premises, but the others do serious research with their experiments." He paused as a family walked past on the street. The mother and father were arguing about being late, while the little boy played make-believe with a toy Albatros biplane in his hand, diving at his imagined enemy. "They're sort of like the Order of the Seven Stars in that way. They don't like to attract the attention of mortals," Viktor whispered.

"We're not mortals," Josef said, ringing the bell again, curious to know exactly what the people inside and out were so secretive about. He understood the need to be careful with information about magic. He'd been indoctrinated by members of the Order on the matter prior to being released from his shackles. He was a mortal man who'd been drawn into the world of the supernatural by a single bite. No longer able to serve as a soldier—the risk of his relapsing playing on the minds of those in the Order even then—he knew they saw the potential for him to act as a liaison between the world of the supernatural and the mortal conflict playing out between kingdoms. A battle between shadow and reality. *His* former reality, anyway.

"So," Petra said, "if they let us in, we just have to hope König left something behind that will help us uncover the treatment she talked about." She looked up at Josef with that same look of optimism she'd been carrying around ever since she'd spoken with the emperor's witch, believing there was a cure. He was all for chasing down leads, but what good was optimism when the woman who held the answer was dead? They would have to resurrect both her memory and her body of work at this place to make that happen, and he'd had just about enough of the undead rising from their graves to last a lifetime.

"Let us hope you're right," Yanis said to Petra. "Because we only have between now and the next full moon to find the cure before the consequences of this unscheduled detour come back to bite us and we're forced to take other measures."

After waiting for what felt like a full five minutes, someone finally answered the bell. A clean-shaven man wearing wire-rimmed glasses held the door open just wide enough to show his face. "May I help you?"

Josef was certain the man kept his foot firm against the other side of the door in case he had to close it quickly against invasion. Josef put his hand on the door to test the theory, but before he could give it a hard push, Viktor stepped forward, smiling nervously.

"Viktor, what are you doing here?" The man stepped aside, quickly waving everyone in off the street. "I thought you were away assisting in the war effort as the Society's proxy witch."

"I have been, yes." Viktor set his satchel down on a dusty chair. "Still am, but we were unexpectedly turned back when the enemy advanced and we had to make other plans."

Viktor directed his companions into the dimly lit front room. As Josef had seen through the window, the area was starkly furnished with a round table with two hard-back chairs pushed up against the wall, a brochure stand advertising nearby libraries and colleges, and a decorative wooden lectern that looked like it had been salvaged from a cathedral a century earlier, only to gather dust from disuse in its new home.

There was a bookshelf on one wall that was sparsely populated with reference books and a heavy door at the end of a short hallway opposite the entry that could lead to either a closet or an array of mystical rooms. With this lot, it was a flip of the coin what you might get.

The man closed and locked the front door behind them. "We aren't open to unscheduled visitors," he said to Viktor, barely concealing his displeasure. He shut the single curtain over the window with a harsh snap. His tone suggested he didn't yet know who or what he was dealing with: a witch or mortal invasion. Did he close the curtain to hide them from the outside world, or what he was about to do to them? Josef let his hand drift to his pistol.

"My apologies, Ernst," Viktor said. "I know you don't like surprises."

The man relented and tried to pretend like he wasn't perturbed by the sudden influx of visitors Viktor had brought back with him. "Well, I'm glad you're back safe and sound," he said without much sincerity, folding his arms in front of him as he made small talk. "Will you be returning to work here, or will you be off on another assignment?" He nodded toward the others.

"Yes, um, my companions and I are still working on something, actually," Viktor said. "That's sort of why we're here. We were hoping we might make use of the research library."

Ernst met Viktor's remark with a tight smile. "May I have a word?" he asked. "In private?"

"It's all right," he said. "They're with me."

"Now!"

While Viktor and Ernst disappeared through the door at the end of the hallway, Yanis rolled his eyes before thumbing through a brochure. "This place seems to have a nice collection," he said, pointing to a description of the Saint Clement library. "At three hundred years old, I suppose they're only getting started, but I wouldn't mind seeing their section on magic."

Petra leaned over the sorcerer's shoulder to read for herself. "It's an old church library. What makes you think they have books on magic?"

"They always confiscate the best ones." Yanis folded the brochure and stuffed it inside his robes for later.

Josef had never even considered visiting the library they spoke of, though he'd passed it often enough. He'd never had any reason to go inside. It was a place for scholars. Intellectuals. Professor types. He was a baker's son. His world consisted of early mornings, hot ovens, and eternally burned fingers. He'd never dreamed magic was real, that writings on magic were secretly housed behind ordinary walls inside his city, that matter could be manipulated with a single touch, or that a man's body could be turned inside out and made into the shape of a wolf. He'd had to learn quickly there existed a hidden world within the one he'd always presumed he lived in, one full of mystery and beauty, but also danger. Always danger.

Viktor and Ernst returned from the back room. All pretense had slipped away from the man's face. He no longer pretended to be running a reception room for an academic society. "Everyone, this is Ernst Bergmann. He's an apprentice researcher here at the Libuše Society." Viktor then introduced the others by name as they crowded around to shake the man's hand.

Ernst took a more relaxed posture while he explained his earlier response to their arrival. "Viktor says you're looking for something that once belonged to Ava König. It's true she worked here many years ago, but I doubt very much we have what you're after. Regardless, it's not customary to share another witch's notes with those who aren't somehow related to the subject matter or connected to the facility through authorized research projects."

"Frau König told me she and my father once worked together," Petra said. "At university. He was interested in alchemy too. Isn't that part of what you do here?"

"You've spoken to Ava?" The man seemed perplexed. "When was this?"

"Yesterday," Petra said. "Before she was killed by the tsar's mystic, Grigori Zimin."

"He's also dead, by the way," Josef added, enjoying the taste of the words in his mouth.

"Is this true?" Ernst looked sharply at Viktor, who assured him the report was correct. "This is terrible. The others will be devastated." The man shook his head, frowning as one does when they hear bad news about other people, then turned back to Petra. "I'm sorry, who did you say your father is?"

"My father was Honza Stamitz."

While the news of Ava König's death was awful, something else entirely shifted inside Ernst after he heard Petra's father's name. "You're Petra Stamitz?" he asked with a heavy dose of doubt. When she nodded, the man made a sharper inspection of the group standing in front of him. "Impossible. His child died years ago. Viktor, what are you playing at?"

Petra held her ground. "I'm not dead, and I'm not a girl anymore."

Ernst crossed his arms and pulled out what he thought was his ace card. "If you're Petra Stamitz, then there's an easy way to prove it," he said with a nudge of his chin.

Viktor exhaled at the growing tension. "Ernst, she is who she says she is."

Petra locked eyes with Ernst. "It's all right, Viktor. I know what he wants to see."

Josef watched Petra take from her pocket the amulet of linden leaves, the one she'd carried since he'd first found her wandering the Old Town Square at midnight taking photos of the dead. He inhaled the citrusy scent, relishing the pleasant memory that came with it, while she cupped the leaves between her hands and closed her eyes. When she opened her hands again, the amulet had been transformed into a small wooden picture frame with a faded photo in it. She held it up to show the man, who went pale with disbelief.

"It's merely an illusion," Ernst said.

Petra handed him the frame. "Here, hold it. The frame is real."

Ernst inspected the frame, then stared at the black-and-white photo of the face held inside. "Honza Stamitz." The man stopped fussing and conceded Petra was who she said she was with a single nod. "I see we'll need to make an exception to our unannounced visitor policy," he said, extending his arm to the door at the back of the hallway. "If you'll come with me."

A mix of sulfur, salt, blood, copper, and the dried husks of flowers seeped out from behind the door the man led them to. The small hairs inside Josef's nose collected the scent information and stowed it away. He had the distinct impression they were entering a hidden lair of the forbidden that only the rare mortal ever entered. He couldn't help wondering how many had ever walked out again. He checked his pistol *and* knife this time just in case.

Ernst walked them down the narrow flagstone hallway, but instead of a closet or mysterious magician's lair, they were led inside a formal study with a large desk, impressive floor-to-ceiling bookshelves, and an Old World fireplace with a colorful winged crest painted above it. The formidable desk in the center of the study was cluttered with the usual—a lamp, books, a paperweight. To Josef's eye it was just another room like any you'd find in the old part of the city. Not worth the effort Ernst had shown to keep them out earlier.

Josef fought to hide his initial disappointment until a second glance revealed another layer to the room. The lamp, standard in any office, had been molded in the shape of a brass dragon protecting an egg. The oddity of it made him inspect the other details of his surroundings more closely until he noticed the ancient-looking books bore titles about amphibian toxicity in potions, healing herbs, the use of psychic powers in self-defense, and something called *Lady Everly's Grimoire*. An hourglass the size of a milk can nearly obscured the presence of half a dozen star maps and astrological documents rolled up and tied with leather strings on a side table. The paperweight on the desk might have been an actual crystal ball. A shield and axe had been affixed to the wall behind the desk, a curved dagger with a jewel-encrusted haft hung above the pile of maps, and what he believed were a pair of wands with foreign symbols carved into their sides rested under a glass dome on the fireplace's mantel.

And there were bottles. So many bottles. Bottles the size of wine decanters, smaller vials that resembled delicate perfume atomizers, and several that looked like fat glass gourds with long, skinny necks. They were scattered on the bookshelves, the windowsill, and the floor. Some with small metal tags held on with wax, some containing amber fluid, some with herbs swimming inside, and one that appeared to have shimmering flakes of gold that had settled to the bottom.

"Love spells are common," Petra said, reading the label of a tiny bottle with a silver moon charm hung around its neck as if the glass surface were a woman's neckline. "But the larger flasks of elixir on this bookshelf are different than any I've seen." She ran her finger along the books and bottles there with a sort of curious reverence.

Josef joined Petra at the bookshelf while Yanis examined the curved dagger on the wall in awe, judging by the way his mouth hung open. "Did you have to study all these books growing up to become a witch?" Josef asked her, gazing at what he assumed passed as an occult library. He knew his ignorance about witches ran deep and wide, but he found himself curious to know how Petra had lived before hiding her magic and assuming the life of a mortal.

"I don't know anybody who's read this many books," she said. "But my father did own several botany books he read out loud to me."

"My father made me read that toad book when I was about ten," Viktor said. "Not as much fun as catching them in the pond. I think he was hoping I'd go to university, but studying dry old texts under lamplight late into the night was never for me. Still can't distill a decent poison."

Josef reached for the nearest bottle on the shelf with new interest. The label claimed the contents to be an elixir of eternal youth. His former mortal instincts warned him the place had to be a sham run by charlatans who sold flavored alcohol to people looking for a cure-all at three times the cost. But as he turned the bottle of elixir over in his hand, experience told him a cursed man could no longer afford to discount anything in the realm of the supernatural. Hadn't he been at least partially saved from ruin by the contents of a similar bottle half the size of this one?

What peculiar mixtures madmen and witches conjure in their minds to distill into stoppered bottles, he thought as he held the contents up to the light and gave them a swirl. He set the bottle down and marveled again at the hidden magical world at work behind the shabby walls of the city he'd thought he'd known all his life.

CHAPTER FOUR

The room leaned more on the mystical side than Petra's first impression had revealed, yet it was far from worthy of the staunch protection their host had exhibited. It could have belonged to any historian in the city with a mild interest in the occult.

Petra began to think Viktor had wasted their time bringing them there, so why did he look so smug with his cat eyes gleaming full of pride? Even if Ava König had worked in the building, he'd been less than honest by letting them believe something remained of her work that would be of value to their mission. There was hardly anything of consequence in the room, aside from the floor-to-ceiling bookshelves, but even those were filled with the same sort of generic tomes found at the university library.

Yanis betrayed the same expression of disappointment in his downcast eyes, as if the entire trip to the city had been a bad decision he'd been forced to go along with. And yet Josef prowled the room, expectant. His eyes searched for some unseen threat or reward as he leaned over to look behind the desk, the curtains, and even the door they'd come through. Perhaps to the once-mortal eye, the room did have an unsettling occult aesthetic, but it was as mundane as day-old potato soup for the others.

Petra's optimism curdled into a sour look to match Yanis's. They'd have to start over. Try and find some other lead or else turn back for the mountains. The task felt impossible. And with nothing to show for their disobedience toward the Order, Petra shivered at the thought of what consequences she might have incurred for the group.

Ernst smiled humbly, as though aware of the underwhelming impression the room presented to the modern witch's eye. "The study was quite the centerpiece in its day," he assured them. "Three hundred years ago the house belonged to an important adviser to the king. A man with a sophisticated scientific mind. He was an astronomer, mathematician, botanist, and chemist, but he was a true mystic at heart. An alchemist." He pointed to a small figurine on the bookshelf of a man in a long cape with his hand resting atop a globe that had apparently been done in the man's likeness. "Many of his contemporaries visited him here in this very room. Some quite well known throughout the continent at the time. All with a desire to achieve the unachievable."

Their host's remarks were met with fake smiles from an underwhelmed audience not wishing to be rude. Ernst responded in kind and said, "Follow me."

"Is there more upstairs?" Petra asked Viktor as they followed him out through a side hallway at the back of the room. "I thought they would have more grimoires and potions for us to sort through."

"Some, though I've rarely been upstairs," Viktor said, seemingly oblivious to her disappointment.

At the end of the short hall, they came upon a room that might have been a bedroom in the original layout of the house but was now being used as a modern office. The scent of strong espresso brewing in a pot permeated the air.

A woman in a navy-blue suit with a high collar had her back to them. She poured herself a demitasse of coffee as she hummed an upbeat song popular with musicians playing in the beer gardens. The woman turned around, holding the cup in a gloved hand while she read a newspaper. Ernst tapped on the door lightly. She looked up and nearly spit out her coffee after being caught unawares by the group.

"Ernst? Viktor? What are you doing here?" The woman wiped down the dribbles on the front of her jacket with her gloved hand as she tried to make sense of the three new faces staring back at her. "Who are these people?"

"Please excuse the intrusion, Martina." Ernst shepherded them all inside the room. "Viktor has brought some unlikely visitors back from the front with him who ask for our assistance." He gestured to Petra, who bristled at being singled out. "I think you might be especially interested to meet this young lady."

Martina appeared unimpressed by Petra's attire and made no effort to hide her opinion. And why not? Petra was still wearing the cloak and dress she'd made by transforming her husband's clothes at Zimin's request. Though the outfit was a lush plum color, she knew the mud, blood, and filth of the last twenty-four hours must be plain to see above her hem.

"We don't generally entertain curious country witches in our laboratory, Ernst, even if they are friends of employees." After insulting Petra, the woman walked past her to size up Josef. She narrowed her eyes, scanning him with her third-eye vision. She was checking for the faint purple aura attached to all witches, but she'd not find one on him. Yet the woman did see *something* invisible to the naked eye, by the way her brows tightened in interest.

"This one's no witch," Martina said, nostrils aflare in victory. "But he's no longer mortal either." Disregarding the norms of etiquette, she leaned her face closer to Josef's to peer into his eyes. He leaned back at having his personal space so blatantly invaded. "His blood is tainted with a common curse, but I'd wager it's in some sort of remission." She picked up her cup and swallowed the espresso inside in one swig. "And this one." She wiped the corner of her mouth, then pointed to Yanis while still holding the demitasse in her hand. "He smells of common healing herbs and wolf's blood. Makes them a pair, I take it. So, what is this all about, Ernst? Why have you allowed these people past the front room and into my office?"

Ernst cleared his throat, hiding a secret-keeper's smile behind his fist. "I thought," he said, making a dramatic gesture of presentation with his left hand, "you might care to meet Honza's daughter?"

"Honza?" Martina set her cup down on the worktable and gazed at Petra through a haze of disbelief, as though she'd just been introduced to a ghost. And perhaps she had. For ten years Petra had happily let the world speculate about whether she was dead or alive.

"It's really her," Ernst said.

Petra feared she'd be asked to do more parlor tricks to prove herself. Instead, Martina dug through the clutter on the worktable until she found a pair of green-tinted eyeglasses. She slipped them on, keeping her gloved hands cupped to the sides to block out any interference from peripheral light. The woman didn't lean in as close as she had with Josef, but her intense gaze still left Petra backing away slightly.

"Petra Stamitz. I don't believe it." Martina removed the tinted glasses while one half of her upper lip spread in a toothy smile. "Please, take a seat." She gestured to the pair of upholstered chairs in front of her desk. "But how did you get here?" the woman asked. "Where have you been? I . . . we all searched for you after your mother's death. Just in case. They never did find a body. Not a whole one, anyway. Just a few charred bones in a heap." She looked up at Ernst in alarm. "I'm saying too much again, aren't I?"

The man leaned against the door and shrugged like they'd had the same conversation about inappropriate subjects a dozen times before.

Petra took the chair offered to her. Josef stood behind her, looming with his arms crossed. Petra, though, was curious to hear more. Something about the woman struck her as vaguely familiar. Her voice, perhaps. The way she'd spoken her name with a hint of an accent, rolling the r. She'd heard the woman say it that way before. When she was a child.

"Forgive me . . . I feel like I should know who you are, but I can't recall where or why," Petra said to Martina.

"Ah, that's remarkable that you remember. It was such a long time ago. I'm Martina Danek, a senior researcher at the institution. Do you remember that name?" The woman waited a beat, but all she got was the shake of Petra's head. "You see, I knew Honza many, many years ago.

Since before you were born. Long before he decided to leave the city for the quiet country life." The woman locked eyes with Ernst before adding, "But I still occasionally saw him after that. One day I took the train to visit him and had the pleasure of meeting you in your colorful *kroj* with your scarf tied under your chin. You couldn't have been more than five or six years old."

"It was Easter," Petra said, stunned by how quickly the recollection flashed in her mind of a younger version of Martina, before her hair had streaks of gray.

"Yes, you decorated eggs with your mother while your father and I chatted in his study."

The jagged shape of a memory floated in the back of Petra's thoughts but refused to materialize fully.

"How did you know it was me just now?" Petra hoped to inspect the tinted glasses for herself, but Martina scooped them up and tucked the lenses in her pocket. "Are they enchanted to view deeper into auras?" she asked.

After a pause, Martina's eyes refocused as though she'd been thinking about something far away. "No, no, I simply do not see well, and the light gives me headaches, hence the slight tint. Viktor made them for me ages ago. But I am otherwise quite good at seeing with my *other* sight, especially through simple illusions like yours." She pointed to her cheek to indicate she'd seen the scar beneath Petra's spell. "Pavel Radek bragged in prison about burning your face with a poker. He also insisted you were alive, even though the bones in the fire attempted to tell a different story. If Petra Stamitz had survived, she ought to have a significant scar. And there it is."

Petra reflexively covered the old wound on her jawline with her palm even though the illusion was still in place. She'd kept the spell over her burn scar for years to hide her identity for just that reason. She'd believed she'd killed Pavel and would be hanged for murder if the mortals caught her. And if the witches found the girl who could turn wood to stone or copper to gold, she'd be hunted to the end of her days for her rare gift. Zimin had only reinforced that notion. The tsar's mystic had even tried to sell her to the highest bidder as one of the spoils of war.

Petra's comrades raised their brows at her mild deception. "It's just an old scar," she said.

"So, Petra Stamitz, what is it that you and your friends hope to find here?" Martina asked. "The elixir of life? The philosopher's stone?" The woman was being flippant, as though they'd undertaken a supernatural scavenger hunt.

"The wolf curse." Josef let an inflection of seriousness resonate in his voice like a slight growl that made gooseflesh of Petra's neck and Martina sit up straighter.

"Ava König's notes, more specifically," Viktor said. "If it wouldn't be too inconvenient, we'd like access to her early notebooks."

"If we can figure out how she conceived the spell, we might be able to disassemble it in reverse," Petra added.

"What makes you think we have that specific information here?" Martina fidgeted with the papers on her desk, stacking them in a neat pile. "Why not go see her yourself in the capital?"

"They claim she's dead," Ernst said with a quirk of his eyebrow that suggested he hadn't seen any proof of it himself. "Killed by Grigori Zimin."

"I see." Martina stopped fidgeting with the papers and folded her fingers in front of her on the table. "How unfortunate. We had our differences at times in the past, but there was no question she was an exceptionally talented witch."

"Before she was killed, she assured me there was a way to rid Josef of his curse," Petra said. "It's imperative we find a solution. We believe her notes might lead us toward the answer. If we could just see the chain of work behind her experiments, we might be able to decipher the spellwork for ourselves. We're already familiar with an elixir that tames the worst effects of the curse."

"You mean the herbs and wolf's blood I smelled on his robes?" she said with a look toward Yanis. "You must have caught the vlkodlak that bit your friend. That's the only tempering cure I know, but you must understand it's only sustainable as long as you have the blood from the original beast."

Yanis nudged Petra on the shoulder. "Ask her how she knew about his curse just by looking at him."

The sorcerer had remained stoically silent since they'd entered the woman's office. Petra knew she'd challenged his sense of authority earlier at the train station, but she hoped he'd see that she was right to defy their instructions for Josef's sake. The upíri had been an imminent threat, conditioned to kill on command, but this new threat with the half men, half wolves was more complicated—logistically, supernaturally, and perhaps morally too. She was pleased to see him engage with Martina on the subject, but why was he asking her to speak for him?

The Lingua Franca spell.

Petra had become so accustomed to understanding everything he said, she'd forgotten it required a spell. "My companion would like to know—"

"Your translation isn't necessary." Martina then addressed Yanis directly. "I understood you perfectly," she said, swirling her empty coffee cup to indicate its contents had been enchanted. "We often have a need to understand a variety of individuals seeking assistance from the Society during these tumultuous times."

"Ah," Yanis said with a slight bow. "Very thoughtful."

"As to your question . . ." The woman hesitated, as though wondering how much to say. "There are flecks of . . . moon shadow in the young man's eyes. It's there if you know what to look for. It's enough to give him away for what he is, but perhaps not enough to trigger an involuntary impulse to transform when the moon is full. Do I have that right?"

Josef reluctantly nodded, while Viktor did a poor job of nonchalantly inspecting his comrade's eyes for the splinter of moonlight. "The elixir stabilizes the worst impulses of the curse," he said, pushing Viktor out of his face with a small nudge.

Martina looked over the ragtag group, seemingly still unimpressed by their appearance, until her eye settled on Petra. She drummed her gloved fingers on the desk, thinking. "We'll consider your request. It's true, we do have some of Ava König's early writings, though I don't know how useful they'll be in this situation. She only conducted preliminary work here for some of the things she became famous for later. Most of the writings are from her years at university, but that is where the first inklings of her madness were born."

. "We would certainly appreciate access to those notes given the time-sensitive nature of our mission," Yanis said.

"I understand, but the decision isn't up to Ernst and myself. We'll have to consult with the others."

"The research fellows," Viktor said, noticing his companions were confused. "The other academics who work here."

Petra gazed up at the ceiling, wondering again how much access there was to be gained given how small the footprint of the premises was, but she supposed even a small box of related notes could be helpful.

"I wish I could be of more assistance in this moment," Martina said with gauzy sympathy for their situation. "But some of their research work might be intertwined with the pages you wish to see, so I must confer with them first on such a delicate matter. Come back tomorrow and we'll have a better answer for you then."

With that, Martina stood and asked Ernst to show them out the same way they'd come in. *So much for urgency,* Petra thought. If their request got denied, then what would they do? They'd be no closer to finding a cure than they had been in the frozen mountains. She held out hope that Josef would get the help he needed in this unusual building with its brusque and secretive occupants, but their quick dismissal to the street left her feeling an odd sort of déjà vu. She'd been tossed out of her apartment only days before with nowhere to go. Now, here she was back in the city with even fewer prospects than she'd had when she left with a single valise to join Josef as one of his last recruits to fight the undead.

Yet there was something different this time. Something that itched under her collar. A vague feeling of fate holding its hand out to her rather than shooing her away. Yes, an invitation hung in the air, but to what, she wondered, as the door shut behind them and they faced the bustle of the city streets again.

CHAPTER FIVE

Josef slid the storeroom door open, letting the wood slam against the wall. The echo only emphasized the emptiness of the space. It wasn't much. A small cookstove, a washbasin and toilet, a storage cupboard, a rack of wooden shelves with a few restaurant supplies on them, and a single window overlooking the side street. But they'd sheltered in worse. Besides, it was his responsibility as team leader to keep them together, to provide a roof over their heads and food in their stomachs.

"Is this yours?" Viktor asked, swiping at cobwebs in the window.

"My uncle owns it, but I still have a key." Josef tried the light switch. A single bulb behind a wire cage buzzed to life overhead to reveal a decent-size room with peeling paint, sagging wood floors, and a plain tick mattress in the corner with a threadbare blanket. "He used to store the overstock for his café in here until the war started. Most of his supplies have been cleaned out, and now he only comes here when he's drunk and needs a place to hide from his wife after she's kicked him out. He doesn't have any sons, so my father loaned me out to work for him a few summers ago. I think I hauled so many sacks of flour from here to his restaurant, I walked with one shoulder higher than the other for a month afterward."

Josef slipped the key back in his pocket and looked around, reacquainting himself with the space. Located on a quiet backstreet, the storeroom was only a five-minute walk to the building that housed the mysterious Libuše Society. The space would do for living quarters, if they could get past the musty odor. All the old scents arose fresh for him again, but he knew they would fade after he'd spent some time in the room. In familiar places, the nose forgot what the nose already knew. At least it had when he was still a normal mortal man. These days one scent was traded for another, cataloging them in his brain like a librarian with an individual card to indicate where each book should go on the shelf. The smell of his uncle's storeroom got housed in the past with his memories of stolen cigarettes and first kisses.

Petra walked to the sink and turned on the faucet. Rusty water spurted out of the spout a full five seconds before it cleared. He wondered what she thought of the place, what she saw through her eyes. For reasons he hadn't quite sorted out, he cared what her opinion was about his judgment, about this place, and even about the ridiculous quality of the water coming out of the tap.

"It's cold," Petra said, shaking her fingers off.

"I can fix that with a spell later," Viktor said. The glassmaker blew a puff of breath over his hand, producing a ball of flame that floated in the air for a mere two seconds before it evaporated. The room immediately warmed to a comfortable temperature. Josef had become accustomed to seeing the unexplainable before his eyes, but it hadn't diminished his awe at watching the glassmaker's fire magic.

"This will do nicely." Yanis set his satchel down on the floor near the cot, along with the bread, cheese, and beer they'd picked up at a corner shop on their way over. "I was doubtful before that this would be a good idea, but perhaps we can make something of this venture."

Josef wasn't sure whether Yanis was talking about the storage room or Petra's commandeered mission to the city. He'd built a friendship with the sorcerer by fighting a common enemy in the mountains, but the relationship was tenuous at best, dependent on the existence of that mutual goal. If that shared objective shifted and they found themselves on opposite sides over the parameters of this new mission, it pained him to know he'd have to keep open the possibility of killing the priest. "It's important we stick together for safety," he said as Yanis responded with a sideways smile that suggested the sorcerer might be having similar thoughts.

It also didn't hurt that Josef knew this part of the city as well as he knew the ridges and scars of his scraped knuckles—from the burn when he'd pulled the pan of *chleba* out of the oven too quickly at twelve years old to the cuts on his fingers, hand, and arm from trying to block the vlkodlak's teeth that had poisoned his blood. Becoming a creature that turns one's body inside out to take the shape of an animal had made him appreciate the otherwise ordinary features of his skin, hair, and eyes. Odd that the woman had so easily noticed the fleck of silver light in his irises. Moon shadow, she'd said. He'd regarded the phenomenon as a sort of wound leftover from the curse. Like a bruise or a blood-shot eye. Something that would go away eventually. Now he wasn't so sure. It made him queasy to think it might be similar to the shadow that flitted under the membranes of the eyes in the upíri, that he had somehow been marked in the same way by a speck of moonlight. If that silver gleam was the difference between beast and man—cursed and favored—getting him cast in with the devils by the Order, at least he had a good idea of which way to run through the city to buy himself time to escape.

Josef and the others worked through the afternoon, scrubbing the floor with an old rag, taking a broom to the windows to clear away the spiderwebs, tossing out the dozen or more beer bottles scattered in the corners, and tightening the screws on the rickety wooden shelves so they could store enough supplies to last them the month, if needed. Afterward, they drew up a map of the city. Not of streets, houses, and restaurants but one made up of the collective knowledge of where to buy herbs, amulets, gemstones, essential oils, parchment for spells, and vials for mixing and stoppering whatever solution they found. When they finished, they had the framework for where to start if they got approval from the alchemists to study Ava König's work. But after a cold meal of bread and cheese, the yawns became infectious and they had to set their work aside.

"Should I make us blankets?" Petra asked when there seemed little else to do but lie down. "We can't all sleep on the one mattress."

Josef stirred out of his thoughts, pleased to have his gaze land on her face. Her smile was the only distraction that could draw him off his spiraling mood recently. "Yes, good idea," he said. "What do you need?"

Petra searched the room with her bottom lip firmly pinned down by her upper tooth. Not only could she manipulate objects, but she also manipulated his emotions in ways he could never see coming, often taking him from sullen and hopeless to filled with optimism the world would somehow right itself again. All by a mere facial expression that rendered him captivated and hungry for more. "I need something roughly the same size or shape," she said.

Josef opened a cupboard door next to the sink and handed her a stack of old flour sacks still covered in dust. "These might do."

With only the touch of her hand, the interwoven threads holding the flour sacks together lost their bonds. The material frayed and swelled at her command, rearranging into fluffy down comforters. Two for each of them with a pillow and mattress to match.

How could such magic exist in the world? How had she ever found the strength to give up the ability in the name of anonymity? Suffering with want and cold, and who knows what other torment she endured as a young girl, while living as a fugitive. That she had survived was an enigma to Josef. A treasure too. The others used spells and herbs to aid their magic, but her enchantments went beyond incantations and charmed gemstones. They were in her, part of her, like hair color or a dimpled chin, residing in the touch of her skin.

He caught himself staring at her, wondering about the scar on her cheek that she kept hidden. He'd known about it from the old woman who'd healed him. Hana had once filled his head with stories of a girl who could transform anything she touched. A girl who was supposed to have died in a fire, yet the rumors said otherwise. At times the idea that such a girl might have survived, that she might be able to transform him back into the man he'd once been, was all that had kept Josef from hanging himself with his straitjacket when the pain of transformation seared through his misshapen limbs in those first days. It had proved a fool's dream in the end, but he suspected being offered that kind of hope to hold on to on his worst nights had been part of the old woman's treatment too.

Exhausted from their ordeal of the past several days, the others collapsed on their beds, while Josef paced the room's perimeter to take the edge off the pleading from his legs to run one last time before morning.

"What's the longest you've gone without transforming?" Yanis asked after the third time he'd walked past him.

Josef paused, appreciating that he should probably make up an excuse to leave the storeroom to work out the buzzing in his body. "I have about three weeks before the urge will become unbearable. Before this week, Valentina always left me with an extra bottle of elixir in reserve. I've never really had to worry about the consequences of changing without the cure somewhere nearby. This time, though . . ." He peered out the window at the glow of a streetlamp at the end of the lane. "I'm not sure what will happen."

"I'll begin working out her formula in the morning," Yanis said. "You can hold out a little while longer, yes?"

Josef wasn't sure, but he nodded as his muscles twitched with the need to elongate in a run. Viktor and Petra had fallen asleep the minute their heads touched their pillows. He wished he could find such peace, but it wasn't only the ache in his legs that gnawed at him. His conscience made other demands as well. "I'm going for a walk," he said to Yanis with a parting look at his sleeping colleagues. "I won't be gone long."

Outside, the city greeted Josef like an intimate friend as the night hung like a canopy over the narrow streets with her coverlet of late-winter stars. The river, silent yet alive with movement, reflected the lamplight on its surface as he crossed the old bridge to the Lesser Town, the district of the city that sat below the castle on the hill. The scent of fish and rotted grass swirled off the bank to torment his nose, but he quickly forgot his discomfort as he glanced up at the spires of the castle cathedral, lightly aglow against the deep blue of evening. It was there he walked with purpose, letting his natural stride carry him easily over the cobblestones and up the steep hill.

The air was brisk as the road to the castle widened and grew stingy with its sheltered niches, but he no longer felt the cold as he once had as a young man. Caught up in wondering if he was permanently affected that way or if the discomfort of being out at night without a scarf might someday return should they uncover a true cure, he nearly walked into a couple strolling home after a late supper. Or maybe they were on their way to catch a film at the movie house at the bottom of the lane. He preferred the comedies himself. He enjoyed watching the trickster get revenge on the villain by pretending to be the dolt, only to later turn the tables and snap the trap. Sometimes the hero won through his own dumb luck, but the reward of seeing the character prevail always put Josef in a good mood. He glanced over his shoulder at the couple to make up his mind about them, catching a whiff of garlic on the man's breath and a common rose perfume on the woman, but they were already lost to the darkness.

Near the top of the lane, just before reaching the unfortunate quarter of tiny houses where so many of the city's poor congregated in crowded living conditions outside the palace walls, Josef found the house he was looking for: number 11. A flower box with the woody remains of a dead geranium still clung to the railing out front. Upstairs, the windows were covered with thin drapes, but lamplight burned brightly enough in the room that he detected the silhouette of a woman when she passed. A child squealed with laughter as though they were playing a game before bed. The toxic mixture of fear and shame nearly had him turn back at the thought of the child. He didn't know if he could endure the effort of getting the words out. To put his name to the deed.

Josef knocked despite the late hour. A minute later the woman opened the door. Her puzzlement at seeing him on her threshold was plain in the way she pleaded for an explanation with her eyes wide yet wary.

"Yes?" she asked out of polite curiosity when he said nothing.

Josef almost lost his nerve. She glanced in both directions on the street before making a move to go back inside. He pressed his hand against the door before she could close it. "Wait," he said. "I have news about your husband. About Karl. I was the one who recruited him for the mission."

"Where is he?" the wife asked, searching the lane behind Josef with her eyes.

"He fought bravely and was a credit to his kind," he said and then emptied his heart of the burden it had carried home since having to strike the stake into the man's heart.

When he'd finished and the woman had accepted the return of her husband's carving knife through her tears, Josef escaped into the lane and ran back to the storeroom, taking the long way around the city, circling its center until his legs nearly gave out from the exhaustion. He was near the square in front of the old clock when a ruffle of warning hit the back of his neck. A scent familiar but not yet categorized carried on the wind. A man's breath from eating too much garlic mixed with the soft scent of roses. He spun around, catching a glimpse of the couple he'd seen earlier in the night—the man in a black bowler hat and the woman in a fur stole. He was certain the man had been watching him before he abruptly pulled the woman closer and kissed her. A kiss absent of passion. Bodies rigid, hands held still and proper like shop mannequins. While the man kept his head bent toward the woman, Josef slipped into the shadows and stayed there until the pair walked past, their eyes searching for someone who was no longer there.

CHAPTER SIX

The *starshina* inhaled slowly, letting the information penetrate the insides of his nostrils before taking the breath deeper into his lungs. The scent trail of linden leaves and wolfskin was still strong days later. He worried his heightened senses had been dulled after two kills, but he'd been unable to resist the urge to bite once the taste for blood had flooded his mouth. Besides, the latest one, the villager, shouldn't have been so drunk that he didn't believe his own eyes when a vlkodlak stood before him bathed in the strong light of a full moon.

Like his first kill, the starshina had left the villager's body in the road. *Let them see what I can do.* Afterward, he'd followed the man's unwashed stench back to his front door. The house had proved a typical hovel for an unmarried middle-aged man who gets drunk every night, but there'd been clean clothes in the wardrobe: a pair of boots with frayed laces, a white shirt with all its buttons, and trousers to replace the ones he'd ruined earlier while running away from the battle on all fours. The civilian clothes weren't a perfect fit, but he had not minded shedding his uniform. He now fought for only himself.

After counting the coins he'd found stashed in the man's "secret" box in the cupboard, the box that also hid his crude photographs of women in provocative poses, the starshina had climbed out the back window and down the unpaved road. He'd thought at the time to burn down the man's home before he left, but the moon had still been engorged and shining bright in the sky over the towering pines, luring him into the woods. And so, he'd made room in his head for what peace he could recover from that night and walked west toward the outlying forest.

Now, two days later and two hundred kilometers closer to his objective, the starshina approached the train station with the caution of a man planning to rob a bank. He'd found a creek to wash the blood from his hair and nails, but he worried the scent of death still clung to his skin. He watched everyone who passed, looking for the scrunch of their nose, the stitched-together brows, the curious glance over the shoulder. Everyone ignored him or was too busy with their own worries to pay him any attention. Even a small girl holding her mother's hand smiled at him.

He fit in. He was one of them still. That's when he knew with certainty he walked in two worlds.

"Ticket, please." His voice sounded normal. Not too eager, not too aggressive. An ordinary man going on a short trip to visit his ailing father. Or an aunt, maybe. Yes, a great-aunt who lived in the west. *What big teeth you have, plemyannik!* He envisioned a terrified old woman's face and stifled the urge to laugh at his own joke.

The starshina paid the necessary coins for the trip, then found his place on the platform while the wind hissed in his ear. The scent trail had shifted on him briefly, but he knew which direction they'd gone. He traced their movements on the crude map he'd drawn sitting by the campfire the night before. He had a good idea of where they were going, and soon he would catch up. When he did, he would take everything from them.

His mouth salivated at the thought.

CHAPTER SEVEN

Petra had never heard anyone refer to her father as an "alchemist" until Ava König had called him one of the most accomplished she'd known. He'd been a university-educated witch with a reputation verging on greatness in some people's eyes. Important people in the Empire. He'd worked within some department at the Ministerial Council for Magical Affairs until he'd retired to the countryside to live a simpler life with his wife and daughter. Afterward, he'd puttered around the house like an old man using innocuous spells to fix a leaky roof without having to get on a ladder and getting his hair to regrow where it had begun to thin on top of his head. Petra smiled, remembering the smell of rosemary and mint in the potion he rubbed on his scalp at night.

Reminiscing about her former life, Petra realized her father would have been only thirty-two years old when he'd given up his coveted career with the Ministerial Council. Forty when he died. She'd been too young to know his moods well enough to understand his motivation then, but he'd always been a man on edge, as though waiting for something to happen. And then it finally did, when he dropped to the floor of his study and died of a heart attack on a Sunday morning. An owl outside the window had found him and hooted a death knell as the sun came up. Later, Petra had to explain to her mortal mother why the bird had kept up its calling long after the coroner had come out to pronounce her father officially dead, for owls always mourned for a full day after a witch died. Not understanding, her mother had shooed Petra away and told her to leave her alone to think.

Petra blew on her second cup of hot tea and watched the steam fog over the windowpane. Beside her, Yanis and Viktor took turns getting cleaned up at the sink, while Josef finally stirred awake after coming in the night before with his shirt drenched in sweat. How strange, she thought, to be living in a room with three men she'd met only a week before and be so perfectly at ease, as if it were the most natural thing a woman might do after learning her husband had been killed in war.

"Here." She handed Josef a cup of tea. He'd been out late. She'd heard him come in well past midnight, settling into his comforter with the exhaustion of a man who'd been exorcising demons. The night air still clung to his hair and skin. He'd been down by the river. She didn't think he'd been foolish enough to transform without his elixir, but she didn't fully understand how much control he had over his urge to change. "How are you feeling?" she asked as he sat up.

"Better," he said with clear eyes and no hint of a fever in his cheeks. His hands cupped hers briefly as he accepted the mug of tea. He drank and took notice of the changes she'd added to the room. "You made chairs. And a table."

"I hope you don't mind." She took a quick sip and set her cup aside. "We only used half of the shelving for our supplies, so I made practical use of the rest of the wood." She rubbed her wrists when reminded of the twinge in the muscle she'd felt after changing so many items at once. She hadn't used her innate magic in so long that she'd started to feel as if she were straining herself. She just needed to remind herself not to overdo it. "I'll put it back when we're done here," she said when his brows pinched in a vexing manner.

"No, it's fine," he said, tossing his comforter off. He still wore his uniform trousers from the day before and an undershirt that revealed just enough definition of the taut muscles beneath that she nearly knocked her cup over pretending not to look. "It's just . . . it's hard to wrap my head around how you're able to do these things," he said, pointing to where she sat. "Is the table still the shelf? Or have the shelves somehow been swapped out, and now they're somewhere else? Or has the wood in the shelves been rearranged into a table?" He shook his head as if the thought gave him a hangover.

Viktor paused in the middle of shaving his neck as he cleaned up his beard. He rinsed his razor off, then tapped it against the sink as he waited for her to explain. Yanis, too, stopped sweeping the dirt from his robes with a boar-bristle brush. If her magic was difficult for other witches to understand, it must verge on the impossible for a mortal to comprehend.

"A little of both," Petra said. "The shelves have changed but also remain the same." She tried to describe the process as best she could, though words sometimes failed to capture the essence of her magic. "The way my father explained it is that everything is made up of tiny particles of matter. This chair, the shelf, a book. They're all made of tiny individual cells that are smaller than the eye can see. The particles are bonded to each other in different configurations. Tension and attraction hold them together. The way those connections assemble themselves is what makes an object appear rigid or flexible. Plush or prickly. It's like different patterns in stitchwork. Or brickwork. Depending on how they're put together, things might look different, even though the building materials are the same. Even the color of something is determined by the order the particles are in when they bond together." She retrieved her cup and swallowed the last of her tea, then held the teacup in her palm. She ran a finger along the rim and the porcelain transformed into a mirror, with all the particles breaking apart and rearranging themselves in an order that made sense for the image in her mind. "My father said my magic works like a solvent, loosening the bond between particles enough so that they can be reorganized into whatever shape my mind envisions. It's best if the mass remains roughly equal."

The three men stared back at her, not quite able to close their mouths all the way. Viktor blinked first, wiping soap away from his neck with a small cloth. "That's the kind of thing the researchers at the Society are trying to understand. The ones interested in alchemy, that is."

"Didn't the alchemists try to make gold out of lead?" Josef asked.

"Yes, but there was always more to it than the gold," Viktor said. "They're searching for the origins of magic. That's their whole mission, really. To trace spellwork back to the beginning to figure out how it works, how to harness magic in different ways. But especially the manipulation of matter. Petra is the only known witch on the continent who can change a solid object into something else. Not just change how it appears with an illusion but actually alter its physical makeup. She's famous for it among the members of the Society."

Yanis brushed a final bit of stubborn mud from the hem of his robe. "The jinn do a similar manipulation of matter, but theirs is an old and hidden magic not easily accessed by outsiders." He lifted the robe to inspect it before slipping it over his shoulders. "Perhaps the fire in their blood works to break the bond and rearrange these particles the same way your magic does."

"Anyway," Viktor continued, "they've talked about Petra as long as I've worked there. Some were certain you were dead. Martina stubbornly believed the rumors that you'd escaped the fire." He stared at the mirror in Petra's hand as she changed it back into a cup. "If they let us have access to König's notes, it will be because of you," he said and hung his towel beside the sink.

"I can't imagine there'd be much there for us to see," Petra said. "I thought the place would be a little more . . ."

"Impressive?" Viktor combed his hair, unbothered with her assessment. "That's what everyone says."

"It just wasn't what I was expecting," she said, but she got no sympathy for her disappointment from the glassmaker. Odd, though, that Viktor talked about the place like it was one of the grand libraries of the Empire when inside it proved to be a slightly tilted-on-its-foundation house that was a prime candidate for demolition.

An hour later, the group stood before the crooked front door of the Libuše Society and rang the bell as they'd been instructed. Ernst greeted them as he had the day before, only this time he let his guests in right away with a sweep of his arm and directed them to the back room. Martina met the group in the study with the bookcases, maps, and giant hourglass. Petra had merely thought it a strange quirk the day before, but the woman was again dressed in an ensemble with a collar that reached up to her chin and dark gloves over her hands.

"Welcome back," Martina said, all smiles and handshakes. "Please, do come in."

The group squeezed into the crowded study, careful not to knock into any of the fragile bottles, scales, or scrying stones on the credenza. Josef stood beside Petra, nostrils flaring, eyes searching. Something about the room made him uneasy. While Yanis and Martina exchanged greetings, he subtly lifted his nose in the air as if following a scent again. He shrugged at Petra when he caught her watching him.

Martina clapped her hands together and leaned against the desk. "Well, I won't keep you waiting. I have good news. The others have agreed that your mission is of a high-enough priority to merit use of the facility." Viktor beamed and thanked Martina for the generosity before she held up a finger. "However, there is something we would ask for in exchange," she said, letting her eyes rest on Petra. "Something we've waited a very long time for."

Petra noted the familiar hunger in the woman's gaze. The overly curious and hopeful look full of expectation. Perhaps not for gold this time, but for something else she deemed valuable.

"We wish to study the properties of your unique talent," Martina said. "Perhaps do a few experiments—blood tests, hair and nail samples, kinetic testing of your reflexes."

"I'm to be one of your test subjects." Petra had expected the stipulation. She'd known it was coming since the moment they'd learned who she was. Just as Grigori Zimin and Ava König had both fought for control over which kingdom would benefit from her magic, these people wanted her under their charge. Would they, too, seek a way to profit from her abilities? Or was their interest purely scientific? If unraveling the origins of her magic was their goal, there was little she could do to enlighten them. The hows and whys of where her powers came from were as big a mystery to Petra as they were to everyone else.

She wondered if Martina was aware that her body had gone rigid while holding her breath. Petra had no desire to be pricked and prodded like a frog flayed open on a dissecting table for study, but if the barter gained her team access to a possible cure for Josef's curse, there was no option but to allow the exchange. She'd been the one, after all, who'd pushed the idea of returning to the city in defiance of their orders. "Agreed," she said, letting Martina relax as the air gushed out of the woman in a grateful thank-you.

"Petra, are you sure?" Josef asked. He eyed the pair of researchers with that overprotective scowl of his. His hackles were up, though she wasn't sure what he was reacting to. Perhaps his respectable mortal parents had ingrained in him the need to avoid entering into a bargain before knowing the full weight of the consequences, but Petra had always flown by her instincts alone. The group needed access to König's research, and this was the way to get it.

"Can we begin today?" Petra asked Martina.

"Of course," the woman said. "Ernst, will you do the honors?"

Petra had expected they would be shown to yet another back room, given the key to an understated library across town where they could do their research, or shown a winding staircase leading to a garret full of dusty, old notebooks. Instead, their host cut between Viktor and Yanis to get to the wall of books at their backs. There he reached for the small figurine on the shelf of the man in a long cape with his hand resting on the globe—the astronomer and alchemist who'd originally lived in the house. Ernst bent the statuette forward and a latch gave way, splitting the bookcase apart. One third of it opened on a hinge to reveal a hidden passageway with stone steps leading belowground.

"Let's go find the others and tell them the news," Ernst said. "I think they'll be quite eager to meet your friends, Viktor."

Josef positioned himself between Ernst and Petra. She noticed he kept his hand close to the hip where he kept his knife. Her instincts hadn't been ruffled like his, and she wondered again what had him on edge. Had he been thrown off by a room full of the eerie and unfamiliar as he had earlier with her magic? By an unfamiliar scent from a brewing potion? Objects of the occult? If his mortal intuition knew any better, he'd realize his physical weapons would do him little good in a place so steeped in shadow and illusions.

Artificial light buzzed to life on the wall where Petra imagined metal sconces had once held fat, dripping candles. Insulated copper wires wrapped around porcelain knobs connected one light to the next for several meters down a meandering underground passageway. "We had electric lights installed about two years ago." Martina flicked the switch off and on again. "We're quite modern now compared to when the tunnels were first carved out. At least in some important ways. Please follow me. Watch your step."

The passage was narrow and cut from stone, but the play of the artificial light against the darkness interfered with Petra's vision, making it difficult to see just how far the tunnel went. Martina led them another three meters into the passageway before they came to a carved-out room on their right. The ceiling clearance was understandably low, but the scent wafting out was superb. Dried bundles of herbs, grasses, flowers, and twiggy stems hung from a wooden rack suspended from the ceiling. There were baskets of fruit pits, brass scales, flower presses, and ribbons of twine on giant spools. Painted on the wall was a mural of an anthropomorphic sun and moon dancing around a flame-colored bird, peeling now from age and moisture.

"The botanical room," Viktor said rather obviously. "A leftover from the original alchemists who built the tunnels hundreds of years ago."

"Why did they put all this underground?" Josef asked innocently enough, but the others already knew. Persecution had always been the hound at the heel for those who pushed the boundaries of what mortals considered normal. "Occult" carried a double-sided meaning: practicing the supernatural arts and keeping things hidden from view.

"The tunnels were necessary to keep people safe so they could do their experiments free of persecution," Martina explained. "You are still new to our world, so it's understandable you might not be aware of the atrocities witches and seekers of the occult have experienced at the hands of the ignorant. But even you must recognize how your brief crossover into our world has put your safety in peril at times." The witch walked on without waiting for a reply.

"Many members still prefer to use the original botanical room for the calming ambiance," Ernst said of the cozy space. "The shape of the room funnels the city's underlying energy, boosting the potency of the herbs." He let them take a look around before beckoning the group forward again.

Petra lingered a moment to inhale the bundles of lavender hanging overhead. The scents invigorated her desire to work with plants again as she had when she was a girl under the tutelage of her father and Hana. Josef stayed back with her, the top of his head grazing the ceiling.

"What's going on with you?" she said, tipping jars of dried fruit pits to read their labels. "You've been on edge ever since we arrived."

"Just wary." He shook his head at the array of aromatic plants. "This room is full of the scents of flowers and crushed herbs, but it isn't strong enough to mask the harsher smells coming from somewhere deeper in the tunnel. Sulfur, char . . ." He inhaled. "Ammonia." He inspected a string of garlic with far too much interest before plucking a stem of lavender loose from the nearest bundle and handing it to her. "I suspected there was more to this place when we were upstairs, but I couldn't figure out why the scent was coming from the bookcase until it opened. I thought maybe one of the bottles on the shelf had leaked."

The curse had left him with heightened animalistic qualities that stayed with him even when he was in his human form. His ability to track a scent, his superhuman strength, and the quick pace he moved at when he didn't have to hold himself back for others were the result of the wolf's influence in his blood. She had to wonder if he ever considered his newly attained abilities a gift. "They must do all kinds of experiments with botanicals down here," she said, wafting the lavender under her nose and wondering what he wasn't telling her. "If they go through as many beakers as Viktor claims."

"This way, please," Ernst said, urging them to keep up with the others. "Much to see."

Beckoned forward, they passed two other rooms of a similar primitive construction, spaces dug out of the rock with picks and shovels centuries ago that had been bolstered by haphazard brickwork. One room housed a brass vat that sat over a firepit on a three-pronged stand. Distillation tubing wound out of the cover on top and spiraled into a pair of large beakers on a workbench. The bottles had skinny necks and fat bottoms like the ones in the study, each filled with an amber liquid. A final drip from the tubing splashed into a bottle on the table as Viktor proudly turned their attention to the room opposite.

"This is the glassworks, where I make the bottles," Viktor said. He bent to inspect a shelf of glass beakers with tubes coming out of them, small vials capped with cork stoppers, and more of the gourd-like flagons in various sizes.

The room felt smaller than it was because of the large furnace that took up the center. Around it, stacked against the wall, were tubes of colored glass, buckets of sand, long metal punties, metal prongs, stacks of newspaper, and a row of blowpipes. A window set high in the wall was open to the street above to vent the space, which must have gotten unimaginably hot when the fires were blaring, but it didn't account for the shockingly cold air inside the room compared to the rest of the tunnel. The chill air was an unwanted reminder of the haunted frozen mountains they'd recently fled.

"Looks like you're still well stocked," Viktor said, nodding at the inventory on the shelf.

"You did leave us nicely prepared for your long absence." Martina hugged her arms to warm them against the room's nippy air. "Shall we move on," she said, checking the small pocket watch pinned to her jacket. "I always regret stopping in front of this section of the tunnel for too long without a coat. We use charms to keep it deliberately cold so our poor glassblower doesn't keel over from the heat of the furnace when he's hard at work."

"I guess someone forgot to disable the charms after he left," Yanis said. He kept his hands clasped behind his back as though he were a tourist on a tour of a subterranean archaeological site. His casual stance made for an impression of someone harmless, but the sorcerer took in every nook and niche of the place as though studying an enemy for the weak point to strike. Josef always entered a room in the same manner, though he was much less effective at pretending to be harmless.

"This way." Martina left the sorcerer's comment hanging in the frosty air as she led them down a set of stairs to another level.

The stonework on the lower section appeared newer. The walls were straighter, the lighting stronger, and the rooms larger. They'd entered a workspace as impressive as any to be found at a university, with work-tables, books, cauldrons, beakers with colorful contents, skulls with markings on them to differentiate the various parts of the brain, plants growing in big brass pots with halos of spell light hovering over them, boxes containing dozens of vials with peeling labels, and a huge vault, like the one Petra had seen in the National Trade Bank, only this one had a radiating metal sun for a handle.

A group of three men in white lab coats lifted their heads as Martina led them inside the workroom. The first man was bald on top but sported a long reddish beard. Another, at least a decade younger, wore gold-rimmed glasses and appeared to use a heavy dose of pomade to tame the chestnut hair that sprouted out of his head in thick waves. The third man peered at them through the fogged-over lenses of his gas mask as he sprinkled powder into a beaker of bubbling liquid.

The man pulled the mask up, letting it rest atop his head as he waved his hand over the cloud of gases rising from the beaker. "Are these our new guests, Martina?" He scanned the group until he found Petra. The corners of his eyes creased ever so slightly, as though he was excited but didn't wish to show it. He stepped away from the worktable with another wave of his hand. The gas retreated into the glass container on command, where it roiled like an angry cloud in the belly of the bottle.

"May I introduce you to pan Brunner," Martina said. "He is the senior researcher of our small group. He's been with the Society for nearly thirty years."

"Please, call me Augustus. Welcome to our laboratory." He removed a pair of safety gloves so he could shake everyone's hands. With the mask off, he resembled an elder statesman with his tufts of reddish-blond hair, full mustache, and neatly trimmed beard that came to a perfect point on his chin. "We hope we might be of some service to your endeavor."

The two others, introduced as Max Decker and Franz Burián, had much the same reaction as the senior researcher, showing intense interest in Petra while pretending they were equally glad to meet Josef and Yanis.

"Paní Kurková, what a pleasure to meet you at last," Max said, taking her hand and burying it in both of his calloused palms. His long beard bounced with every word he said. "As you might imagine, we're all more than a little curious to get to know you better. Your talents are of the deepest interest to our Society, as I'm sure Martina explained."

Petra understood what he meant. He wanted to know how she ticked, how she could manipulate matter the way she did when others couldn't. She held none of the answers he was seeking, but perhaps the mystery really was buried under her dirty fingernails or in her unwashed hair as Martina had suggested. "A pleasure to meet you all," she said, forcing a genial smile.

"We've not had a visitor from the Order of the Seven Stars in quite some time," Franz said, eyeing Yanis's robes through his gold spectacles. "A pleasure to welcome someone with such a breadth of worldly experience. I hope that we might find time to talk later and compare notes."

"Ah, thank you. Yes, of course." Yanis had replied with stiff formality, even for him. "Our visit was hastily planned, but we very much appreciate you allowing us to conduct our research on behalf of the Order's interests."

"Which almost always benefit our own as well, as students of the occult," Franz said, maintaining the air of cordiality in the room that everyone seemed pleased to hold up like a spell wall binding all of them together under the illusion of cooperation.

After a single handclap from Augustus to say there'd been quite enough small talk, Franz cleared his throat and invited them down a short hallway that led to a separate workroom in the back where a dozen floor-to-ceiling bookshelves with glass doors lined the wall. "I imagine you're eager to get started," he said, taking a key from his suit pocket and opening the third cabinet from the right. "I believe Ava's notebooks are mostly kept in here." He flipped through a few leather-bound books and stacks of papers held together with paperclips as though checking to make sure he had the right cabinet. "We were all quite disturbed to learn of Frau König's fate. So many good people have been lost in this war already."

Petra thought to impart that the woman had died bravely fighting the undead, but sometimes people said a thing only to be polite and weren't truly interested in the details that might force their actual acknowledgment of the depth of a tragedy. At least that was the feeling she took from Franz, as he didn't bother to look up from the stained pages of a notebook as he expressed his regret over the famed witch's death.

Max and Martina entered the study room and quickly cleared away the scalpels, tongs, rubber tubing, and petri dishes cluttering up the end of the worktable in front of the bookcase. "Please, feel free to use this room for your research," Max said. "We have paper, fountain pens, ink, whatever you might need for note-taking. All we ask is you not mark in the books themselves."

Yanis gave them his assurance as a representative of the oldest clandestine magical society in the world that they would take the utmost care with the documents. He waited for them to acknowledge his promise with a nod before he asked, "I don't wish to impose so early into our new arrangement, but while we're sorting out the details, would it be possible to have access to the other materials you use here at the Society?" He eyed the hallway, implicating the well-stocked lab they'd just come from. "Herbs, extracts, oils? The Order will gladly compensate the cost of any supplies we might use."

The alchemists conferred with Martina via raised eyebrows and caught-off-guard shrugs.

"Yes, of course," the woman said after no objection was raised. "I assume this, too, is for the benefit of your friend here?" Martina let her eye land on Josef briefly. "With the full moon having just passed, he'll be starting a new phase."

"Exactly," Yanis said. "His unique situation requires an elixir be administered occasionally during the month, but we've regrettably run out."

"You'll need calendula for that." Martina tapped a finger against her lips. "And perhaps a pinch of borage?"

"I'll write up a full list of what we'll require," Yanis said with humble palms pressed together in thanks. "In the meantime, could you also spare a few grams of eyebright for our research?"

"For the notebooks?" she asked, though Petra didn't know what was meant by her conclusion.

When Yanis said she was correct, Martina casually glanced back at her coworkers, giving them an almost imperceptible nod to fulfill the request. Max left, taking it upon himself to personally gather the ingredient they'd asked for. "Please let us know how we can be of further assistance," Martina said. "Franz is our main caretaker of the library. If you don't find what you're looking for in the notebooks, simply let him know and he may be able to assist you."

"Yes, of course," Franz said, still young enough to be eager to please. "Happy to be of assistance."

"Thank you for letting us have use of the study room." Viktor shrugged off his coat and threw it over the back of a chair. "I can finish getting them settled in from here."

Max returned with a small pouch containing the requested eye-bright, and then he and Franz both gave a quick bow and returned to their work in the main laboratory. Their hostess, however, waited at the entrance to the reading room, casting a sly glance in Petra's direction. "If you wouldn't mind, Augustus and I would like to begin our inquiries now too." Martina had spoken in a tone that suggested she wasn't making a request but rather was demanding payment for what the others had just been given access to.

Petra stuffed her natural resistance to being scrutinized deep inside her chest and followed the woman into the hallway. If sacrificing her comfort contributed to them finding a cure for Josef, she'd gladly submit to a thousand examinations. It was the least she could do for a man who'd saved her life by giving her a purpose. A way to use her magic for a more noble purpose than flipping brass coins in the air and changing them to gold. She'd gone to the mountains not knowing what to expect from war, from her fellow recruits, or from herself. Josef had believed in her magic when others had doubted a woman's presence on the team. He'd believed in her, and given her a chance. How could she do any less for him?

CHAPTER EIGHT

Josef dug his thumbnail against the edge of the table until a thin groove began to form in the wood. He didn't like the idea of paying for the privilege of reading a witch's dusty old school notebooks by having Petra treated as a guinea pig. Nevertheless, Yanis shoved a stack of notebooks in front of him. He reluctantly sat forward with the same enthusiasm he'd often shown in school when the teacher assigned them blocks of reading from some long-dead philosopher.

"They've waited a long time to finally have the chance to meet her," Viktor said. He seemed to be thinking about something as he continued staring at the doorway where Petra had left with Martina. "And hopefully we'll find something here about the curse. And if we don't, we'll appeal to the Order on Josef's behalf. There must be a way, right, Yanis?"

The sorcerer glanced up without comment, offering that same look of commitment to his orders that overrode friendship or camaraderie in the name of public safety, before going back to reading the spines on the notebooks.

Josef hadn't mentioned the run-in with the couple from the night before to the others. He suspected they'd tailed him, though he wasn't entirely convinced he'd got it right. While it was an odd coincidence to run into the same pair twice in one night, it was just as likely they had followed the flow of the main artery through the city just as he had. It was the scent of the garlic in the botanical room that had thrown him. For a moment he'd thought the couple might have come from the Society. If the Order of the Seven Stars wanted all evidence of Ava König's monsters killed, perhaps others did too. But after meeting those inside, he was more inclined to believe he was being paranoid.

And yet the place still gave him pause. He lifted his nose and inhaled in the direction of the hallway. The faint scents of char and sulfur wafted up again, and another odor he couldn't quite place. Something caustic and abrasive like the cleaning fluid his father used in the bakery once a month to scour the floors and worktables. The combination of scents unsettled him, though he couldn't say why other than the odors irritated his nostrils to the point he had to rub his nose with the back of his hand. But the whole underground warren for witches had made his skin itch with a sort of aversion ever since they'd first entered the front door. The others showed no signs of discomfort, so he chalked up his reaction to his sheltered mortal upbringing.

"Best get to it," Yanis said, shoving a pair of notebooks toward Viktor.

Viktor and Josef both cracked open the leather-bound books in front of them. The date inside the copy Josef was given suggested Ava's notes were taken four years before he was born. But the date was as far as he got before it became obvious he wouldn't be able to read any further. "I can't make out more than a word or two. Not without a translator."

Viktor agreed and suggested they try using a spell to rearrange the letters before Yanis stopped him, claiming they weren't allowed to mark the notebooks.

"So how are we supposed to read the text?"

"Your instincts are correct," Yanis said to Viktor. "A spell is in order, but not one to alter the letters. One to alter the eye." The sorcerer took his fountain pen and drew a handful of geometric symbols on a piece of paper, then attached a word to each one. At least Josef believed they were words. Like the notebooks, the text was written in a language foreign to him. "These symbols work together like your incantations,"

Yanis said to Viktor. "Only we burn the paper they are written on and let their intention infiltrate the space to carry the magic."

Yanis folded the piece of paper four times until he made a small square, which he then held up before Viktor. "A small flame, if you will, glassmaker." Viktor snapped a spark to life on his fingertips and lit the paper on fire.

The edges glowed orange and black as the smoke rose. Yanis blew on the smoldering paper until it ignited. Josef narrowed his eyes as he watched the sorcerer hold the paper until the last of it burned to ash. Yanis then opened the small pouch of herbs he'd requested. He crushed the dried leaves between his palms, releasing a sharp, bitter aroma that stung the inside of Josef's nose momentarily.

"What is that stuff?" he asked, feeling his eyes water as he waved the scent away along with the smoke.

"It's only a bit of eyebright," Yanis said, looking perplexed by Josef's reaction. "Is it bothering you?"

"It's . . . sharp," he said.

"The herb will help us decode the language in the pages. We can't touch the books, but we can alter the eye to see better."

Before Josef could object, Yanis held his palm flat and blew the crushed herbs into the air. The powder formed a cloud with the smoke from the paper. The airborne mixture hit all three of them in the face, seeping into their lungs and watering their eyes.

Josef blinked and coughed into the crook of his elbow. When he looked again at the page before him, the handwritten words seemed to float just above the paper. And he could read and understand them. "How'd you do that?"

"Eyebright fools the eye," Yanis said, pulling a book closer for inspection. "The floating letters are only an illusion, but they've deciphered the language for us, much like the Lingua Franca spell did for the spoken word."

They'd been at it only a few moments when Viktor raised his hand. "I think I already found something," he said, moving his fingers in the air as though playing a quick scale on the piano. "These notes have to be over twenty years old," he said, flipping the book closed to look for a clue on the cover to support his guess. "It's not really a Book of Shadows. More like a diary from when she was at university."

"And?"

"There are a few paragraphs here that mention transformation theory." He scanned farther down the page as the crease between his brows deepened. "It's difficult to read Ava's handwriting through the effects of the translation spell, but I think it says 'blood moon'?"

Yanis spun the notebook around to try to decipher the line Viktor pointed to. "Blood *magic*," he said. "She's written about transformation being achieved through the use of a few drops of blood."

"That's a *g*?" Viktor squinted at the letter, then ran his finger down the page. "All right, but look at this," he said. "She's drawn a moon and sun. It says 'moon plus sun equals everything.' What does that mean?"

Josef tilted his head to read the page, baffled by the statement yet compelled to know what she meant as the hairs on his skin shivered beneath his clothing.

"Two halves of something make a whole?" Yanis asked, thinking out loud. "Night and day? Above and below the horizon?" He shook his head, unconvinced, and told Viktor to keep reading.

A tingle of foreboding traveled up the back of Josef's neck, spread to his face, and made his mouth salivate as Viktor read out loud.

October 1, 1888. Imperial University lecture. Professor Gruber.

~ When we talk about transformation, we do not refer simply to the physical jumbling of body parts. That does occur, but it is more subtle. The undertaking is more akin to art than science, once the spell invades the body. Limbs, livers, and spleens no longer conform to the mortal concept of biology. Bones and organs morph into pliable tissue that contorts into whatever form the witch predetermines (like a circus performer stuffing herself into a box that appears one-third her size). The predetermination is the most important part to get right. You must have a fixed image in your mind before casting the spell.

~ Before that, however, there is the issue of attaining the subject's blood. It must be drawn out—a drop or two is all that's needed—prior to any transformation spell. Therefore, this is one of the least recommended forms of defense if one does not have time to plan.

~ But can the blood and the spell be mixed at the same time? If blood can be drawn *while* defending oneself, is the spell still a viable option? And what about this newfangled electricity everyone is talking about? Conductivity is something that should be explored beyond blood. Both can carry energy! Professor Gruber does not consider all the possibilities. The other students just eat up his spoon-fed magic without question. Only Honza Stamitz seems to share my frustration with the professor's limited imagination.

—⁓—

October 8, 1888. Imperial University guest lecture by Augustus Brunner on the power source of spellwork, based on research done at the Libuše Society.

~ The occipital lobe is not inconsequential in the successful application of spells, but this is especially true in the case of transmogrification. The frontal and temporal sections of the brain play their part as well. The amygdala, however, is everything. Infiltrate that and your subject will no longer bear the wherewithal to resist the spell's intent. The pleasure principle, the tension between want and fulfillment, will relax and the illusion will implant itself in the occipital region. For the common witch, this is achieved through spoken incantation, visualization, and a subconscious channeling of the energy enveloping them, otherwise referred to as the aura. Advanced practitioners of the metaphysical arts, however, may find an easier and quicker method, especially if they intend to pursue the studies of transformation, electro transference, or spontaneous combustion. (Which I do!)

~ Recent studies have also concluded that a wand or similar implement works to concentrate the stream of spell energy. The prism effect of crystals, in particular, can hone the aim of one's magic down to a target range of a few centimeters, providing a sixfold boost in successful outcomes in the arts of defense and predetermined hexes. Given the small size of the aforementioned amygdala, a tool like this could only enhance one's chances of success. (What fool wouldn't want one?)

* Reminder to go to the Okkutladen to purchase six-sided crystal for walking stick!

"Let us hope Frau König's cure was not bound up in the crystal affixed to her walking stick," Yanis said.

Josef tried not to focus too long on the image of the woman's singed body after the tsar's mystic had shot her with a bolt of lightning, shattering the crystal wand in her hand. As it was, the smell of her incinerated skin and hair would haunt him the rest of his life.

He often didn't know what to make of this world he'd been cast into. König's notes on how to stun people with spells, or use their blood to transform them into animals, and magic wands that shoot hexes like bullets made him feel vulnerable. Afraid. As though he had no control over his own fate. Not when there were beings in the world who could come along at any moment with their curses and enchantments to turn his life upside down and empty his pockets of everything he ever thought was true.

But then there was Petra. And Yanis. Josef was amazed and astonished by the things they could do. Or that they even existed in this world. Viktor, too, with his ability to call fire casually onto his fingertips or draw down rays of moonlight. They'd taken him into this underworld where the extraordinary was commonplace. And now he found himself a part of it. A man who walked in two worlds. But how long could he expect to straddle the indefinable without risking falling into the abyss?

CHAPTER NINE

Petra was taken deeper into the alchemist tunnels to a small study located behind the laboratory. She couldn't see any farther, as the blackness was denser than any she'd encountered, yet she sensed the passageway continued, feeling its cool breath exhale in the beyond. Inside the room, she was instructed to sit on a green velvet settee. Martina closed a pair of curtains to give them some privacy from the rest of the underground facility while Augustus boiled water for tea over a small orb of green spellfire.

Martina sat on a cushioned chair opposite Petra. She held a notebook and a small leather carrying case on her lap like the one the doctor had brought to Petra's house after her father collapsed in his study. Martina undid the latch on the case and made a quick inventory of the items inside before setting it aside. "Are you comfortable?"

"I'm fine, thank you," Petra said, though she was far from all right. Every nerve ending under her skin told her this was going to be an unpleasant experience, a feeling that only increased every time Augustus Brunner smiled at her. But the longer she could keep them engaged in here with questions about herself, the longer Yanis, Viktor, and Josef had to dig through Ava's past notes without interference.

"Let's start with some simple questions," Augustus said, handing Petra a warm cup with floating leaves.

"Yes, for instance, when did you first know you had magical abilities?" Martina asked, leaning forward while her fountain pen hovered in her hand over a blank page.

When *did* she first notice? "I think I was three years old." Petra eased back on the settee to maintain a more comfortable distance between herself and her interrogators. "I remember it was laundry day. *Maminka* was pinning my father's clean shirts on the clothesline when one of them slipped free and fell in the dirt. She tried to brush it off, but it only made the stain worse. My mother started to cry, so I fixed the shirt for her."

"What do you mean by 'fixed'?" Augustus asked after blowing on his tea. "I know you were young, but can you be any more specific?"

Petra thought back to that morning. She'd not done magic before, and her mother had seemed ill prepared for when it emerged, clutching at the amulet she wore around her neck. "I tried to do what my mother had done. I shook the shirtsleeve to clean it, and all the dirt disappeared."

"Your mother is a mortal woman, is she not?" Martina asked without looking up from her writing.

"She was, yes." Petra let her eye fall on Martina's notebook as the woman wrote a half page of furiously detailed notes complete with a rough drawing of a man's soiled shirt.

Augustus cleared his throat and the woman finally glanced up, as though her mind had been in another room the whole time. "Oh, I am sorry," she said. "I didn't mean to be insensitive."

"Do you recall if you recited a spell, or did you conjure a picture in your head?" the man asked, getting off the subject of dead mothers. "Many young witches often begin with simple imagery."

Petra let an uncomfortable pause sit between them before answering. "Images do form in my mind, yes, but my magic has always been tactile, even then," she said before sniffing her tea. *Chamomile and lavender to calm me?* She sipped and changed the contents to espresso when it hit her lips. "I need to touch an object in order to alter it."

Martina gave a sidelong glance at her partner with a barely perceptible *I told you so* smirk. She wrote down more notes.

"What about later? Did your father encourage you to explore your world using your tactile magic?"

That had always been a yes-and-no answer. Sometimes when Petra's mother was away and it was just father and daughter, he would indulge her curiosity about her unique gift. Other times he made it clear she was not supposed to transform objects. Not in front of her mother or any other villagers. Only himself and members of his family. Namely, other witches.

"My father tutored me in magic when he could," Petra answered. "He'd let me read his books, and whenever *maminka* was away, we would practice changing objects. It seemed to make him happy whenever I did something I hadn't done before, and yet it was also a secret."

"Did he ever ask you to change objects into precious metals, for example?"

"Martina." Augustus chastised his coworker with a firm frown.

Petra studied the tension between the two. Both wanted to know the answer to the question, but only one had been willing to ask. "No, never."

A censured Martina asked, "What about other materials? What kind of objects did you practice on while you were younger?"

"Shoes, keys, dishes." Petra was getting bored. "It was fun at first to surprise my father with what I could do. I once turned his ladder into a small windmill, until he made me undo the transformation before anyone saw."

"Any chance we could have a small demonstration?" the woman asked.

Now was the time to be coy. "It doesn't always work," Petra said. "But I'll try." She rubbed one wrist and then the other. "What would you like to see me change?"

Martina was momentarily flummoxed while she looked around for a suitable object. "Will this do?" she asked, grabbing the teakettle.

"It's pure copper, a base metal, so whatever the exchange of energy, it ought to be a straightforward substitution." The last part she'd said to Augustus as though hoping to confirm some hypothesis.

"That will work." Petra set the kettle, still warm, on the marble table between them and cupped her hands around the belly, where water sloshed inside. She wanted to impress but not overdo it. Considering Martina's remark about base metals, Petra envisioned a blacksmith's fire in her mind's third eye and transformed the copper kettle into an iron mortar and pestle. The water that had been inside the kettle now filled the mortar to the brim.

Martina furiously scribbled down her observations in her note-book while Augustus examined the mortar by tapping on its side with the pestle as though listening for a particular sound. "It could still be copper disguised in an illusion," he said. Wearing a mask of indiffer-ence to hide his intentions, he dug in a drawer until he found what he was looking for: a horseshoe-shaped magnet. He returned and held the magnet near the metal, where it was immediately pulled to the side of the mortar. "It's iron," he said, testing the magnet's attraction again. "It's really iron."

Martina beamed at Petra before sketching a quick representation of the kettle's transformation in her book. When she was done, she clasped her hands together over the drawing. "Can you describe the sensation of changing objects? For instance, is there a burning feeling? Any pain involved?"

Petra rotated her wrist, noticing a slight ache that seemed to occur after each transformation lately. She'd ignored her magic for too long, and now her body was paying the price. "There's a tingling sensation," she said. "The magic flickers in my chest like a mini sunburst and then usually travels down my arms and through my fingers."

"You say 'usually'?"

"My skin needs to make contact with the object, but it doesn't have to be my fingers."

"And afterward? I noticed you flexing your wrist."

They really were watching everything. "I've just overdone it the last few days." She rotated her wrist one more time before pulling her hand inside her coat sleeve.

Martina pursed her lips and tilted her head slightly. "Do you mind if we take some physical samples for our studies now?"

Petra was curious to know just how intrusive their examination would be. "What kind of samples?"

Augustus took out a stethoscope, some intimidating calipers, and a pair of tiny scissors. "We'd like to get a sample of your blood, hair, and nails. Test your reflexes, both physical and metaphysical. Compare heartbeats before and after casting your magic. We'll swab your temples and wrists for perspiration." He held up the shiny metal instruments as if they were harmless party favors. "Perhaps a saliva test wouldn't be out of the question either. And then we'll look at it all under the microscope."

"Ours is lit with an aura amplifier," Martina added, in case that wasn't obvious.

Petra slid her hand forward on the table. There was nothing unusual to discover. She was almost certain of it. She'd always assumed her magic worked the way it did for the same reason her eyes were amber, her hair was brown, and she couldn't tolerate the taste of beets on her tongue: too metallic. Her traits, physical and metaphysical, were a matter of the genes she'd inherited from her father.

And yet, as Augustus snipped a half-moon of fingernail from her left hand and Martina plucked three hairs from the top of her head, she wondered what anomaly might show up on their instruments to explain her unique talent for manipulating matter. She supposed she'd been looking for some sort of answer all her life, or at least since her father—the one person who didn't think her magic strange—had died and left her to fend for herself alone among covetous witches and incurious mortals, all with the common gleam of avarice in their eyes.

CHAPTER TEN

The sun had come out and the café was busy with people eager to leave the house on a late winter afternoon. Josef felt almost himself again as he sliced off a large piece of schnitzel and tore into it with his teeth. Since his injury, his appetite had sometimes been difficult to control when there was no distraction to take his mind off the thought of meat. At certain times of the month, he craved the stuff until his mouth watered from the want. He hated to concede the behavior coincided with the phases of the moon. He'd been assured time and again by Hana that that part of his curse had been tamped out. Any killing instinct he had was purely human. And for the most part she'd been right. He experienced no overriding desire to maim or kill, but a residual influence remained, despite the witch's guarantees. One that left a craving on the tongue that could not be sated with a bowl of erbswurst. Given all the shortages that had hit the city since the start of the war, he'd been surprised to find a place that still had meat on the menu until Viktor informed him it was run by witches. He tore off another chunk and swallowed it down with pleasure, not caring if the meat was an illusion or a feast conjured by a master magician.

"They're hiding something," Yanis said. He inspected the breading on his meat with a knife and fork, seemingly unsure of what he'd just been served.

"What makes you say that?" Petra asked before Viktor could object about the characterization of his employers.

Yanis took a tentative bite of the schnitzel they'd ordered for him. He nodded to himself as though pleased before cutting off a bigger chunk, which he balanced on the end of his fork while he answered. "The cabinet that contained Ava König's notebooks. It was the only shelf out of twelve where the dust had been disturbed."

Viktor shook his head, confused. "Which means?"

"You think they sorted through the notes before we arrived?" Petra asked. She'd not eaten much, pushing her spoon around in her bowl of half-eaten goulash without taking a bite.

Viktor reached in his jacket for a folded-up newspaper he'd bought on the street. "What makes you think that?"

Yanis held up a finger while he swallowed. "Because none of the other cabinets had been opened recently before they allowed us in their library. Only the shelf containing Ava König's work. They wanted to make sure we wouldn't stumble on anything potentially problematic."

"We did find *some* useful information, though," Viktor said. "We saw how her mind works. How she thought about magic."

"But no notes on how to cure a vlkodlak," Josef said. He scraped his knife and fork over his empty plate to get the last crumbs of meat and potato. The whiff of garlic hit his nose. At first he assumed it was from the kitchen, but when it was paired with a distinct rose-scented perfume, he leaned back in his chair and nonchalantly checked the faces of the café patrons while the glassmaker folded his newspaper into a tight quarter section for easier reading.

"No, not yet," Viktor admitted. "But we didn't get through all the notebooks. Tomorrow we might find something we can use."

"Exactly," Yanis said, pointing the end of his fork at Viktor. "And that is why we also need to figure out where they are hiding the rest of her notes."

"The rest?"

"The ones you said they have referred to when doing other work in the lab."

"Did I say that?" Viktor slid his plate of devoured duck breast out of the way and leaned his newspaper against the table.

"You did," Yanis said. "And, in fact, there was a small gap on the middle shelf where it's possible a notebook or two were missing."

Petra slid her untouched bread toward Josef, who accepted with a nod. "They couldn't possibly house all her important writings here in the city," she said. "But I agree with Yanis. They're hiding something from us." She leaned forward to be discreet so the other diners wouldn't overhear. "I think they know a lot more than they let on about the curse König developed. Martina knew just from looking at Josef's eyes that he'd been afflicted. That can only mean they've read enough about her wolves to know they'd have a glint of moon shadow in their eye, or else they've seen the results of the curse for themselves. Up close."

Josef gave up his suspicions of the restaurant crowd when he found no familiar faces. "So why tell us we can have access to her notebooks if it's all a charade?" he asked.

"They obviously want to keep Petra coming in so they can learn her secrets," Yanis said. "She's why they tolerated us inside their lair today, but they won't actually share anything useful with us if they think they can get away with it. They're humoring us to get to her."

Petra folded her arms over her stomach. "I could refuse to let them study me anymore. That might shake free any documents they're keeping back from us."

"How did the, er, interview go, by the way?" Viktor asked.

"Not as bad as I'd imagined," she said. "But they were curious about everything. They even took a sample of my blood to look at under the microscope." She seemed to deflect from saying more by sipping her coffee. "At least they didn't attach any electrodes to my temples," she added with a shrug.

Josef recognized the inflection of hope in the lift of her shoulder. Something inside her had shifted. She'd lost some of her defensiveness. He'd experienced the same sort of reluctant curiosity to know more about the curse that afflicted him, too, once he accepted the premise that magic existed in the first place. Petra was apparently unique even among her own kind. All those years she had to wonder what was different about her and why. And even though she complained about the Society being intrusive, a part of her must also view their scrutiny as an opportunity to unearth a level of truth.

"They do have those," Viktor said, looking up from his newspaper. "The electrodes. They've done experiments with electricity before. I heard Augustus mention once that Ava König had the idea years ago that magic and electricity were related. Her notes today hinted at it."

"And?" Yanis asked.

"I never heard any more about it, but I think they did some experiments and found a connection," Viktor said. "But that's how they are. The researchers will follow all kinds of ideas just to see what they can discover. It's how their minds work."

Viktor ordered a cup of coffee from the waiter and shifted his attention back to his newspaper while the others finished eating. It was only a few minutes later when something he'd read made him hold his head in his hand, sweeping the hair back from his forehead. "Veles's blood," he said.

"What is it?" Josef leaned across the table to read the headline.

"Listen to this." Viktor cleared his throat. "A man was found dead last night after a brutal attack left him decapitated and half his torso eviscerated." Viktor stretched the newspaper out to read the rest of the article under the fold. "Authorities suspect a brown bear may have attacked the man as he walked home after visiting a well-known pub in town."

"Where was this?" Josef held his hand out to see the article for himself.

Viktor turned the paper around and tapped his finger on the name of the town. "Isn't that where we spent our first night on the road when we left for the front?" he asked. "We met Yanis in the café there."

"Could be just a coincidence," Josef said, scanning the article.

Yanis stabbed a chunk of meat and a potato together on his fork. "I'm not as familiar with the local wildlife as you are, but don't bears hibernate in the winter?"

"Another upír attack?" Viktor exhaled through his teeth like a man wanting to crawl back into a cave of denial.

Josef shook his head. "Upíri go for the throat, but they don't usually take a man's head off. And as Yanis pointed out, it's too early for bears to be out."

"So," Petra said, leaning in next to Josef to read the article for herself, "did the Order have a legitimate reason for wanting us to go back right away? Was this a vlkodlak attack? I'm such a fool. I should have listened and done what they'd said."

"Wait, this was one of König's monsters?" Viktor exhaled in disbelief, then whispered, "You think a vlkodlak killed this man?"

"We just passed the full moon, did we not?" Yanis cast his eyes to the sky. "But you're wrong to question our decision to come here, Petra. Even if we'd gone back like the Order wanted, it would have been nearly impossible to prevent the attack without knowing where there'd been other recent activity. It's part of the creatures' shifting nature. Once the moon passes, it becomes very difficult to cull them from the rest of the population. We can't be everywhere at once on the full moon. There was little we could have done to prevent this, if, indeed, it was a vlkodlak. Though I suppose there's an argument for the information we might have gathered from seeing the evidence for ourselves."

"Then what does the Order want us to do?"

"You have to remember that we work on shifting sand," Yanis said, pushing his plate away. "What was called for yesterday might prove shortsighted today. This mauling demonstrates there is an active casualty of the vlkodlak curse wandering around out there. Maybe more than one."

"If it was one of König's, it must have come from the fighting on the front. So how did he escape so quickly after the Empire's army retreated from the pass?" Viktor asked. "He'd have had to travel, what, nearly a hundred kilometers to get to that town? Is that normal—for a vlkodlak to move that fast in a day? How will we ever cover a range that wide to catch him?"

"Traveling that distance in a day would not be unusual for a creature like that," Josef said, handing the paper back to Viktor. "Using the wolf's agility is how I was able to get over the ridge to the tsar's camp and back in a night."

"How does the Order expect us to find something that can move that fast?" Viktor halfheartedly skimmed the information in the article again. "Even if we do uncover some useful methodology buried in the Society's library, we can't do much with it to stop any of them from changing, unless we can locate them. And we can't do that unless they attack and give away their position."

Yanis, with his half-priest, half-warrior demeanor, gently corrected them. "The cure isn't for them. It's for our friend Josef. The others, however many there are, are beyond our help. Trapping and killing them is our only option."

Josef and Yanis exchanged a look of brief acknowledgment at the truth of the matter.

"But to do that we do need to find the others first," Josef said. He rubbed his elbow, recalling the ache in his legs and arms the night before. The strain of the moon pulling on his blood like a riptide. Had he not been weaned off the worst parts of the curse, he too would have been out hunting to satisfy the wolf's lust. But while he did not suffer the curse's most extreme effects, he did share certain characteristics with those who became full vlkodlaci. Some he was ashamed to mention, but others might help them look a stranger in the eye and judge him by the gleam set there by magic. "Martina knew I was cursed by the glint of moon shadow in my eyes. Maybe it's something physical we can use to identify possible subjects."

"I'm not getting close enough to a vlkodlak to check the color of his eyes," Viktor said, folding the newspaper back up.

"It's not only the eyes that changed for me," Josef said. "There's the elevated sense of smell. An increase in strength. But there's also the intense need to run. None of it would be easy to hide from someone who knows to look for those particular traits in a man." Josef leaned forward on the table and kept his voice low so as not to be overheard. "If this proves to be one of König's beasts, then we know the whereabouts of at least one of her cursed men besides me. Now that he's killed, he shouldn't be so quick to move. He may even rejoin his comrades. I tried to return to my unit until it proved too difficult to fit in anymore as a mortal, knowing what I'd learned of your world. So we do what we can here with the time we have between now and the next moon, and then we track down any others we can find before they have the chance to kill again."

The others agreed as their plates were cleared from the table.

"Now what?" Petra asked when they reached the street.

The air was cold as the scents of the city hit Josef's nose in layers. The cooking smells always hit first, then the women's perfume, the animal scents below that, then lastly the grime on the street from people—with their dirty shoes, emptied bladders that were once full of beer, and their discarded cigarettes. He tried to locate the rose perfume scent again, but if it was there, it had been overpowered by the rest.

"Another member of the Order makes their home here," Yanis said, wrapping his robes closed. "I need to drop in and let him know we're here and see if he has any advice on our mission going forward."

"Is it far?" Petra asked. "Do you want us to come along to help you find it?"

"No, no, I'm quite all right on my own in the city."

"And I have to go check in on my sister," Viktor said. "Should probably let her know I'm still alive. I'll see you back at the storeroom."

The two men took off in different directions, leaving Josef and Petra standing on the sidewalk alone.

"What about you?" Petra asked. "Don't you need to let your family know you're all right?"

Josef shook his head and shoved his hands in his pockets. "I saw my parents and sister at the bakery the morning we left for the front," he said, giving a nod toward their shop a few lanes over. "What about you?" he asked and immediately regretted it. Her husband had died in the war, something she'd discovered only days before. He knew nothing of the man, nothing about their relationship, but he didn't mean to be so tactless.

Petra fidgeted with her coat buttons, taking her time before having to face the chilly air. "There is someone I should go see, but I'm avoiding it."

She said no more, so the pair strolled away from the café, following the narrow lane together—hands in pockets, their breath rising in the cold air, arms bumping together every couple of steps they took. They did not travel in the direction that would lead them directly back to the storeroom. The thought of going back there alone with Petra set off a flare in Josef's chest. Fear, desire, hunger. The urges conflated sometimes until he lost track of which instinct he should follow. Which one was the right thing to do in the moment. Instead, he was relieved when they simply let the flow of the medieval streets guide their steps, passing jewelry shops and milliners closing for the day, and restaurants just opening their doors for the evening crowd.

"Is it your husband's family you're avoiding?" Josef asked after the silence grew too long between them.

Petra nodded. "I'm afraid to tell them what little I know about Marek's death. They're apt to call me a liar and slam the door in my face." She waited until a man in a bowler hat passed before she added, "They don't know about my . . . abilities. They wouldn't understand how I could know a thing like that when the army doesn't."

"I could go with you, if you think it would help." Again Josef regretted his mouth uttering words that were better left unsaid.

Petra stopped and looked him in the eye. Her lips were on the verge of accepting his offer, but then her mind seemed to catch up to the reality of how that might look and stifled the impulse. "Major Bako put in an official request to uncover the details of Marek's death. The army will send a telegram to his parents once they sort it out, won't they? They'll let them know? After that, I can go see them."

Josef assured her the army would notify the family, but he didn't tell her it may take months or years for them to discover the truth of who died fighting the tsar's army in the winter mountains. The men wore metal tags around their necks to identify them, but the system was only as good as the man who found your body and recorded your tag number before you were dumped in the earth for a quick burial. "They'll let them know what happened to their son as soon as they know."

Petra chewed her thumbnail. Guilt? Habit? Or was it just plain worry? Josef gently placed his hand on her back and directed her across the cobblestones to the other side of the street. They were near the river now. The noise of trams rolling over the old king's bridge always made him feel at ease. At home. He was glad the group had returned to the city, even if their time there would be brief. No one knew what the next day would bring in wartime. Long-term plans were for optimistic fools, so you learned to suck the juice out of the good here-and-now moments.

"Do you think Major Bako made it out with the others?" Petra asked somewhat randomly.

They'd seen him driving behind the convoy of trucks retreating from the mountains as they flew home. They had no way to get in touch with the hussar who'd fought with them in the mountains, but Josef didn't doubt their comrade would survive. "If anyone could make that drive alone, it's Bako."

A small boat passed between arches under the bridge. The pair leaned against the railing overlooking the river to watch it float by when Petra removed her camera from her pocket. The handheld device had endured the trip to the eastern front despite the bitter cold, battles with the upíri who'd infiltrated the soldiers' ranks, and a confrontation with a crazed zduhać intent on selling her to the highest bidder. In fact, the camera was her only possession to survive the ordeal. As she enjoyed the familiar feel of the camera in her hands again, her intuition flared, her eye focusing on the riverbank below as she extended the lens and snapped a photo.

"Is there someone there?" Josef asked, squinting through the twi-light as though he might make out the outline of the unseen entity walking along the water's edge. He saw nothing, but he thought he, too, felt a small thread of electricity in the air just before the faintest trace of rose perfume reemerged.

"Yes, but I won't know who they are until I'm able to develop the film," Petra said. "But who knows when that will be again." She put the camera away and cleared her throat. "By the way, I took your photo," she said in a tone bearing the weight of a confession.

"You did?" The only photo he could remember her taking was when she'd wished to commemorate their newly formed group. When Karl and Dragoş were just two more recruits he'd picked up on the streets of the city to fight the upíri. "When was this?" he asked.

"That day at the café. Before we climbed into the truck and drove to the front."

Josef was confused. Why was she confessing something they both already knew? He turned from the railing to face her. "Why are you mentioning it now as if it was a secret?"

She stared at him hard, as though daring herself to peer into his eyes and beyond to something deeper inside. "The flecks of moon shadow," she said, moving closer with her lips slightly parted. Her gaze softened, and he felt his abdomen tighten. "I see them now. Like silver sparks. That must be what showed up on the photograph as eyeshine. When I first saw it, I thought—"

"You thought I was upír like the others in the photographs?" He didn't know why, but he found the revelation amusing. He was a mon-ster, yes, but not a throat-ripping killer. *The thoughts she must have had about me.* And yet maybe he was fooling himself. He swallowed a lump in his chest. After all, he was only one dose of elixir away from becom-ing the thing she'd once feared about him.

"At first I did," she confessed. "But then it became obvious there was no light in *their* eyes. It was merely the moonlight reflecting off a flat surface behind their irises."

"And mine?"

"Yours? Oh, I think they still shine from within," she said.

With little regard for where they stood or who was nearby, he had the strongest urge to lean in and kiss her. He nearly acted on it when he spied the couple from the night before out of the corner of his eye. They stood on the bridge, leaning against the railing. They'd thought the life-size bronze statue of a saint would hide them, but Josef's eyes were sharper than most.

"Did I say something wrong?" Petra asked.

Josef caught himself glaring at the bridge with a desire to leap over the barriers and take the couple by the throat until they confessed they were following him. "No, no, of course not," he said, still distracted by the sudden intrusion. There was no more coincidence about it. The pair had been following him. "Would you mind if we walk some more? I need to stretch my legs."

"It's hard for you to stay still for long, isn't it?"

"One of the unfortunate side effects of being bitten by a cursed wolf." He held out his arm and she took it, resting her hand in the crook of his elbow as they veered back toward the center of the Old Town district. The king's road was still busy with pedestrians and traffic, far too busy for what he had in mind, so he suggested they cut through a small, winding side street where his mother had once made him take piano lessons. The lane was barely wide enough for two couples to pass each other without one stepping out of the other's way. Just before they made the turn, he caught sight of the man's bowler hat half a block behind them in the reflection of a store window.

Petra glanced over her shoulder. "You're distracted by something."

"Keep walking forward. Don't look back again."

She gripped his arm a little tighter. "What's going on?"

"Do you have a weapon on you?"

"No. Do I need one?"

"Here, take my knife, but don't let go of my arm," he said, reaching under his coat to slip the handle into her free hand while their bodies shielded the exchange.

"Who is it?" she asked.

Josef leaned his head closer to Petra's, as though they enjoyed lovers' talk. If the other couple could pretend, so could he. "The man in the bowler hat and the woman in the fur wrap that looks like a wolfskin. They've been following me around the city for two days now."

"Who are they? What do they want?" Petra asked. She'd instinctively changed her gait to walk more like a woman in love, with an idle coquettish stride that had her leaning into him every few steps. He half wished it were for real.

"No idea, but we're about to find out," he said. "Be ready." He nudged her through an archway into a small courtyard, where he hoped pan Jenik would not look down from his second-floor window to see his former pupil encouraging a young woman to hide in a darkened alcove. He slipped his ushanka off as the small hairs on his back prickled with anticipation, waiting to see if the man and woman followed around the corner.

He detected their footsteps getting nearer as their scent moved in like fog. He squeezed in against Petra in the alcove until their bodies were pressed together, whispering in her ear to remain silent.

"Where'd he go?" the woman in the courtyard whispered. The man replied by flicking open a spring-loaded knife.

Josef waited until the couple passed by them in the alcove. Carefully and quietly he backed into the courtyard, knowing he had them bottled up between him and the archway leading back out.

"Call me paranoid, but I get the feeling you've been following me." Josef stood with his long coat open and his pistol drawn as the pair spun around three meters in front of him. They immediately separated so he could aim his gun at only one of them at a time. He chose the man.

"Where's your lady friend?" the woman asked, moving farther to his right.

Josef ignored her and spoke to the man. "Drop the knife on the ground."

The man did as he was told and raised his hands in the air. The woman stood unperturbed.

"What do you want with me?"

"Your head." The man gave a small shrug. "Orders."

Josef was confused until the woman lifted the tail of her fur wrap to reveal a juvenile wolf's head resting against her chest beneath it. Clamped in its teeth was a photo of him stamped König's, with an order to kill printed below it. "Bounty hunters?" he asked.

"Word went out two days ago," the man said. "Nice spot of luck seeing you walk down the lane in that fur hat soon after."

"He's not a vlkodlak!" Petra had stepped out of the alcove to stand behind him.

"Our employer doesn't split hairs." The woman snapped her teeth at them.

Josef nearly succumbed to the urge to transform and rip his claws into the pair. He had to steady the gun with both hands until the wave passed. "I need you to back up against the far wall," he said, raising the barrel of the pistol so it was level with the man's head. "Both of you."

"Can't do that," the man said. A shimmering wall of energy rose up like a curtain to surround the four of them inside the courtyard.

Josef turned his head slightly to speak to Petra. "What's he doing?"

"He's building a spell wall around us so no mortals will see what he's about to do to us," she said, but her voice was steady. Calm. He tried to remain the same.

The man laughed. But the woman merely sneered and pushed her sleeve up to reveal a miniature crossbow attached to her arm with a single arrow primed for release. Petra walked up beside Josef, holding his knife out in front of her like it was some kind of torch. His confidence that they might walk out of the situation in one piece sank. He turned his gun on the woman, staring her down. But then Petra stepped between them. The knife in her hand transformed into a black walking stick with a crystal on top. Ava König's wand.

The woman gasped. Petra lowered the crystal tip and the man dropped his arms, stretching his hands out in front of him to defend himself. The woman brought her arm up, but before she could release the arrow, Petra sent a stream of hot, white electricity shooting out from the crystal. It forked in two, zapping the man and the woman at once. Both were thrown back and knocked to the ground. The spell wall the man had created swirled once, then collapsed.

Josef gaped at Petra. "Are they dead?" He did a quick search of the apartment windows above, but no one raised their shade to investigate.

Petra knelt beside the woman, pressing her fingers against her neck. "Still alive," she said. "But we should probably go before anyone sees us." She changed the walking stick back into a knife and returned it to him.

Josef snatched the photo of himself out of the wolf's teeth. The Order hadn't wasted any time. Now that König was dead and all hope of a cure forgotten, he'd been tossed in with the beasts and killers. How long before the real huntsmen—men like Yanis—came for him?

CHAPTER ELEVEN

Petra's skin thrummed from the contact with the replica of König's wand in her hands.

"How did you know to do that?" Josef asked as they hurried down the narrow lane before anyone associated them with the two bodies in the courtyard.

"I once saw Ava use her wand to incinerate a man. I knew I could channel my energy through the crystal to do more with it than a mere spell thrown at them."

"That's what we read about in König's notes today," Josef said, leading them around the corner. "That's the whole reason why she bought the crystal for her walking stick—to increase her power."

"I think her reputation preceded me. Did you see the look on that man's face when I produced the wand?"

"I thought he was going to trip over himself trying to get away from you."

Petra laughed as they clasped hands and ran the rest of the way to the main square.

Out of breath, Petra begged Josef to stop for a minute. She leaned against the base of the newly erected statue on the far side of the square, laughing and holding her side until the ache there subsided.

"A dissenter and a rebel," Josef said, with a nod of approval toward the man idealized in bronze behind them.

Petra glanced up, admiring the fierce stare of resistance in the martyr's demeanor. "Burned at the stake, the way I heard it." She let out a breath and looked up at the stars. Josef did the same, but when he lowered his head again, the starlight still reflected from the flecks in his irises. *Silver* flecks, she noted. Her back straightened with the revelation. "Your eyes," she said, considering his glittering feature from a different angle. "The color is more subtle in the daytime."

He blinked, aware something had shifted between them. "Um . . . it is?"

"That's what the film picked up on," she said, following her train of thought. "Or at least with the help of my magic it did." She turned his face toward her and peered into his eyes while the moon was at her back. "The flecks fade when the sun is out, but under the moon, they're much more striking."

And beautiful.

"Petra, what are you doing?" He glanced at the people who passed as though he were embarrassed to have them see a woman hold his face so publicly.

"The flecks are silver. Like the moon." She let go of his chin, still drawn by the revelation and the lure she found there. "All this alchemy talk makes me wonder if there's some connection between the moon, the sun, and the silver in your eyes."

"Just one more mystery of the curse, I suppose." Obviously disinterested in her hypothesis, Josef stood and pulled his collar up before suggesting they return to the storeroom. "The others ought to be back by now. We need to return and tell them what happened."

Feeling a slight sting of rejection at her idea, Petra deliberately walked at a martyr's pace, forcing Josef to either drag his feet in annoyance or go ahead without her. When they arrived back at the storeroom five minutes later, they found the door open a crack. With no lights on and no sign the others had returned, Josef put an arm in front of her and told her to stay back.

"A break-in?" she whispered.

Josef removed the pistol from his belt. He swung the door open, making as little noise as possible. Before he switched the light on, Petra's eyes saw in the darkness what had happened. The mattresses and bedding had been flipped over and sliced open, the shelves where they kept their meager supplies had been rummaged through, and Josef's uncle's stored cartons of candles and coffee had been gutted down the middle and their contents spilled on the floor.

"Was it them? The couple in the courtyard?"

Josef shook his head, unsure. "Whoever they were, they were looking for something." He checked the water closet to make sure there wasn't an intruder still hiding somewhere. When he came out, he picked up a soiled mattress covered in coffee grounds.

"Your uncle?" Petra asked. "Could he have come by, thinking someone was squatting?"

"Uh, I don't think it was the uncle." Viktor, back from visiting his sister, stood on the threshold, examining the damaged doorjamb. "Looks like the door was kicked in." He set his satchel down and entered the room with the same look of disbelief Petra had minutes earlier. "Are you two all right?"

"We're fine," Josef said. "We only just returned ourselves."

Petra repaired the damaged mattress with a swipe of her hand. "What could they have been looking for? Money?" She let her fingers find the gold ducat sunk deep in her pocket.

"Hard to believe anyone would think four people crowded into a storeroom would have anything worth stealing," Viktor said. He righted the small kitchen table and set the broken cups on top.

"What's happened here?" Yanis slipped inside the door as Viktor had, having just returned from his trip across the city. His face was flushed from a long walk in the night air as he took in the frenzied destruction.

"Someone kicked their way in," Petra said. She closed the door behind Yanis and studied the doorjamb a second before repairing the splintered wood by running a finger along the edge.

"Was anything taken?" the sorcerer asked, seemingly as surprised as the rest of them that anyone would think they had anything of value.

"Anyone missing anything?" Josef asked. He'd reverted to using his scowling warrior face again, as he had nearly every day while they'd been encamped in the upíri-infested mountains.

When everyone shook their heads, Yanis swept the room with his eyes. "Then they were looking for something besides valuables. Something they thought only we would have."

"But no one even knows we're here." Viktor checked the street through the curtains covering the one small window.

"Perhaps an opportunistic thief, then, but that feels a little too random to me." The sorcerer set his satchel down on a wooden chair. "There was real desperation to find whatever it was they were searching for." He picked up two pieces of a broken plate. "Rage when they didn't find it."

"That's not all," Josef said. "A man and woman started following me yesterday. I wasn't sure at first, but Petra and I just confronted them in a courtyard."

Viktor picked up a white shirt of his that had been shredded down the back. "You think they did this?" His expression suggested he questioned the motive for ruining a perfectly good shirt.

"I don't, actually," Josef said, shaking his head. "These people weren't looking to steal anything."

"Then what did they want?"

"My head." Josef reached in his coat for the photo he'd taken off the woman and tossed it on the table next to Yanis. "Know anything about this?"

Yanis cleared his throat after barely looking at the photo. Most people would be afraid of Josef's mood, but the sorcerer calmly handed the photo back and said, "It's a kill order."

"A what?" Viktor dropped his shredded shirt and came over to see the photo.

"A kill order," Yanis repeated.

"I'm guessing it means we're not the only team who were given orders to destroy König's vlkodlaci."

Petra tugged on the sorcerer's sleeve. "Is that true?"

Yanis righted a chair and sat down. "There was a general order given, yes. Josef is one of the few cursed men they can identify by face and name. But as I said, I went to go see another member of the Order who lives in the city tonight. My superior, actually. I went there to explain Josef's unique position. About the elixir. About how he's been cursed and yet also works with us against the undead. Knowing there is a possible cure, he's agreed to rescind the directive. For now."

"Which means until the next full moon," Josef said.

The sorcerer swept broken glass off the tabletop into a bin. "Correct."

"Then tell me who trashed the place." Viktor held up his last clean pair of trousers and shook his head at the grimy boot print on them.

"Whoever did this wasn't looking to kill anyone. They were after something of value." Yanis surveyed the damage until his eyes landed on Petra. "And yet the only thing of any substantial value in this room is what she is able to do."

"Well, I don't think they were searching for Petra inside this," Viktor pointed out, flipping his shredded mattress over.

"Which suggests they sought something small and tangible," Yanis said with a shrug. "Something of some worth that could be hidden inside something else. And yet we remain ignorant of what it could be."

"So, maybe it's something they expected us to have, but we don't," Petra said. "Which suggests someone knows more about our visit to the city than we do."

And while Petra agreed the thief had to have been looking for an object, she couldn't help feeling she might still be the target of the break-in as the sorcerer suggested. She touched the cool gold in her pocket. The ducat was worth something, yes, but it was the magic that created it that had already proven a thing worth stealing.

And yet it wasn't just the break-in, or the attack in the courtyard, that had Petra on edge. She'd been on the verge of uncovering something interesting in Josef's eyes earlier. There was a connection between his curse and this alchemist business they'd been digging up. Something that swam in the subconscious of her intuition. A notion that recognized the significance of the silver in his eyes against the moonlight. But there was another connection just as mysterious: the curious way she felt after staring into those eyes.

CHAPTER TWELVE

Josef stared at another of Ava König's notebooks, thinking about what Petra had said about his eyes the night before. He'd never been one to lose control of his heart easily, but when she'd grabbed his chin in the public square and stared into his eyes, something restless had passed between them.

Friends he'd known at school could gawp at a girl's silky hair tied up in ribbons, slobber over a peek at her ankle beneath her skirt, prop their chins in their hands and watch a girl flutter her eyelashes at them, and then proclaim their undying love for her. And while he appreciated a pretty face as much as any man, he'd always wondered if his friends were afflicted with some veil behind the eyes that prevented them from seeing through the artifice of certain attractions. He'd rarely pursued the girls at school. Klára had been his main exception. She'd had a brooding outlook on life that he'd found entertaining in someone as young as himself. He'd brought her summer flowers tied with ribbon and sweet, fruit-filled *koláče* from his parents' bakery, and she'd read him poetry from a leather-bound book she carried with her everywhere. They spent a summer of easy evenings dedicated to each other until Klára got sick and died of consumption later that winter.

His mother had called him merely circumspect when it came to other young women after that. "Josef," she said as she kneaded the soft, white dough with her hands covered in flour to her wrists. "You may not fall in love with the next girl you meet, or even the one after that, but you, my son, will marry well." His mother could not have known that he would one day go off to war, only to be injured and maimed with an injury like no other. A curse that had embedded a noticeable glint in his eye and a splinter of resentment in his heart. One he may never be rid of, now that the emperor's witch was dead.

But then he'd met Petra. First through a story about her and then in a hidden courtyard not five streets away from where he'd grown up, when he'd gone to convince her to join a somewhat doomed mission to fight the undead. He'd felt no real attraction to her at first. After all, she was married and belonged to another. Besides, he'd already been down the long trail of thought about his life that had led him to believe there was little hope for a man forced to spend a good amount of time as a four-footed beast. But if he could find love, a witch might have an inkling of understanding of the creature he'd become. And if not, then perhaps it no longer mattered if they found a cure in a dead witch's notebooks. But as Klára had taught him from reading her poetry books, hope was the thing that perched in the heart, waiting to take wing.

"The trick is to get the heat right," Yanis said.

Beside him, the sorcerer used a pair of tongs to hold a glass beaker over a gas burner to warm a mixture of herbs. The smell was nearly a match to what Hana's elixir had tasted like—the bitter green-weed flavor that set the saliva glands watering—but something was still missing. The sorcerer added a pinch of some dried brown leaf and nodded.

"I only saw Valentina make her aunt's potion the one time," Yanis said. "It may yet take some trial and error to get the right proportions of herbs." Smoke swelled in the belly of the beaker until it rose through the neck and burped. "And too," he said, waving away the foul stench left behind, "she may have deliberately left something out of the recipe to protect her aunt's creation while I watched her make it."

Petra studied the ingredients laid out on the table that the sorcerer had requested from the Society's stores. "König said Hana used a small dose of the wolf's blood to inoculate Josef, which we don't have."

"What exactly would that do?" Viktor asked. He'd been reading and taking notes, not paying much attention to the potion-making when he looked up at the mention of inoculation.

"It would desensitize him somewhat to whatever triggers the transformation," Yanis said. "The part that's carried in the blood to transmit the curse. I'm not sure how to compensate for that in potion form."

Viktor lifted his glasses and rested them on top of his head. "It's just that I was reading Ava's second-year notes on a transmogrification class she took. There's a part here where she talks about full transformation versus illusion." He looked at Petra. "She mentions your father again too."

"My father?" Petra reached for the notebook. She leaned close enough to Josef that their shoulders met, and they read the passage together.

November 7, 1888. Imperial University Lecture on Transmogrification with Professor Gruber.

- Honza is right. These professors are all talk and little action. If they tried half the spells that they advocate for inducing transformation on themselves, they'd wind up with a crooked spine and covered in scales. Blood is the key. Not just a drop or two, but taking full advantage of the five liters in the body. It already carries the information through the body on a continuous cycle. Like a tram car following its route around the city all day long, only the blood never has to make unnecessary stops. It pumps and pumps and pumps. All the latest research points to this. They're right, the subject's flesh, bone, and mind must be altered with the spell's intention, of course, but why would the spellcaster wish to bypass the circulatory system when it will do all the work for them, no illusion necessary?

Honza was one of the first to recognize the importance of the subject's natural biology in implementing sustainable transformation. Finding the right vehicle to carry the spell through the blood, however, is proving the biggest hurdle witches face when it comes to mastery of transmogrification. But I've no doubt it can be done. Honza is already experimenting with different elements. One of us will unlock the magic!

Petra ran her finger down to the bottom of the handwritten page. "She gives my father credit for being on the verge of some discovery, but he never talked about knowing any transformation spells. At least, he didn't with me."

"I think Ava had an eye for your father," Viktor said, turning the notebook back around to face him. "After second year, she mentions him almost every day."

Petra's and Josef's eyes met. "Maybe they worked closely together on some project," Josef said.

"They did," Martina said from the doorway. "Here in this very room." The alchemist stood with her arms folded, leaning against the jamb. Almost as though she were trying to hide the gloves she was wearing.

Petra straightened. "I don't understand. My father never worked here."

"Oh, but he did, though you may have been too young to remember your time in the city. He left for the quiet countryside when you were just a smidge of a girl." Martina hugged her middle and stared at the toe of her shoe. "A small controversy brewed up during his appointment here. Accusations. Never proven, but nonetheless he decided to leave the Society for the good of his name. It's why I didn't mention it earlier. In case you didn't know."

Josef could see Petra struggling with the new information. Her eyes stared at the wall as she tried to remember, hoping to find a clue in her memory that supported what the woman was telling her.

"Come with me," Martina said, extending a gloved hand to Petra. "I'll show you. In fact, it may even prove useful to your endeavor here, now that you've discovered the bond Ava and Honza shared."

Josef tapped Petra's shoulder to say they were all going with her. They followed the woman through a maze of hallways until they came to a door none of them had been shown before. Inside, the room was lit with soft lamplight that reminded Josef of his *babička's* house—always dark, always dusty, but full of books. Curtains on the walls suggested faux windows, while four fat upholstered chairs had been arranged in a circle over a plush rug. A celestial globe on a wooden stand glowed in the corner. Martina ran her finger over the leather and cloth spines of the books lining a built-in shelf. She stopped with her back to them and pried a volume loose from the others. She turned around and fanned the pages open to reveal several diagrams inside.

Petra gasped. "My father's grimoire. I recognize the drawings. His handwriting." She looked up at Martina in disbelief, as though the researcher had somehow resurrected the man himself. "How did you get his book of spells?"

"It was brought to our attention after your father's untimely death. The authorities naturally contacted us, once they understood they were dealing with a member of the supernatural community," she said, taking a sniff of the book's cover. "You can still smell Honza's pipe smoke embedded in the leather."

Josef thought she might be exaggerating. His nose detected only the scent of brittle paper and dust, but he kept his thoughts to himself as Petra closed her eyes and held the book to her face. She inhaled and almost immediately wept.

"It's him," she said, wiping a spent tear from her cheek with her sleeve. "It's my father."

Martina helped Petra settle on one of the soft chairs, making a soft tutting sound with her tongue. While her back was turned, Yanis examined the rest of the bookshelf, tilting his head to read the titles on the spines.

Josef reached for his handkerchief and handed it to Petra as he knelt beside her chair. He regretted it had been in his pocket through weeks of travel on the road and fighting upíri in the mountains, but she quietly changed it from a square of rough linen to a soft cotton cloth anyway and dabbed her eyes.

"So, what was it about the book you wished to show her?" Yanis asked, prying himself away from the shelf.

"Ah, yes. May I?" Martina held her hands out to Petra, who reluctantly surrendered the book after flipping through all the pages.

Viktor rubbed his hands together the way he did when he was about to create a ball of fire to read by, but Martina gave him a mild scolding with a twitch of her finger and told him to fetch an oil lamp instead. "Viktor is very trustworthy with fire, but in this room, we don't take any unnecessary risks."

"You have many one-of-a-kind copies of grimoires and codices housed here," Yanis said. "*The Book of Ancient Talismans and Amulets*. I haven't seen a copy of that one since I was an acolyte with the Order."

"We have many rare books indeed," Martina said, sitting in the chair beside Petra. "But what I wanted to share with you was this passage in Honza's spell book." She carefully turned the pages of the grimoire until she came to a section with drawings of beakers connected by elaborate glass tubing. She called the bottles "alembics" as she pointed to the flow from the first bottle to the last. There, the artist had drawn lines radiating around the final product, the way children draw the sun with lines to show how bright it is.

"What is the drawing referring to?" Petra asked.

"Read the ingredients," Martina said, pointing to the notes below. "It's instructions for a potion your father was working on. This symbol, with the circles and triangles, tells us it is related to transmutation or change, so there might be parts of it that are transferable to what you're trying to achieve."

Petra read the passage with her lips moving as she scanned her father's handwriting. She tapped her finger on the diagram when she was finished. "She's right. I think there might be a solution to at least part of our problem. My father talks about the power of using blood in certain spells."

Viktor agreed. "That's what Ava wrote too."

"But," Petra added, "he says that if the required blood isn't available, the distillation process can provide a reasonable substitute using hair, nails, or even saliva."

"In Josef's case, that would still mean having access to the host animal, which we don't." Yanis scratched his chin as though thinking about how he might circumvent that requirement to make the potion.

"You mean like its fur?" Josef pulled the folded-up ushanka out of his coat. "Hana instructed the men who shot the vlkodlak that bit me to make a hat out of his fur. She told me to keep it and wear it as a reminder of what I might become."

"Perhaps there was more to Hana's instructions than mere life advice," Yanis said, picking up the hat to feel the fur between his thumb and finger.

"Distilling the essence from a few hairs off the host animal might work as a substitution, though it's possible it would be less potent," Martina warned. She held her hand out for the grimoire. "Worth a try, though."

Petra's fingers lingered on the book, as if she did not wish to let it go. She stroked the cover, flipped through the pages again, then took a final sniff of the leather before handing it over. "Thank you," she said.

"Anytime you would like to see it again, just ask," Martina said. "I'd be happy to escort you to the library."

There was a slight tremor in Petra's shoulders, as though she shook off a shiver under the collar. Josef let his eyes roam around the room, wondering whose ghosts prowled the deep halls of the alchemists' lair to give her such a chill.

CHAPTER THIRTEEN

Petra desperately wanted to go with the others back to the lab to try out the distillation process. Instead, she was directed to return to the lab room with Martina, where Augustus waited for them with a request to conduct more examinations. Before being forced to part from the others, she sidled up to Josef, close enough that their hips touched, and slipped her hand in his coat pocket. She punctuated the brief encounter with a meaningful look in his eyes when he nearly questioned the move in front of the others. "Good luck," she said. He patted his pocket and raised an eyebrow at her before leaving with the others. The slightly confused grin on his face was worth all the risk.

Resigned to submitting to more interrogation, Petra returned to the lab where Augustus had set up a large microscope with a faint blue light hovering around the base. She took her usual seat and accepted a cup of tea when one was offered, feeling the notable absence from her now empty coat pocket.

"Ah, I'm glad you're here," Augustus said, looking up from his worktable. "I have some interesting results to share with you concerning the samples we took yesterday."

Martina sat on the edge of her seat to await the news with an eager, open face. Petra, too, was curious, but more reserved about what to expect. After all, what could something too small to be seen with the human eye reveal about anything?

Augustus passed out a sheet of paper with typewritten notes on it. "You'll notice the hair samples were completely normal for someone of your age and gender; however, there was one slight inconsistency I'd like to follow up on."

"Yes?" Martina asked. She held her fingers interlaced tightly together in her lap like a woman bracing for bad news.

"What is it?" Petra asked when the researcher seemed to lose his nerve.

"It's delicate," he said. "You see, all mammals have hair or fur, as you know. Human hair is different from a dog, or a cat, or a goat. You can see the difference with the microscope. Here, I'll show you." Augustus led Petra to his worktable. He slipped a glass slide on the microscope's platform where the lens magnified the object, while Petra pressed her eye to the other lens at the top. Once things came into focus, she saw three distinct hairs of different thicknesses. At least, she assumed they were hairs. Each looked like a sample of rope under the magnification, with some of them appearing frayed.

"And *my* hair?" she asked, lifting her head to read his expression.

"Well, with mortals it's all very straightforward," he said as he switched the slides. "Their hair is very ordinary. There is no shimmer or shine. Mere functionality." Petra looked at the example he'd given her through the microscope. The hair resembled rubber tubing like a bicycle tire. "But," he said, barely able to conceal the thrill of discovery, "a witch's hair will have small traces of illumination. A result of the minor current flowing through our bodies. It's rather new research, but it appears electrical impulses within the body work as a conduit for our magic. For creating fire, et cetera." When Petra scrunched up her nose in confusion, he added, "Oh, yes, it's quite proven. We all have electrons floating through our bodies." He tilted his head from side to side. "Positive. Negative. But witches even more so."

Petra pulled at the strands of hair that had come loose from her bun, trying to see with her eye the things he was talking about.

"It's important to understand, however, we witches are not as common in the world as mortals for a reason. Our traits are recessive, which makes them much rarer."

"Less likely to be passed on," she said, seeing his logic. It was part of why witches had to learn to protect themselves by keeping a low profile, by agreeing to hundred-year-old covenants that restricted their power, and, sometimes, by marrying mortals to lend them cover.

"For whatever reason, certain mortal traits are dominant," Augustus said. "Therefore, if a witch and mortal create a child together, the mortal traits, for example in their hair, would present as lackluster, even if she's born a witch." Petra nodded along with the explanation, waiting for him to make his larger point. "But if two witches produce a child, their offspring will carry both their ensorcelled genes." He slipped a new slide under the microscope. "And, in that case, their child's hair would have the sparkle of magic embedded in the strands."

Petra looked through the eyepiece and saw exactly what he was talking about. The hair had small threads that shimmered throughout. It was remarkable the way the luminescence was embedded in the hair. She squinted at the sample, a little envious of its brilliant shine. "So my hair is one of the dull ones," she said, lifting her head again.

"No, my dear, that is my point." Augustus gestured to the slide under the microscope. "*That* strand is the sample we took from you."

Martina gasped and covered her mouth with her hand to silence her surprise.

Petra was confused after the explanation he'd just given. "There must be a mistake," she said. "My mother was a mortal, so shouldn't my hair be dull?"

"I've devoted my life to magic," the researcher said. "To discovering its origins, its characteristics, its secrets. But, like my predecessors, I've done that, in part, by relying on the validity of science. Something that can be proven through testing. That's why I'm confident in saying your mother and father were both witches."

"That would go a long way toward explaining why your magic manifests as it does," Martina said, staring at Petra as though a missing puzzle piece had suddenly fallen into place. "And perhaps how you came to possess such a unique talent."

"But that's impossible." Petra knew who her mother was. From her earliest memory, her mother had been there. "I look just like my mother's side of the family. I have her nose, her eyes."

"But not her magic."

Martina's remark slid between Petra's ribs like a hot knife. No, her mother had been a mortal. A woman with no magic who'd been left alone with a young daughter after her husband died. A woman who had only her wits to live by, however flawed, when she'd let Pavel Radek into their lives. But it was her mortal mother's initial survival that led Petra to believe she could live on her own without magic after the murder. And for a decade she'd done just that, until the war had colluded with her past to rip into her Achilles' heel and take down her sham of a life.

"I'm still waiting to test the blood sample we took yesterday," Augustus said. "It will tell us more about your magical heritage, but the evidence is very clear. If there's anything unusual in the blood sample findings, I'll of course let you know. In the meantime, I'd like to test your magic again on various elements to see how they react to being transformed at your touch." He held his hand out to invite Petra to sit at the worktable.

Petra didn't believe a word of it, but she recognized the precarious position she was in as Augustus and Martina watched and waited for her to respond. If she stopped cooperating, they might refuse the team access to the only lead they had in finding a solution to Josef's growing problem. Each day that passed without him changing into a wolf voluntarily was another day closer to him being forced to do it under the full moon—the consequences of which could be deadly to him and others, judging by the attack they'd thwarted in the courtyard the night before. But without the elixir to help him recover, he couldn't risk transforming on his own terms either. So, with little choice, Petra sat at the worktable and began changing aluminum into pottery, copper into granite, and a magnet into a brass candleholder until her wrist ached.

And then came the request Petra had been waiting for from the moment she'd walked into the underground vault of the old alchemists' lab.

"I can't do that," she said.

"Why not?" Martina asked. "You've done it before."

"Is that the rumor?"

"According to Pavel Radek, it's more than a rumor. He claims you turned a heller into a ducat." Martina thought she'd surprised Petra with the news, but she certainly wasn't the first to listen to the tale from that wretch of a man in prison. She wondered how long after Martina's conversation with Pavel he'd had the coin cut loose from his stomach by Grigori Zimin.

Petra felt the weight of the coin in her pocket tugging at her. Such tales the ducat had told since it fell into Pavel Radek's hands. "Or maybe that was just a story spread by a desperate liar," she said. "After all, no witch is allowed to use their magic to benefit their own wealth or status. It would be against the law for someone like me to create something as precious as gold out of a lead slug." She pushed away the glob of metal before her.

"I'm afraid I must insist you try," Augustus said. "These are controlled circumstances. For the benefit of scientific understanding of magic. We have the full authority of the Ministerial Council for Magical Affairs behind our work."

"You must understand we aren't under any obligation to follow the normal rules of society, given our mission here at the Libuše Society," Martina said. "We don't intend to use it for our own indulgence. Besides, we already have access to a fair amount of gold for use in our experiments. Though not as much as we once did." She'd said the last part as a whispered aside, indulging in some need to let the statement leave her mouth in front of her present company.

Petra gave in to her need to impress by flicking a finger against a paperclip instead and turning it into a gold wire. "If you say so."

The sight of the precious metal brought out the predictable reaction, even in a pair of witches who claimed to be interested in only the science behind the magic. First their eyes couldn't turn away from the shining gold metal on the table, then their lips grew damp with sweat as the possibilities of what else might be achieved so obviously cycled through their thoughts.

And yet all Petra could think about was how that shimmer of gold had shown up in the sample of her hair, knowing her mother was no witch.

CHAPTER FOURTEEN

The starshina gazed out the passenger car window at the rising moon as his bloodlust engorged, swelling on the back of his tongue. His mouth watered when the image of his last victim reemerged in his thoughts. Curious, though, how the moon's light had little effect on him. He'd been told it would, like in the old tales, if he didn't take the elixir the old woman had fed him. He'd swallowed the drink the first few times, but the taste didn't agree with him, so he'd spit the rest out whenever she turned away. But he'd still not lost his mind to any moon madness, only to the hunger. He'd been able to transform at will, succumbing to nothing, whether the moon was full or as she was now—an orb past her prime, turning away from those on earth who now ignored her for another month.

His lips quivered at the thought of all he'd done since, and he had to control the giddy laughter roiling up inside him. He covered the near outburst by coughing into his fist. "Pardon me," he said like any normal gentleman.

The man sitting across from him in the train car gave him an uneasy feeling. His fellow passenger smelled of cigar smoke, exhaust fumes, and cheap peach brandy, fermented and sweet the way they make it in the west. The man had barely said a word to the starshina, yet his eye looked up from his newspaper article—the same one he'd been reading since they boarded the train—to watch him whenever he crossed a leg or chewed on a torn fingernail with his teeth.

The starshina felt the same uneasiness with everyone. He always had, even before he'd crossed over into whatever existence he was in now. Yet this fellow had a way about him that attached to the intuition like a bur in the mind.

He took his eye off the moon to make a closer inspection of the man in civilian clothes. Too young to have been excluded from duty in the service during wartime. Too old to be anything less than an officer. His mustache was thick and drooped over the lips. One hand bore a recent wound: a thin cut from a sharp blade. The starshina could no longer smell the blood beneath the wound where the skin was thinnest, but the idea was delicious. Nearly floating away in a grisly fantasy, he found himself chewing on his thumbnail again until he coolly slipped it out from between his teeth and stroked his chin with his fingers instead.

"We must be nearing the station," the starshina said.

The passenger lifted his head, looked at his watch, and agreed. "Yes."

A single word spoken sheepishly with a foreign accent.

The man had understood him well enough to look at his watch before he'd replied, yet he was no supporter of the tsarist regime. Just like the man in the attic with the fur ushanka who'd understood everything he'd said, even while he'd thrashed in the depths of his worst delirium, calling out for salvation. Yet the tall man in the ushanka could not speak a word of the tsar's tongue, gesturing with his hands when he needed to communicate with him—eat, drink, shit in the can. The starshina had done the same, thrashing his head from left to right, asking for food or water by humiliatingly pantomiming his needs while his hands and arms were restrained in a straitjacket.

Until the tall one, Josef, brought him a cup of coffee.

It tasted like gutter water, but some strange magic had been stirred into the cup. After he'd drained the dregs, the starshina could understand every word Josef said, even when his lips were out of harmony with the words he was speaking. Curious how this man here could do the same.

"It's said there is a famous church in this town," the starshina commented as the outline of a steeple came into view in the distance. "Decorated with the bones of the dead." The mere idea of something so grotesque had him fighting to hide his smile from the stranger again.

The passenger across from him raised his head, feigned ignorance, and then folded his newspaper up. The starshina could see the soldier's demeanor hidden beneath the civilian veneer. He wore a cheap suit with the well-heeled boots of the hussar on his feet. He ought to kill the man, this old enemy of his. One swipe of the claw across the throat would do it. He let the blood rise, tempting the transformation, and then changed his mind. His hunger was not fully ripe, and anyway, they were pulling into the station, where he needed to locate the scent trail again. He smacked his tongue against the roof of his mouth as his fellow passenger stood and exited the car.

Soon, he thought, inhaling the local air and finding the scent of her. Soon he would find the young woman who could change objects with her magic. He would find Petra, this conjurer of riches, and see what she could do.

It was not far from the train station to the graveyard. Her scent lingered on the stone pavement, the grass, and the wooden door to the church. *Their* stench was there too—the sorcerer with the dark circles under his eyes and Josef with the dead wolfskin on his head. And another perhaps, though the crosshatch of scents could be confusing sometimes where so many people trampled the ground. The starshina knew they would go there, to the bone church. The line they were traveling on had become indelible in his mind.

He pushed the church door open and followed the scent downstairs. There, a symphony played in his head at the sight of so many bones hung in glory to the dead.

"Welcome to the ossuary, though I must advise you we'll be closing for the day in a few minutes." The caretaker, a petite woman in a black skirt and white blouse with hair pinned up like a cinnamon *plushki* on her head, carried her authority like an accessory dangling from the crook of her arm. "Feel free to have a look around, but I'll have to ask you to be quick about it," she said, looking at the watch pinned over her heart.

"Oh, I will," the starshina assured her. The caretaker, doused in lilac soap, pretended like she didn't understand him, recoiling slightly as she walked away. Never mind her, he thought, as his nose found a rich vein of Petra's scent. It was everywhere on the tiles between a fragment of leg bone awkwardly stuffed in among the others and a small altar at the back of the room. He was so close. A day away from his prize at most.

He deserved a reward for his diligence.

The starshina took a final deep inhale inside the bone church, then bid good evening to the caretaker, so eager to lock the door behind him. Outside, he went around to the side of the building and lit a cigarette as the sun set and the clouds came up to obscure the moon. *Good, I like it dark.* While he smoked, he skulked beside the graveyard where an old wagon sat half-rotted in an adjacent field. He didn't question why he'd taken so easily to this new way of life. The old witch woman had tried to "bleed" the killing instinct out of him in the attic with her herbs and oils, but the instinct had been buried too deep inside him for her magic to reach it. He'd known that before she'd even tried. So had the three *prostitutki* he'd killed before the war started. And then his country had forced him to join the army and shoot men for money in the name of the tsar? Too rich.

It took only a few minutes longer before the caretaker left her sanctuary. The starshina tossed his cigarette aside and took his clothes off. He would need them later, and it was too much trouble to steal a new set when he needed to be on the move again quickly. While he was still lucid enough to think ahead, he folded the shirt, trousers, and jacket and set them atop a tombstone with his underwear. His shoes he set on the patch of grass on the grave itself and stuffed his socks inside to keep the bugs out. The air was cool and invigorating against his bare skin, but not for long. Soon he'd be overcome with the heat of the hunt.

The woman had locked the front door and walked away. The click of her heels against the cobblestones rang like a dinner bell in his ear. He threw his head back and let the bloodlust swell inside him. Fur erupted on his arms and chest; his fingernails hardened and elongated into claws. His front teeth extended into flesh-tearing fangs as his snout stretched out and filled his nostrils with the scent of lilac soap. The muscles in his legs enlarged, lean and strong, ready to run.

He dropped on all fours and chased down his prey while the waning moon vanished behind the clouds.

CHAPTER FIFTEEN

"It's cloudy tonight." Moonlight reflected off Viktor's wire-rimmed glasses as he peered up at the sky. "She doesn't like to come down in the rain."

The glassmaker was talking about his *bella luna*. Josef sat beside him on a bench in a small square outside the Libuše Society house while Yanis had gone to check in with his city acquaintance again. Honestly, most days he believed Viktor was the one with the moon-affected curse, not him. He looked up at the silvery backlight forming around the clouds above. "It isn't raining," Josef pointed out, though he knew it would soon. He could smell the moisture skirting the belly of the clouds.

They both waited for Petra, who'd been asked to stay behind a little longer by Martina and Augustus. More experiments, they'd said. Josef had no reason to worry, and yet his thoughts kept returning to her when he wasn't being drawn into frivolous conversations. Thoughts brought on by the thing weighing down his pocket.

"It's a shame," Viktor said. "I had an idea to ask her for help." He pivoted on the bench to check the street behind them. "I got the idea when we were in the library earlier. From that part in Honza's grimoire about using blood substitutions to inoculate."

Josef adjusted his weight to disguise the fact that he really wanted to double-check the thing was still in his pocket. He didn't know what Petra was up to stealing the book, but he knew it was his responsibility to keep it secret and safe. "I see." He didn't bother looking at Viktor when he spoke, hoping his comrade would drop the subject. He liked Viktor well enough when they were on any other subject, but this talk of the moon as though she were a living being exhausted and confused him. "Why do you go on about the moon like a man in love all the time?" he asked, unable to hide his annoyance any longer.

Viktor shoved his hands deeper in his pockets. "It isn't love in the way you're thinking."

"I hope not. That would be really odd, Viktor. Because you can't have a relationship with the moon. You know that, right?"

"Depends." Viktor tilted his face up to the sky. "My mother had been sick for a long time with cancer. My father had already passed, and my sister was recently married with a new baby, so it was just the two of us. Toward the end, I used to sit with her in her room at night, waiting for her to fall asleep. Those few hours were the only time she seemed to find any peace."

Josef sat up a little straighter, as though his slouching were too disrespectful for the turn the conversation had taken. "I'm sorry. I didn't know."

"In the last days before she died, a beam of moonlight, stronger than I'd ever known, kept shining through the window each night at midnight, casting a glow over the bed. It felt like a presence, almost like the moon was keeping vigil with me. Like I wasn't so alone." Viktor reached in his satchel and unwrapped a small cut-glass vase just large enough to hold a single flower. The same sort Josef's own mother kept on the dining room table. "After my mother passed, she showed me this."

"Your mother?"

Viktor corrected him. "My *bella luna*. She shone her moonbeam on the vase as it sat next to my mother's bed, spilling her silvery radiance into it and making all these intricate cuts glint and sparkle like refracted diamond light." He smiled as if he didn't care what Josef thought as he wrapped the vase back up and put it away. "She's the reason why I became a glassmaker. I felt like the moon was telling me what to do with the rest of my life in that moment, showing me the beauty of glass and a way to use my talent in the saddest moment of my life. I honor her for that."

Josef didn't know if he should feel sorry for the man or revere him for believing in something so strongly. But as he stared up at the silver light peeking out from behind the clouds, he knew he wouldn't tolerate anyone mocking the man's moon-eyed talk ever again.

Viktor didn't say anything again for a long time. People came and went on the sidewalk in front of them, everyone busy, hurrying home or to the theater or to the butcher for a pair of pork knuckles. Josef's legs twitched from the need to move after watching so many people bustling about, so he stood and paced in front of the bench.

Viktor watched him with what looked like concern. "You haven't changed in a few days. Does the urge build up?"

Josef shoved his hands in his coat pockets. "I'll be all right." He looked up at the sky. "I have a few more weeks."

"But see, that's just it." Viktor stood to pace with him. "I think the cure is tied to the—"

Petra burst out of the front door and ran across the small square. "Do you have it?" she asked, nearly breathless. Before Josef could answer, she hooked her arm around his and tugged both men away from the square. Once they were far enough away and could no longer be seen by anyone at the Society, Petra stopped and held her hand out. "Do you have it? Let me see."

"Have what?" a confused Viktor asked.

Petra rubbed her hands together. "The book, Viktor. My dad's grimoire."

"How did you . . ." Viktor held up his hands and cradled his head. "You stole the book?"

Josef slipped the small leather-bound book out of his pocket and handed it to Petra.

"They'll know, Petra," Viktor said. "They have spells protecting everything in that place. They'll trace it right to us. We'll go to jail."

"Calm down, Viktor. It's only a copy." Petra exhaled and slowly opened the book. "It cost me dearly, but I sacrificed my camera for this while Martina wasn't looking."

"You turned your camera into a book?" Viktor rubbed his forehead with the heel of his palm.

"By rights, my father's spell book should be mine. It should have come to me when he died," she said, defending herself. "More importantly, there has to be something in here that will help us. Ava and my father worked closely together for years. They were on the same research path. Until something happened. But I'm sure we'll find information in here we can use. These aren't student notes. These are tested spells. Come on, let's get back home."

For once the others moved at Josef's pace as they hurried down the side street on their way back to the storeroom, in part out of excitement at what Petra had done and also to get off the street in case Viktor's warnings about tracking spells had somehow been copied along with the book. They were nearly back to the lane where the storeroom was located when a woman waved to get their attention.

"Petra? Is that you, my dear?"

Petra's feet came to a stop. She spun around, and the color drained from her face when she saw who'd called out. Her posture shrank and her eyes searched for an escape as the woman approached. The stranger wore a black wool overcoat with a lush mink collar. Her wide-brimmed hat was trimmed in matching fur, and her handbag was polished leather. She appeared to Josef as a woman who paid for whatever authority she carried with the trappings of wealth. The kind of woman he'd seen come into the bakery and make demands no other customer would and expect quick service or else simply because her husband made a little more money than most.

Petra finally found her tongue. "*Matka*, what are you doing here?"

"Oh, Petra, tell me it isn't true," the woman said. She did not lean in for a kiss or offer her hand to her daughter-in-law. Instead, the line between her eyes tightened. "You've been evicted from your apartment. Why didn't you come to me? What is my son supposed to do when he returns? How is he supposed to find his wife when she's busy running around the city with strange men?" The woman glared at Viktor, then Josef.

"I . . . I've been working," Petra said. The woman raised an eyebrow. "For the war effort."

"You?" Helene Kurková gave Petra a disbelieving once-over as she was introduced to Josef and Viktor. "Don't talk nonsense. Gather your things. You're coming home with me."

Petra looked to Josef, pleading with her eyes.

"What are you looking at him for?" Paní Kurková's posture tensed with superiority. "Or perhaps the filthy rumor I was told about you is true. I told them it was nonsense, that you would never sully our family name, but here you are, walking the streets with this pair of stragglers."

"That's not fair," Petra said. Her hands had clenched into fists. Josef didn't know what might happen with her magic if her temper got the better of her. He only knew paní Kurková was a mortal who was ignorant about her daughter-in-law's hidden abilities.

"I warned Marek not to marry you." The woman, too, was on the verge of casting out words she would later regret. Or perhaps not, but the confrontation was drawing attention from passersby.

Josef intervened between the women with his body. "There was heavy fighting in the mountains three days ago," he said to the woman, softening his voice to convey his sympathy. "The tsar's army broke through the pass, as I'm sure you must have read about in the papers. I think it's best you go home, paní Kurková. Marek is going to need you to be there. For when there is news."

"What news? Who are you? What are you doing with my daughter-in-law? Why are you talking about my son?" The woman's voice had risen an octave by the time she'd finished her string of questions. Fear flooded her eyes with a soft sheen when she realized what he was saying. "My son?"

Petra walked forward. "I tried to find Marek at the front, but he was already gone," she said. "I'm sorry I didn't come to you sooner. I didn't know how to explain what I'd learned. About what happened to Marek. The army will send an official telegram when they know more."

"Your son helped us save lives," Viktor added, though there was little more he could say without revealing the details of the upíri attacks in the camp.

"Without his help, many more would have suffered," Petra said, holding back the knowledge that Marek's help had come from his ghostly form showing up on the film in her darkroom. She tried to take her mother-in-law's hand to offer comfort, but the woman shook her head.

"No." Paní Kurková continued shaking her head in disbelief as she backed up. She turned and walked away—slowly at first and then in quick, angry steps—clutching her coat closed at her throat.

Petra watched the woman go until she turned a corner and disappeared. She wiped an eye with the palm of her hand and said, "Come on, we have work to do."

Josef hung his head and exhaled. So many sons and mothers.

CHAPTER SIXTEEN

Petra sat at the table, studying her father's grimoire, while the scent of fresh-baked bread made her stomach grumble. Josef, too agitated to ever sit still for long, had decided to work off his excess energy by baking with the small sack of flour they'd managed to find in a shop around the corner. He occasionally interrupted her reading to ask if she would mind transforming a measuring cup into another loaf pan, which she did by barely looking up from the page, too engrossed in the puzzle that was her father, Honza Stamitz.

Her father's handwriting was uniformly neat as she remembered but with a fanciful flair added, like a curved tail of ink across the page whenever he wrote certain capital letters, like *W* or *F*. She didn't know why exactly, but the small quirk made her smile, thinking her father had once indulged the whimsical side to his otherwise fatalistic nature. That was the part she didn't quite understand. He'd always been gentle with her. Patient, too, understanding the underpinnings of her gift in a way no one else ever had. But his last years had also been filled with a palpable distance that even a ten-year-old could feel—from her, from his wife, from other members of the village. Almost as though he'd been forced to live someone else's life while observing the world through a lens coated with memories of what used to be.

Viktor sat across from Petra at the table, chewing on a slice of bread. A smudge of butter smeared the corner of his mouth. "Any discoveries?" he asked. He took another bite, then licked the butter with his tongue.

"Maybe," Petra said. "I don't know." She laid the copy of her father's grimoire open on the table. "There are all kinds of spells written down. A lot of experimental stuff, too, from when he worked at the Libuše Society." She pointed to an illustrated page where he'd used watercolors to paint a yellow sun and silver moon couple. The page had been enchanted so that the images rotated around each other. "What do you make of this?" she asked, knowing Viktor's affinity for all things moon related. "It looks like one of his usual entries, but there's no incantation to go with it, no directions, no ingredients for a potion."

Viktor took a closer look, his brows pinching together while he finished chewing his bread. He brushed off his fingers, then slipped on his dark glasses, lifting and then lowering the frames several times to see how they affected his vision. With a curious grunt, he flipped to the back cover of the book. He did that several times before closing the grimoire and sliding it forward upside down. "There are pages missing," he said. "Are you sure you copied the entire book before you stole it?"

"For the thousandth time, I didn't steal it. The original copy is still in the Society's library. They'll never miss a thing." Petra tilted her head to examine the closed book again, only this time she noticed the slight gap in pages about two-thirds through the book. Like Viktor, she opened and closed the book several times. Once she was aware of it, the space became as noticeable as a missing front tooth. "You're right. There are pages missing, but it isn't because of the way I copied it." On closer inspection she could see the slight stubble where the torn paper remained. "He'd written more than what's here."

"So, who removed them?" Josef asked, looking up after punching the bread dough.

Petra shook her head in ignorance. "And what might have been written on them?"

"I'm guessing it was something about the moon and the sun's effects on transformation," Viktor said. He handed Petra his dark glasses and told her to have a look at the illustration again. "Or rather silver and gold."

Petra put on the glasses and held the illustration up. The image still moved from the enchantment, but the dark lenses revealed added details in the picture. A golden circle and dot radiated in the center of the sun, and a silver crescent shone with the moon.

"The alchemical symbols for gold and silver," Viktor said. He pointed to the third symbol that had been placed above the sun and below the moon. "That's Pisces."

Petra blew out a frustrated breath. "Why Pisces?"

"Because in alchemy, that symbol also represents projection."

Josef wiped dough off his fingers with a dish cloth as he looked over Petra's shoulder. "You mean like a movie projector?" he asked. He borrowed the glasses to see the illustration for himself.

"Actually, projection represents the end step in the ultimate process the alchemists had tried to achieve."

"Turning lead into gold," Petra said.

Viktor nodded. "Silver and gold are two of the most important elements in old alchemy." He bit his lip and turned away briefly, as though conflicted over what to say next. "Petra . . . Franz told me something about your father today while you were with Martina and Augustus."

"What did he say?"

"He was explaining why the Society was being so cautious with us. Not allowing us the same degree of freedom they allow other researchers." He rubbed his hands together and shrugged. "He said your father did work at the Society years ago but that he was let go for stealing gold. Actually, he was swallowing it."

"Swallowing gold?" Josef ignored the slight burned smell seeping out of the oven. "Why would someone do that? Is that something you witches normally do?"

"No, it's something people who believe in the power of elixirs do," Viktor snapped. He seemed to regret his tone when Josef scowled at him. "Sorry, it's just that gold was a staple ingredient in longevity potions. Eternal life, that sort of thing. People really believed a precious metal could prolong life. But that was hundreds of years ago. No one makes potions like that anymore. Well, a few charlatans might try concocting bottles to sell to gullible mortals, but your father was no impostor. He was a recognized scholar. But he must have been experimenting with gold. Maybe he took more than he needed."

"Martina said he resigned quietly in exchange for preserving his reputation." Petra studied the drawing again. None of it aligned with her memories of the father she knew. "You think this illustration has something to do with him getting dismissed over the gold?"

"Gold and silver . . ." Viktor paused, scratching at his beard while thinking. "Did you happen to notice the drawing painted on the wall in the society's botanical room? It's of a man and a woman. The man has a sun for a head, and the woman's is the moon. They're holding hands under the heavens to indicate they're joined in marriage. Or at least lovers."

Petra blushed, recalling they were also depicted in the nude.

Josef pushed Viktor's colored glasses up higher on his nose and leaned against the table, putting his weight on his knuckles, seemingly mesmerized by the moving image on the page. "The sun and the moon are lovers? Is this the same moon you talk to every night?"

Petra put her hand on Josef's arm briefly to caution him from saying more. "So, the relationship depicted could be symbolic?" she asked.

"Or maybe it really is about gold and silver being used in harmony together in some sort of spell," Viktor said. "Without the rest of your father's notes, there's no way to say for sure. But one thing is certain. Honza Stamitz was the only one to ever have a daughter who could turn ordinary objects into gold. Kind of the ultimate projection in human form."

A shiver crept among the soft hairs on the back of Petra's neck. She covered her mouth with her hand and shut her eyes.

"What is it? Have you remembered something?"

"Augustus took samples from me," Petra said, opening her eyes. "Strands of hair. A few clipped fingernails. A small vial of blood. He showed me my hair under the microscope and said the shimmer proved both my parents were witches. He's wrong. I know he is. My mother was a mortal. We have the same eyes, same nose, same hair." Her heart was pounding like a scared rabbit when she considered the possible meaning behind her father's illustration again. "You said earlier you got the impression after reading Ava's journal entries that she fancied my father. What if *they're* the sun and moon couple in this drawing? What if they were lovers?"

"Are you saying you suspect Ava could have been your mother?" Viktor asked.

Josef put his hand on her shoulder and sat down. "Is it possible?" he asked.

Petra slowly shook her head. "She just couldn't have been. Ava never reacted to me like I was anything more to her than a colleague's daughter. But what if they were lovers? What if they were working together late at night, their chemistry affecting their mingling thoughts and emotions. Their ideas."

"Urging them to take chances others might not, if not for their intimate relationship," Josef said.

Viktor, no stranger to inexplicable love, pointed to the drawing again. "What if they unlocked a hidden aspect of alchemy and witchcraft that no one had discovered before?"

"They could have made some breakthrough together," Petra agreed. "Think about it. My father has a child who can turn objects into gold or anything else she wants. And Ava König creates a wolf curse that can be rendered resistant to the effects of the moon. Something no one else had ever done. Sun and moon." She looked in Josef's eyes. "Gold and silver."

"Lovers *and* collaborators." Josef held her gaze briefly before going back to his bread.

Petra's head swam in uncertain waters. Dizzy from their speculation about her father and hollowed out from the Society's scrutiny of her, she couldn't be certain what she'd just stumbled upon. Without the missing pages from the grimoire, none of them could be sure they'd figured out anything that would help Josef recover from the transformation he'd soon be forced to endure. Still, a truth resonated in her body that they were on the right track.

"There's a related concept I've been working on I wanted to run by you both," Viktor said. "For Josef's looming situation." He reached for his vase, the one he used to draw down the moon, or at least the rays of moonlight she sent. "König's university notes talk about using a subject's biology in transmogrification. Hair, blood, saliva, but also an element that they were experimenting with."

"You mean the gold," Petra said.

"Right, but if she was the moon in this picture, they must have also played around with silver. Maybe the elixir requires that element in it to make it work."

"I can't just conjure up silver," Petra said. "I already made a pair of gold coins to pay off Zimin's men. If the Ministerial Council finds out, they'll come looking for me, and I haven't heard good things about conditions at the Old Saint's Prison," she added, reminded of Pavel's stomach.

"Right, I know, but silver and the moon are intertwined in alchemy. Symbolically, at least. And we all know how influential the moon is for those afflicted with the vlkodlak curse."

"And?"

"And you said Ava König had mentioned using the blood of the host to inoculate its victims so they wouldn't change into a full vlkodlak. But what if that isn't the only way to go about it?"

"What do you have in mind?" Josef asked, suddenly calm as he leaned against the counter to listen.

"If we can't use actual silver, maybe we can use the moon." Viktor tapped his knuckle on his vase. "What if we try inoculating Josef against the moon's influence by steadily exposing him to pure silver moonbeams? A little at a time until he builds up enough resistance that he doesn't lose himself to moon madness when she's full. Just in case we can't replicate the elixir in time."

"Would that even work?" Josef crossed his arms defensively.

"Wasn't the reason Hana told you to be certain to change at least once during the middle of the lunar cycle was because she knew it would be easier for you to resist becoming a vlkodlak without the lure of the full moon to distract you?"

"She said the more energy I spent changing into a wolf before the full moon, the less urgency I would feel to become the vlkodlak when it finally arrived. I would be able to resist changing when others who hadn't been treated couldn't. And I've always needed more elixir to recover when I transform closer to the full moon. But sometimes I'm able to get by on less when it's the new moon phase."

Viktor stood and ignited a ball of fire in his palm with the silver gleam of moonlight. "May I?" he asked, holding the light up to Josef's face. "Look straight ahead at Petra."

"What are you looking for?" Petra asked.

"The flecks Martina talked about," Viktor said. "Given what we've learned, I'm willing to bet they're specific to Ava's strain of the curse."

"Silver flecks," Petra said.

Viktor held up the light and examined Josef's eyes. "Yes, I see the silver reflection now." He lowered the firelight. "Hana was right. I have a suspicion the more you willingly changed under the half-moon, the more inured your eyes became to the effects of the full moonlight. The repeated exposure of low light in your wolf form may have made it easier to resist the more rabid parts of the curse later when she was full. Do you want to try a small dose of exposure?"

Josef glanced from Petra to Viktor. "How do we do that?"

"It's still cloudy, but I'm going to try and call down the moon. Ask her for help." Viktor set his special vase near the window and lit a candle. The reverence he showed his celestial love was touching, really, the way he straightened his shirt and smoothed his hair back to make himself presentable. The glassmaker was a modest man, but there was power in his quiet devotion. Watching him prepare to call the moon stirred a yearning inside Petra to dive deeper into her father's book to better understand the rituals behind the magic.

Viktor knelt before the window. He held his open palms up and closed his eyes briefly, inhaling deeply to center his power, before gazing up at the sky and reciting his invocation. "Argent goddess of ethereal light, grace me with your glow tonight. Fill the vessel so I may see, the love and light you stir in me."

Clouds blanketed the night sky, but silver cords of light shone from behind as they scuttled across the window. Petra stood beside Josef, wondering what he would think of the magic, remembering how the moonbeams had made the jinni king lighthearted as a child. Together they watched the luminosity brighten outside the window, as if the moon herself peeked inside the room. The clouds parted, and a single ray of moonlight traveled through the pane of glass and into the vessel.

Viktor thanked his goddess and held up the vase to show off the small trickle of light that had seeped inside. The light pulsed behind the vase like a heartbeat, soft and steady, giving the room a bright, silvery glow.

Josef took in a sharp breath.

"What is it?" Petra rested her hand on his back and felt him tremble.

Josef gripped the table with both hands. "Sometimes when I walk around at night, I can feel the weight of the moon pull against my blood like a tide, urging me to slip out of my skin." He winced as though he'd been punched in the stomach. "Since arriving back in the city, it's never been strong enough to make me give in. But this is too much," he said and sank to his knees. His fingernails thickened and grew. His nose stretched, darkening with fur.

Petra waved at Viktor to lower the vase. "Put it away!"

The flecks in Josef's eyes flashed like diamond light. His body reverberated in a state of change until Viktor cast the light back out the window. Once the moonbeam was gone from his sight, Josef fell on his side, panting while his body reverted to his normal self.

"I almost lost control," he said.

Viktor set the vase down and hurried to his side. "I'm so sorry. What an idiot. I really thought it would work."

Josef reached up and gripped his friend's arm. He caught his breath and exhaled, the worst of the moment over. "No, there's a good chance your theory was right. But too much. Too bright." He flopped onto his back until his breathing calmed down.

"Are you all right?" Petra reached for a wet cloth. "Can I get you anything? Should I call your mother?"

Josef pulled himself up to a sitting position. "I'm fine now. And for God's sake, don't call my mother. I don't want my parents to know anything about this curse."

Viktor scrunched up his face. "So you think the moonlight was working?"

Josef shook his head. "I think it could work, but in smaller doses next time. Like maybe a moon shadow instead of a full beam."

"Next time?" Petra couldn't believe it. "You're willing to go through that pain again?"

"It's no worse than what I've been through already," he said. "Besides, if pain is what it will take to get me back to normal, I'll gladly go meet it head-on."

Viktor tugged at his chin, thinking. "I could make a different vase. One that cuts the intensity of the moon's light. I made an adjustable lantern like that for Martina once, so I know I can do it again. If that works and you get used to the exposure, we can increase the dosage with different colors and thicknesses of glass. My *bella luna* was more than happy to offer a moonbeam for us to train with tonight. It's a good sign."

"Viktor, you're a moon-mad genius," Petra said. It was the first positive breakthrough they'd had. And if the search for König's elusive cure for the curse proved a dead end, at least there was hope of balancing Josef's tightrope walk between worlds. She hadn't been willing to admit it to herself until then, but his stability mattered. It mattered to the attraction brewing in her heart. Without that balance, his life would constantly be threatened with being lost to the madness of the curse. But this beam of moonlight had broken through the cracks to give him a chance.

Where there was hope, there was shelter. And in her short, disjointed life, that's all she'd ever needed.

CHAPTER SEVENTEEN

Josef splashed cold water on his face. He'd nearly lost control, and bitten the side of his tongue trying to hold on. How easily he could slip from one form to another when he knew he had the elixir to revive him, but without that small vial of herbs, he feared the brittle pane separating his wolf persona and the vlkodlak would shatter for good.

What if he'd succumbed and attacked Petra? Or Viktor? Or his family two lanes over? The thought made his stomach rise. The moon's light had been more intense than he'd admitted. It pulled on his insides like a magnet, threatening to wrench the wolf out of him. Halos had dilated in his eyes until he was nearly blinded to reason. Another few minutes and he might have been raving in the streets, demanding blood, because the threat was always there, lurking in the back of his thoughts.

If there was no more elixir, then yes, he'd go through whatever pain it took to be free of that doubt in himself again to protect those around him. If he began with small doses, he thought it just might work. Build up a resistance to the moon's power, the way he'd seen some men's broken bodies develop a tolerance to morphine. *If* it worked, he might finally look at the future through a different lens.

Caught up in his thoughts, Josef nearly missed the arrival of a pigeon inside the storeroom. It landed on the table in the center of the space, strutting and cooing until Petra talked to it.

"Where did that come from?" he asked.

"I let him in after he tapped at the glass," Petra said, bending at the waist to look at the bird eye to eye. "Didn't you hear him? He's brought us a message from Yanis."

"And how do you know that?" Josef asked, but he needn't have. Where witches were concerned, he trusted there was a spell for everything. But he did wonder if they were aware of how discomforting it was to watch someone have a viable conversation with a bird.

Viktor petted the pigeon gently on the back as he listened to the message. "Yanis wants us to meet him at that odd stargazing tower on the other side of the river. Says it's urgent."

Petra straightened. "I know the place he means. It's not far from my old apartment."

After a few final coos and wing flaps from the bird, Viktor extended his hand and carried the messenger to the window, where he let it outside.

"Are you feeling up to a short walk?" Petra asked.

Josef grabbed their coats. "I'll take any excuse to get out in the cool night air and stretch my legs," he said, then shook his head, resigned. "Even if it comes from the mouth of an enchanted flying rat with wings."

They crossed the old king's bridge to the Lesser Town district as a light mist settled over the bronze saints, making halos around the gas streetlights. Petra pulled up her hood and led them along a winding, narrow lane populated with respectable apartment buildings. It was near ten o'clock, and most of the windows had gone dark already, leaving only the eerie glow of lamplight on the wet cobblestones.

"This way," she said, rounding the corner on her right and pushing open a wrought-iron gate.

Yanis awaited their arrival beneath an archway at the entrance to a private enclosure. "I was worried that mangy bird wouldn't fly straight to the storeroom," he said. "It's impossible to find a nice, reliable dove in the cities these days. The war has made beggars of us all. Come, follow me."

The sorcerer slipped through a narrow doorway and up a winding staircase that carried them three levels higher to a garret at the base of the tower above. An older man with thin gray hair swept over the bald spot on top of his head sat at a table, drumming his fingers. He stood when they entered and began to gather coffee cups from a cupboard. He wore a long black frock coat and trousers with a white dress shirt and thin black tie. A wide-brimmed black fedora hung on a peg on the wall behind him. The room smelled overwhelmingly of freshly brewed coffee, but the underlying scents of wet wool and incense that clung to the man's clothes still bled through.

Josef watched Petra do a slow twirl as she gazed up at the expansive room, and he loved her for it. They'd climbed to the rafters of an attic, but unlike any he'd seen before. He no longer had to ask if such a place was related to occult studies. His instincts grasped the truth readily enough when he spotted the astrolabes, a mechanical model of the solar system, and the various star maps pinned to the walls with the astrological names written across the top. There were so many odd contraptions whirring and spinning on tabletops, he half feared he'd get his arm caught in one.

"What is this place?" Petra asked. "I've passed the tower so many times but never knew what it was for." She peered through the south-facing window to take in the view of the night sky. The city glowed below, its spires backlit by silver moonlight.

"My office," the man said, pouring a cup of coffee for each of his guests. "Welcome."

Viktor craned his neck to watch a cogwheel turn a model of the moon around the slowly spinning earth that had been divided into twelve signs of the zodiac. "You study astrology here?"

"At times, yes, but mostly we study people," the man said. "Please, sit where you like. Make yourselves comfortable."

Yanis shrugged off his outer robe. "This is Hugo Reitman, the city acquaintance I told you about," he said. After everyone introduced themselves, he added, "Hugo is the senior envoy assigned to this region for the Order of the Seven Stars."

"A pleasure to meet you all," Hugo said, though there was no accompanying smile to reinforce his words, especially when his eyes landed on Josef.

So this was the man who'd issued the kill order.

Yanis asked them to gather around the table. "He has some news to share that you may find disturbing," he said.

"Which is why I insisted on all of you coming here so I could meet you in person and explain the information myself." Hugo set out a candle on the table and lit it with a quick snap. "You are not the only one with the power to call up a flame, glassmaker," he said to Viktor with a shake of his finger. The remark telegraphed he already knew exactly who and what they each were.

The table was one seat short. Josef pulled over an empty crate to sit on so Petra wouldn't have to transform an extra chair out of a broom. He'd noticed she rubbed her wrists more often, as though she'd strained the delicate muscles there. He didn't know how magic worked exactly, but he imagined channeling all that energy through one's hands after ignoring it for so long might feel like it did for him the first time his father had stayed home sick from the bakery and he'd had to knead all the day's bread dough himself. He was fourteen, and his wrists had ached all the next day.

"So, what's this about?" Viktor asked, still maintaining the optimistic outlook that seemed to float around him like a cloud.

Hugo folded his hands in front of him on the table. "With the exception of Yanis, none of you are fully aware of the role the Order plays in maintaining a proper balance between the universe of magic and the larger mundane world of mortals. The energy between the two has always mingled freely, but because of the nature of magic, there has often been the temptation for some to abuse the gift for their own gain. There are laws in place to prevent chaos from erupting, but there are occasions when we're forced to intervene preemptively. This is the way the Order has worked for centuries." He spread his fingers out and sat back in his chair, as if to say, *Now that that's out of the way, we can talk.* "One of my chief responsibilities occupying this outpost for the Order is to monitor the flux of magic in the city and watch for the illegal use of spells and other forms of malevolent energy."

"I thought that was the Ministerial Council for Magical Affairs who did that," Petra said. "That's who I always feared would find me out. That's what my father had always told me."

"You mean while you were living in your attic apartment with your mortal husband and hoping to evade being recognized as the witch who could turn ordinary objects into precious metals?" Petra's mouth fell open just a little as Hugo shrugged. "There was no need to alert them to where you were hiding. We knew you were living humbly and subsisting on very little magic. We knew, also, that you were coerced into making that gold piece for Pavel Radek." He crooked his finger, and the gold ducat flew out of Petra's pocket. The envoy caught it in his fist like a moth he'd snatched out of the air.

"How did you do that?" Petra didn't take her eye off the coin once he opened his hand to reveal the ducat resting in his palm. "And how did you know where I was living?"

"Your father was not wrong," the envoy said. "We've long worked side by side with the Ministerial Council for Magical Affairs in this region. We generally defer to their judgment on matters of domestic policy, but because of our system, we almost always have first knowledge of a breach of magical integrity, as was the case of your unusual circumstances. The Ministerial Council searched for you relentlessly in and around the city, yet no one ever knocked on my door to ask if the Order had any knowledge of your whereabouts, so we did not see a need to tell them."

A gust of wind hit the window, rattling the glass. The candle on the table flickered. The old man shifted his weight in the chair, as though evaluating how much more to say. Josef got the uneasy feeling he was about to have another illusion about his former life shattered. He'd not known it, but he'd been living in only half a city his entire life, walking around with his eyes shut. He'd never dreamed before he'd been cursed what magical secrets lurked beneath the ordinary mortal existence. He was just another oblivious person eating at sidewalk cafés, waiting for trams to go by so he could cross the road, and working all week in the bakery so he could spend part of his wages on the next silent film to arrive at the cinema. He had to laugh at himself, remembering he'd once considered watching movies at the Lantern Theater in New Town to be the most magical experience a person could have.

"Yours was a high-profile case," Hugo said to Petra. He took a small pad of paper and a pen out of his frock coat pocket. "Naturally, we kept ourselves aware of any fluctuations in the isostatic energy affecting the city's equilibrium." He then removed an astrolabe from a shelf, like the one Yanis had carried with him before Petra had tossed it on a departing train to confuse the Order about their whereabouts. The brass instrument was a miniature version of the city's astronomical clock in the Old Town Square, but in the envoy's hands, it expanded from a flat instrument into a globe-like armillary with multiple rings whose planes intersected through the center pivot point. "We prefer to use a three-dimensional representation of the celestial realm when engaged in this sort of communication." He added, "For the sake of accuracy and ease of understanding."

Hugo set the instrument on the table, and soon pinpoints of light glimmered within the brass armillary, blinking in the representative heavens. The envoy adjusted the rings while making small calculations on the pad of paper until he was satisfied with their positions. He pointed to a single bluish light when he was finished. "There," he said to the group. "That light represents your position. Specifically, at the storeroom you're living in."

"Our position?" Petra shot a look at Yanis. "We're still being tracked?"

"It's protocol," Yanis said with that sullen look of his that communicated both a warning and instruction all at once. "One that has proven to save lives in the past. Hugo has been keeping track of my whereabouts since we left the front, save for that brief unauthorized train ride to the city."

"Which brings me to my point," Hugo said, interrupting. "The other instruments in the observation tower are much more accurate than these traveling ones, but they're occupied with other tasks at the moment. Still, you can see it here." He moved a ring a fraction nearer to another, then pointed to a faint smudge. "There's a gray mist hovering over your position. And it's getting bigger."

"A gray mist?" Viktor gave a shake of his head like he hadn't heard right. "What does that mean?"

Josef leaned in to study the armillary closer. With his wolf-cursed sight he could just make out the faint gray halo. But more than that, he could sense its intent. The cloud pulsed with an odor that wrinkled his nose. "It's some kind of threat," he said.

Hugo confirmed his assumption with a nod. "A mist such as this is almost always present when there is a malevolent supernatural force concentrated in one spot," he said. "It began shortly after you arrived in the city, so I can only assume one of two things: either someone has targeted you since your arrival, or one of you is the source of this energy."

"As a matter of fact, some of us were targeted." Josef didn't regret the bite in his words, knowing it was Hugo who'd given the kill order. He also didn't like the implied accusation that he was still some kind of threat.

Hugo let his eyes linger on Josef. "You're very sure of yourself. Sure of your self-control. But I've seen what the cursed vlkodlak can do. The mangled carcasses they leave behind that even a loved one can't identify. I'll never apologize for taking the right precautions."

"I'm confident it's nothing to do with anyone here," Yanis reassured his colleague.

"In all fairness, I tend to agree," Hugo said, drumming his fingers on the table again. "I've made my own observations since Yanis came to speak to me about the matter, and I'm satisfied you're not the threat I first took you for."

A part of Josef yearned to correct him on his assumption, but it seemed self-defeatist.

"I understand there was a break-in yesterday," the envoy said, changing the trajectory of the conversation.

"Luckily, nothing was taken." Viktor held a protective arm over his satchel.

"You mean nothing was found," Hugo corrected. He tossed Petra's gold coin on the table. "I understand the temptation to think otherwise, but I do not believe they were looking for the person with the skill to transform gold either, or else why break in while no one was there? Surely an ambush on the street would be a better means of snatching someone, if the witch with such a talent was the goal."

"I hadn't thought of that," Petra said. "But then what were they looking for?"

"Something coveted. Something of value. Something thought lost, perhaps."

His conclusions stumped the group, just as theirs had the night before.

"There must be a dozen break-ins in the city every week." Josef bent his head to look at the apparatus on the table from a different angle. "Doesn't seem like the sort of threat that would light up your magic globe."

"No, you're quite right, but there may be a connection," Hugo said.

"Connection between what?" Petra let her question resonate between the Order's envoy and its priest as she looked from one to the other.

"There's been another death," Yanis said. "A woman was found yesterday evening. Her lungs had been ripped out of her chest. Authorities are blaming it on a second rare animal attack. Sound familiar?"

"Where did this happen?" The tiny hairs along Josef's spine, from the base of his skull to his tailbone, lifted in warning, giving him an unmistakable shiver of warning.

"The woman was murdered outside the bone church," Hugo said, pointing to a spot on the armillary just next to the blue light marking their position. "Where I believe all of you took shelter before arriving in the city."

"Hold on, the moon was well past full last night," Viktor said. "It couldn't be a vlkodlak like we thought then . . . could it?"

Hugo adjusted the armillary rings slightly, and a string of blue lights illuminated. "These are the points of the three known attacks. Here, here, and here," he said, pointing, until his finger made the obvious next move in the direction the attacks were traveling.

"He's following us." Josef raised his nose and inhaled but detected nothing out of the ordinary.

Petra looked up, alarmed. "Who's following us?"

"Do you remember the patient in the attic?" Josef thought back to the last day at camp before the tsar's army broke through the pass. The man had still been shackled to the wall, still writhing in the fresh throes of the curse when they'd left to confront the zduhać. "His name is Dimitri. He hadn't finished the moderating protocol yet," he said. "Hana said he wasn't ready to be set free. He hadn't calmed down enough after the dosages she'd given him. But if she and Valentina had to flee the camp to escape the tsar's men, she may have set Dimitri free anyway, hoping he'd consumed enough elixir to protect him from the worst of the moon's effects. Or maybe they had to run and his comrades set him free after they found him."

"So, if this Dimitri only received a partial treatment, does that mean he could have reverted to full vlkodlak?" Petra asked.

Yanis leaned forward on his elbows. "Possibly one that isn't controlled by the moon's phases," he warned.

Josef agreed. "Which would explain the killing after the full moon. He may have received just enough treatment that his transformation isn't dependent on the moon, but definitely not enough to wean him off the killing instinct."

Viktor removed his glasses and rubbed his eyes. "But wait, you said there were three known attacks. We've only heard about two."

"There's something I haven't shared with you yet." Yanis pulled the letter of instructions the jinni had delivered to him out of his haversack. "The information I was given was that the creature's first known victim was a hussar," he said, letting the implication sink in that it might have been their comrade. "There was no way to identify the soldier. There wasn't enough of him left to make a determination."

"You don't think it was Major Bako, do you?" Petra lowered her head.

"We've been trying to locate him," Yanis said with a sidelong glance at Hugo. "They found Zimin's car abandoned on the road, but no one seems to know what happened to the major after we last saw him driving away from the front. We have no confirmed sightings yet."

The group let out a collective sigh. Josef had known the major for only a few short months, but he'd never met anyone with more ingenuity or cunning. He was a survivor. But then every man meets his end one day, and usually on a day he doesn't see it coming. Josef swore if Dimitri proved to be this vlkodlak and he was responsible for Bako's death, he'd skin the man alive and feed him to the pigs.

Viktor studied the armillary up close. "And now we think this Dimitri fellow is coming *here*? Because of this cloud you say is hovering over us?"

"I wanted you to be forewarned of the likelihood," Hugo said and folded up his armillary.

"What does he want with us?" Viktor's eyes widened behind his lenses. "Wait, is that who broke into the storeroom? Does that mean he's already here in the city?"

"That I cannot determine with certainty," Hugo said. "The problem with the vlkodlak is that he walks in the moon's shadow, mystically speaking. It makes him harder to find in both the physical and psychic realms than other creatures, so I cannot answer your question with any conviction. Not until there is another attack to mark his location."

"Upíri are the same," Yanis added. "Which is why the Order keeps organizing small groups like ours to combat the fiends whenever we get confirmation of activity."

"We should have followed orders and gone back like you said in the first place," Petra said, near tears. "But if it is Dimitri, how do we stop him? How do you kill a vlkodlak?"

Josef heard the fear in her voice. Did part of her fear him too? For the things he might soon be capable of doing if they didn't find a cure? He hadn't transformed in days. After the exposure to pure moonlight, he worried his resistance to the moon's influence was more fragile than he'd been led to believe. He'd never truly been tested. He'd always had the option of transforming before the full moon and the luxury of a ready remedy for the side effects when he returned. But what if he'd come to the end of all the half measures keeping him human?

More questions of "what if" gnawed at him. What if they couldn't figure out how to reproduce the right elixir? What if he transformed and lost control? Or couldn't recover? What if he couldn't resist the call of the next full moon? What if he was the next to kill someone? And if it was Dimitri following them and murdering people along the way, what use would he be against him if he had no control over the one thing that qualified him to be in this fight?

CHAPTER EIGHTEEN

The trail of her aroma had grown stronger. The starshina was getting close enough to taste the scent particles on his tongue. Soon he would have his prize, but something in the crosswind ruffled his instincts. He lifted his nose in the air. The smoke from a cigar. Yes, it was coming from somewhere to the west of him. He'd slept in a grove of winter-dead trees whose bark had peeled away. He was always so sleepy after a good kill. Any indentation in the soft ground would do for a doze. Now those trees were his cover as he stood to see who else stalked the hinterland with him.

The hillside vibrated with movement as a flock of blackbirds took to the sky. Did someone hunt him? Did the townspeople seek justice for an old woman whose bones had tasted of dried twigs? No, it was just a tractor in the distance tilling up the late winter soil. And yet the cigar scent was vivid enough in his nostrils he could have exhaled the smoke himself.

Another cluster of trees called to the starshina from across a patch of dead grass. Following the scent, he crossed the open ground in a few easy bounds. He could see the source of the smoke now. A single lit cigar had been stuffed in a rock crevice. Its tip grew heavy with ash while the other end was still wet with saliva. Yet there was no one there. He spun around, inhaling, listening. No one in any direction. Oh, but he knew who the cigar's owner was. The information coalesced in his nose, triggering memory: the man on the train with the thick mustache. He should have swiped a claw across his throat when he'd had the chance.

It mattered not, he told himself. His mission was still clear: find the young woman, kill the men at her side, and live a very happy life drenched in gold and all the glorious things it could buy. He wiped the end of the cigar off on his trousers, stuck it in his mouth, and puffed. A grand life, indeed, for those with the courage to take what they want.

CHAPTER NINETEEN

Hugo led Petra and the others to the back wall of the observation tower. "Fighting is not my specialty," he said to her. "The Order prefers to leave that to men like Yanis, but I always keep a few items on hand, just in case."

Before Josef had recruited Petra to battle the upíri in the mountains, she never would have believed she was a fighter either. For ten years she'd kept her head low, living a quiet life absent of magic. Later, opportunity had her move to the city to take a secretarial course, but then she'd met Marek and they'd married on a whim. He'd asked for her hand after drinking too many beers, and she'd said yes as he twirled her around in his arms. She and Marek had both been lightheaded with desire, mistaking attraction for love. But when the dirty socks piled up and the food ran low, there was little tenderness left to blunt the strain of everyday life. Then after he'd gone off to war, she'd taken up the camera, enjoying the solitude of a night stroll through the city to document those who walked on the other side of the veil, while she waited to learn if her husband would come home. Now? She was examining a curved axe on a wall and wondering how best to swing it to cut the Achilles tendon of a vlkodlak on the move.

"These creatures are not like the undead we've battled before." Yanis took a crossbow down from the wall and ran his finger gently along the flight groove. "They die like any other man, which thankfully is one reason they are not as prolific at reproducing as the upíri are. But they're fast. Strong. Intelligent. They aren't going to be distracted by a few hawthorn berries waved in their face."

"Because of the supernatural strength from the curse," Josef added, "it will require double or even triple the effort to bring a vlkodlak down using conventional weapons."

"Spells will work, but you have to be quicker than lightning to get the upper hand if one is attacking." Yanis aimed his remark at Viktor, knowing his penchant for relying on fire as a defense. "It's been my experience that traps work best—physical and metaphysical."

"Only the victims who survive their bite carry the curse," Hugo said. "It's a blood-borne infection, so the rest of you should start wearing some sort of protection or armor to try and prevent any puncture wounds." He lifted a heavy chain-mail vest, the kind from a bygone era of knights in combat, then put it back. "Though perhaps Petra can sort out a lighter, more suitable armor using her ingenuity. You'll need agility on your side."

Yanis and Josef selected a half dozen weapons from the wall—an extra pair of pistols with ivory-inlaid grips, a sword with a jeweled hilt, a crossbow, a curved axe, and a short-handled pike. The men bundled them up in a pair of old tarps that had been covering a broken whirligig in the corner. "Let's get these back to the storeroom," Yanis said. "At the rate the vlkodlak is moving, he could be here at any time, depending on the urgency of his objective."

Josef swallowed the last of his coffee, then hefted the weapons on his back. Petra hesitated, catching Hugo's attention in private while the others gathered the last of their things. "Is it possible to look for ordinary people with your gadgets?" she asked. "Someone who isn't a high-profile case or member of the Order? A witch?"

"I would need more specifics about who they are to even answer the question," he replied.

Petra waved the others on, saying she'd catch up in the lane. Yanis tried that look of his to give her a stern warning not to bother the Order's envoy, but she had to try. "I'm looking for a healer woman from my village. The woman's name is Hana. She's the only one who's been able to produce the elixir Josef needs to . . . to resist."

"Becoming the vlkodlak?" Hugo gazed at her like a patient father.

Petra nodded. "She was with us at the front, but we don't know what happened to her after the army retreated. We need to find her. We're running out of time and ideas to help Josef before the Order expects us to follow through on our mission."

Hugo raised a sardonic eyebrow, but he took out a pen and paper and wrote down the details about Hana. "I'll see what I can do," he said. "In the meantime, you'd better keep this." He handed the gold coin back to her. "Perhaps the symbolic meaning is worth more to you than the value of the gold itself?"

"I suppose it's become a sort of talisman," Petra said. She gave Hugo a spontaneous kiss on the cheek, thanked him for his offer to help, then ran down the stairs to catch up with her teammates.

An hour later, with the weapons laid out on the storeroom table, Petra was reminded of her first encounter with an upír. The fiend had attacked so fast, she'd barely had time to react, but Josef and Yanis had sprung into action. They'd known exactly what to do because they'd studied their enemy. They'd watched for weaknesses and then learned how to exploit them. Now they—*she*—must do it again with this new unknown enemy.

"We'll take shifts watching the street," Josef said. "We can't afford to get complacent. If it is Dimitri looking for us, he'll find us by smell alone."

"Why would he be after us?" Viktor asked, testing the weight of the short-handled pike. "Does he know who we are? Who we work for?"

Josef paced in front of the window. "We were careful not to say too much in front of him, but he obviously knows what line of work we're in."

"We never mentioned the Order," Yanis said. "But he knew Hana was a healer. A witch."

"Maybe he's looking for a cure," Petra said. "Maybe he thinks we have the elixir he needs, so he's followed us. Maybe *he's* the one who tossed the storeroom looking for it." The thought of a murdering creature like that rummaging through their things put a knot in her stomach.

Yanis swung his head slowly. "If that were the case, it would have been smarter to track Hana instead of us. No, I think it's fair to say he's got something else in mind when he gets to the city. Perhaps he thinks we're somehow responsible for his condition. He might even be under the illusion we abandoned him in the attic."

"Shh." Josef motioned with his hand to douse the lamp. He approached the window, looking out through the small opening in the curtains. "There's someone out there. He's watching the lane."

Yanis limped over. "It's nearly two in the morning. That can't be good." He squinted at the figure. "Grab your weapons, everyone."

"Is it him?" Viktor swallowed and pushed up his sleeves, ready to throw fire.

Josef took a deep inhale as though testing the outside air and cocked his head to the side. "Only one way to find out."

"Are you mad?" Petra darted to the table and picked up the axe. The weapon was heavier than she'd imagined, but she raised the blade using both hands, ready to swing.

"You don't smell that?" Josef opened the front door wide and stuck his head outside. "*Pálinka* and cheap cigars," he said. He grinned and put his hands on his hips as the figure walked toward him. "I began to think I was never going to see you again."

"Your lucky day, I guess."

Major Bako stepped inside the storeroom dressed in civilian clothes and carrying a heavy wooden case with a handle on top. The mismatched image threw Petra off guard until she saw the hussar smile beneath his bushy mustache. "You're alive." She dropped the axe and gave the man a hug.

There was a palpable exhale of relief in the room as Josef bolted the door and told the major to take a seat at the table. "Where've you been? How'd you find us?"

Bako shook hands with everyone, took off his overcoat, and then explained his odd journey to their door. "I found the truck on its side, but you'd already gone. How were you able to get away from the fighting so fast? Did the army take you with them to the trains?"

Viktor cleared his throat. "Flying wagon, actually."

"That's a new one," Bako said, absorbing the information. "Anyway, with the emperor's army in retreat, I followed the convoy out of the valley in Zimin's car, hoping to catch up with you all later when they stopped." He lit a cigar and blew smoke up to the rafters. "But the car ran out of gas quicker than I'd anticipated. Had to pull over before making it to the train station. No one was in any hurry to stop and help, so I started walking with a few others on foot. A group of hussars who'd lost their mounts. The seven of us camped that night in the forest. No fire. No food. Just a few pine boughs for a crude shelter. Sometime in the middle of the night, we were attacked. The damn thing leaped out of nowhere and swiped the first man he met across his chest."

"The vlkodlak," Viktor said.

"So you've heard about him." The major took a puff of his cigar, squinting at the weapons sitting on the table. His comrades confided they'd worried he'd been the victim when they hadn't heard from him. "We fired a few shots at the godforsaken thing, but he dragged that poor bastard off like he had nothing more consequential than a rabbit in his teeth."

Josef wiped a hand over his face, which had gone somewhat pale.

"We believe his name is Dimitri," Yanis said. "The man Hana was treating in the attic."

"Did you notice anything that might confirm his identity? Or which way he was headed?" Josef asked.

"Did better than that." Bako grinned so that his mustache spread wide above his mouth like a raptor's wings. "I tracked him after the others got spooked and started running for the nearest village."

"You tracked a vlkodlak alone?" Yanis stared at him, horror-struck.

"That's the way I was raised. Family business, you might say." Bako hefted his suitcase onto the table and undid the latches. Petra had seen the case before. The last time was when he'd pulled a mallet and wooden stake from it to teach her and the other recruits how to kill an upír by hammering the shaft of wood between the ribs.

"How did you avoid detection?" Yanis, still incredulous, slid the crossbow out of the way on the table to make room for Bako to open his case.

The hussar raised the lid. Inside, they saw the familiar blue velvet interior with the three hawthorn stakes, a mallet, a dagger with the double-raven symbol of the Empire on its handle, and two small-caliber revolvers along with twelve silver bullets lined up in the velvet. Bako pushed a button on the back of the case, and a hidden spring released the tray insert on top. In the space beneath it were two bottles of liquid secured under leather straps, a bundle of dried herbs wrapped in muslin, a clean white shirt that had been neatly folded, a pair of socks, three fresh cigars, and a stick grenade.

"You dragged this thing with you?" Josef asked.

"I wouldn't be alive without this case," Bako said. "Been in my family for generations." He dug out the bundle of dried plants and unfolded the muslin.

"Wolfsbane," Petra said, recognizing the spiked leaves and deep-purple flower petals. A small pouch of crushed leaves had also been secured with a leather thong so it could be worn like a necklace.

"Exactly," the hussar said. He lifted the small pouch from the bundle. "When wearing this, the wolf can't smell you. He can't see you. You're not invisible, but his senses get scrambled so that you might as well be."

Josef confirmed it with a twitch of his nose and a confused nod. "I can still smell the cigar, but I've lost the rest."

"That's right," Bako said, grinning with sinister satisfaction. "Worked like a charm. I got within a few meters of that devil, and he never even sniffed me out."

"How do you know all of this?" Viktor asked. "I don't mean to be rude, but you're the only mortal among us, yet we seem to keep coming to you for advice on how to defend ourselves."

Bako leaned forward, grinning with the stub of the cigar held tight in his teeth. "How do you think I found all of you tonight?"

Viktor scooted his chair back as though he felt mildly threatened. "Lucky guess?"

The hussar laughed. "If a man in my line of work relies on guess-work, he'll end up dead, my friend." Bako stubbed out his half-smoked cigar and put the rest in his pocket for later. "My father was a witch-finder, and his father before him. Our family has been tracking and hunting the supernatural for three centuries."

"The translation spell must be wearing off," Viktor said, touching his ear. "I thought I heard you say you're a *witch*finder."

"Witch hunting is illegal," Petra said, based on her understanding of the covenant agreements with mortals made more than a hundred years earlier.

"The title is a nostalgic throwback more than anything," Bako said, leaning against his seat. "We focus on supernatural murderers and unexplained phenomena these days. Mostly at the behest of confused government officials. That's why the Order tapped me for this liaison assignment with the army. But we still do confront the rogue witch now and again. Some willingly continue to dabble in the forbidden malev-olent arts, covenants or not. In this case, however, I tracked you lovely people by following that maniac out there. He's been headed in this direction for days. I finally put two and two together when he stopped at the church full of bones. By the way, I think you may have dropped this by the altar," he said to Petra. He produced the photo she'd taken of the weeping woman in the Old Town Square.

Petra took the photo from him, wondering how she'd lost it. "Wait, you've been following him while he's been killing people? Don't you have something in your case that will stop him?"

"I do, but even I'm not dumb enough to try and kill a full vlkodlak on my own. He took the train at one point, and I hopped on behind him. After I stole these civilian clothes out of some poor fellow's suit-case, I sat in the same car with him for as long as I could stand it. The man oozes depravity. Almost as if he were born for this cursed life of murdering people."

"The Order has seen the threat coming to us too," Yanis said, gesturing to the weapons on the table.

"If he doesn't stop to kill again, he'll be here by morning," Bako said. "I thought it best to get ahead of him and warn you rather than keep following. This one? He's not reliant on the moon's phases. He changes at will into the full beast. Imagine the havoc his bloodlust will bring to a city of hundreds of thousands."

Josef had listened to Bako's harsh talk in silence, but he spoke up now. "He wasn't able to finish Hana's treatment protocol. She may have created a more dangerous threat because of it."

"Anyone seen her since the army's retreat?" Bako asked. "Or Valentina?" The hussar's question was met with a room full of shaking heads. "What about your supply of elixir?"

Josef rubbed his palms against his thighs. "Gone," he said and stood to pace the room with that animal energy of his.

Bako scratched the back of his head. "But if you don't change with the elixir, won't you be forced into one of those things on the next full moon?"

It was a blunt question. The very one they'd all been dancing around since they'd arrived in the city.

"We're trying to replicate the formula," Yanis explained in answer to Bako's question. "But so far we haven't been confident enough in the results to recommend Josef transform to test it."

Bako dug through his witchfinder case, setting the shirt and socks aside. His fingers reached into a pouch sewn into the velvet where there was some discoloration. His hand came away with a single vial, half-full of liquid. He held it up between his thumb and forefinger. "This what you're looking for?"

"How did you get it?" Josef took the vial and uncorked it.

"Slipped one into the case when we first got to the encampment in the mountains. Must have been three months ago or more. I'd forgotten all about it until I went looking for the wolfsbane in the bottom of the case."

Josef inhaled. "That's the stuff," he said, then passed it under Yanis's nose. "The salty, acidic note is what's missing."

Yanis agreed. "That's probably the wolf's blood, but we'll still try using the fur after its essence has been distilled at the alchemists'."

"Some of it seeped out of the vial," Bako said, feeling the discolored spot on the case's interior. "Hope there's enough left."

Bako might not have realized it, but even with half a bottle, he'd just delivered them another month of hope. Now all they had to do was survive past morning.

CHAPTER TWENTY

Fog had settled in overnight, shrouding the narrow city streets in morning mist. Josef stuck close to Petra as the five of them left the storeroom to walk to the alchemists' tunnels. There'd been no further disturbances during the night after Bako arrived, and there was little point in sitting and waiting for trouble to show up when there was still work to be done. Besides, he suspected Martina had more knowledge about vlkodlaci hidden away in the back of her brain than all of them put together, though perhaps not the practical experience Yanis and Bako had from their past confrontations. Still, they could use all the help they could get, even if it came from academics in white lab coats.

Josef kept his nose in the air as they walked. He'd detected no sign or scent to suggest the vlkodlak was near enough to be an imminent threat. And yet Dimitri could be anywhere on the outskirts of the city, disguised among the population as a normal citizen walking along cobblestone streets. He tried to recall the man's face—a tan mustache, deep furrows in his forehead, and brown eyes devoid of curiosity. He'd marked the lifeless eyes down to the effects of the curse at the time, but then some men willingly walked through life unaware of the wonders around them, letting their own tedium muddy their vision until dullness left a permanent mark in their demeanor.

Josef checked the knife and pistol on his belt for the tenth time. And now he added the less-than-full bottle of elixir in his breast pocket to his checklist of items to worry about. Before leaving the storeroom, they'd all tucked their weapons under their coats. Even Yanis had managed to secure the crossbow under his robes by strapping it to his thigh. The arrows were tucked up his sleeve. If Bako was right about Dimitri planning to ambush them, preparedness was their first defense. And yet, as they walked along the winding streets of Josef's home city, past shops that included the delicatessen selling knish and cured beef that his mother visited every Thursday before the shortages, only the sharpest eye among the city's citizens would have spotted the arsenal the group carried on their persons.

"This is the place?" Bako asked when they arrived in front of the Libuše Society house, safe but on edge. "Looks like a storm could blow it over."

Viktor tapped on the door. "It's an illusion spell," he said. "Puts the mortals off so they don't come knocking."

Bako grumbled, having been tossed into the same group of ignorant people hurrying by on the street.

Ernst answered the door, ready to let the team in until he spotted Bako standing on the pavement. The change in his face from amiable to wary would have been comical if not for the urgency of their visit. "Yes, may I help you?" the caretaker asked, looking from face to face as if he didn't know them.

Viktor scrunched up his nose. "We need to get back to work, Ernst."

Ernst cleared his throat and made an understated gesture with his eyes toward Bako. "I'm sorry, you must have the wrong house, young man."

It took a moment, but Viktor finally caught on. "Ah, yes, Ernst, this is Major Bako. He's a mortal. But he's with us. He's part of the team."

People on the street had started glancing over at the group gathered at the door. They knew there was something odd about the house, something *touched*. Josef had always felt it too. Before he knew the secrets kept beneath the building, he'd thought the place should have been demolished with the rest of the old run-down buildings years ago. He'd never understood how the eyesore had survived. But that was before he believed in magic.

"Oh, very well," Ernst said, waving them in. "You may as well come in before the whole city notices. But you're the one explaining *his* presence to the rest of the staff." With a short huff to express his displeasure, he escorted them to the back study and pulled the lever.

"Curious place you have here," Bako said after slipping through the bookshelf door and entering the lower level. "Might even make a nice little fortress should the need arise."

At the bottom of the stairs leading to the tunnels, the strange mix of ammonia and sulfur hit Josef's nose again. It was stronger this time. Fresher. He stifled a sneeze as Martina approached them, making him wonder what kind of caustic chemicals she'd been working with to have them linger so strongly on her clothing.

"What is it? Has something happened?" Martina asked, noting the strange mortal with them.

"Major Bako is a colleague," Petra said, calming the woman's concerns. "He's been tracking a vlkodlak who appears to have followed us from the eastern front."

"You think a vlkodlak is headed here to the city?" Martina asked.

"That's correct." Bako stood with his hands clasped behind his back. Without his uniform, the major appeared less intimidating than usual, like a salesman or banker perhaps, but Josef knew the man's noble heart was wrapped in barbed wire. Cross it and bleed. "I believe he's been following their scent trail and will be in the vicinity in due time," Bako said. "We ought to take every precaution to prevent a catastrophic encounter inside the city."

"The threat can't be that imminent," Martina scoffed. "We're days past the full moon." She gazed directly into Bako's eyes in that unnervingly piercing way of hers. Josef knew from experience the scrutiny felt like psychic darts shooting under the skin to seek out the hidden truth, but the man held steady. "And, for the record, we don't generally take advice on how to approach the supernatural from mortal witchfinders," she quipped, displaying her uncanny talent with second sight.

Yanis slipped his satchel off his shoulder. "This one went through the elixir protocol, at least partially. We think he's able to change at will like Josef, only he's a full vlkodlak. No elixir needed to recover. He's already killed three people since the full moon." The sorcerer pulled the latest newspaper account out of his bag and showed it to her.

The blood drained from the woman's face. "A full vlkodlak unaffected by the moon? How? It makes no sense."

Josef explained about the man's treatment in the attic and how it had been interrupted by the army's retreat, but she shook her head.

"No, that alone wouldn't do it." Martina went into the research library and pulled a fat journal from the shelf. "The elixir would only treat the aftereffects. It isn't the agent of change. It simply couldn't be. There must have been something else Hana did. Some other elements she introduced to the process."

Petra and Josef exchanged a glance. Just how much did Martina know about these curses? And how much hadn't she told them?

Martina frantically flipped through her journal, looking for a solution. After a few fraught minutes scanning pages, she picked up the book and slammed it against the table. "There's nothing Hana could have done to alter the curse," she fumed. "She's a common hedge witch who drains boils for a living." She bit her lip, grimacing. "How has she altered the basic function of such an ancient hex? Only Ava König has ever been able to do that."

As the woman bristled at her own ignorance, her nose began to bleed. A trickle of blood spilled over her lip and dripped onto the desk. "My apologies. It sometimes happens when I get upset." She dabbed at her face with a handkerchief she kept tucked up her sleeve, then excused herself in a rush, leaving the book open on the table.

Viktor took the researcher's outburst as his own cue to leave, saying he'd be in his hot shop blowing glass to make the moon lantern he'd promised Josef.

"This place is incredible," Bako said after they'd gone. He took a quick inventory of the rest of the books on the shelves, tilting his head to the side as he perused the titles. "Could have used this treatise on southern upíri a month ago. Says here you can use a fishing net as a distraction instead of seeds. They get stuck counting the holes."

"Never mind the undead," Yanis said. "We need to concentrate on confronting a creature that's very much alive and very much has his wits about him."

"We'll need to set a trap," Josef said. "There's no other way." Not with a murdering vlkodlak lurking on the outskirts of the city's heart. Not when there were loved ones in the streets nearby who were unaware that such horrors even existed in the world beyond the realm of folktales, or that their son, brother, or nephew was one of them.

"Traps require bait to work," Bako said over his shoulder.

"Did you get any sense of why he was following us?" Petra asked. "Is there any chance he really is searching for the rest of his treatment? Maybe he knows we're his connection to finding it."

Bako shook his head. "He could have just sniffed out Hana or Valentina, if that's what he wanted. Besides, after observing him for two days, I think he's enjoying it. He licks his lips and smiles to himself like he's remembering what he's done. Turns my stomach to think about what wickedness he's inflicted on his victims."

Josef shrank inside, knowing he was only a full moon away from being the thing that offended the sturdy constitution of a man like Bako.

"Okay, so he enjoys the hunt and the kill," Yanis said. "Still doesn't answer why he's coming after *us*. We did him no wrong. If anything, we saved his life." The sorcerer sat and unstrapped the crossbow from his thigh. "If killing is his goal, there's easier prey to hunt than us in any of the villages he passed."

"Maybe he doesn't see it that way," Bako suggested. "To him it might seem like he was held prisoner in that attic. Tortured even." The hussar pulled down a book on night creatures and thumbed through the illustrations. "Maybe he's simply the type who holds a grudge."

"Or," Petra said, unstrapping the axe from the back of her belt and laying it on the table, "maybe he knows what we do and just wants us out of the picture so he can kill at will."

Josef tried to remember what it felt like to be the man tied down in the attic. How cognizant had he been while in the restraints? Not very, not until Hana began talking to him, telling him stories to encourage him to hold on for one more day when the treatment felt like it would rip his arms off before it made him feel better. The stories were about Petra. About how she could change objects into whatever she wanted. He'd already been forced to accept that spells and curses were real, so by the time he'd heard tales of her magic, he was a true believer. A dreamer, too, believing there might be a way out of his cursed circumstances.

"He's not after us for what happened to him," Josef said, appreciating the wider picture. "He's after Petra. He must have overheard us talking that night in the attic about a girl who could change objects into anything she wants."

Petra took a beat to think about it. "He knows I'm the girl in the story."

The truth ruffled all the little hairs on Josef's arms and chest. "Dimitri knows what you can do. It doesn't take much imagination to assume if you can do all that, you can turn something of no value into a fortune. It has to be you he's after."

Bako flicked an eyebrow at Petra. "Well, I think we just found our bait. Now all we need to do is build the trap," he said and snapped his book on night creatures shut.

CHAPTER TWENTY-ONE

Once the starshina had arrived inside the city, the scent trail nearly fell apart like wet chalk. It mingled with the garbage, the cookstoves, and the sweat of so many humans concentrated in one place—their perfume, aftershave, body odor, sour breath, and clothes that needed washing. The sickening mixture nearly overwhelmed his orientation to the world. The river didn't help either, with its fish gut, muddy bank odor. And yet, among the chaos of smells, his divine nose detected a thin trace of the witch's individual scent like a single red thread unraveling from her coat to trail along the cobbles. Invisible to the mundane mind perhaps, but highly detectible to the hungry eye. All he had to do was keep his nose on the scent and follow the thread to where it grew thick and pungent again with the essence of *her*.

"Do watch where you're going, sir."

The starshina curled his lip at the "gentleman" who'd scolded him after they'd bumped shoulders. He hadn't been to a city with so many people since he'd been a very young man contemplating a life as an ironworker. The discord of so many humans clashing with each other on foot, trams, bicycles, and wagons was like a churning cyclone that threatened his heightened senses, pushing him toward panic. He had to get off the street to get away from the frenzied energy and refocus.

Desperate, he spotted a men's shop across the lane and darted straight for it, barely missing a tram as it rounded the corner. He shut the shop door behind him with an audible sigh. *Better.* His instincts had served him well again. The scent of wool suits and fresh steam always brought comfort. His father had been a tailor, and the smell meant order, organization, dependability. "A man who can sew a neat line with a thin needle can put food on the table," his father had told him when he'd learned of his son's intention to take on factory work. "A wealthy man will pay for a well-made suit that bolsters his position in the eyes of onlookers. Even a tailor of low birth can do that." And while he'd admired and respected his father's talent with the needle, the starshina had never had the patience to do busywork for the benefit of others.

A man emerged from the back of the shop wearing a suit of middling quality. He had a tape measure hung around his neck, and his hands were covered in chalk. "Good day. Is there something I can help you with?"

The starshina managed a brief nod as he admired a dark-gray suit with four buttons down the front. He checked the stitching while the salesman watched his every move.

"All our suits are machine-made in a factory," the man said proudly and nodded toward a sewing machine on display in the corner. "But we can tailor anything off the rack to make a perfect fit." He wiped the chalk off his fingers with a black cloth.

"So you do not make the suits yourself?"

The man shook his head. "I'm sorry, I didn't understand you. I don't speak—"

"You do not seem to understand a lot of things," the starshina said, adding a grunt of dissatisfaction.

The salesman held his hands up in a gesture meant to be a humble admission of his limited understanding of the language being spoken to him. "Again, I'm sorry. I don't understand."

But I can understand you, because witches make playthings of men's lives.

"How much?" he asked the salesman. He held up his fingers and counted one, two, three.

"Ah, you want to know the price?" The salesman lifted the sleeve of the gray suit with a subtle pinstripe and removed a handwritten label that had been fastened to the interior with a string and safety pin.

Was this what the world had come to? No more pride in a man's work? No care with the pins and scissors to fit the cloth to the individual—for the man with the clubfoot who required precise measurements to hide the discrepancy in the uneven trousers, the grandfather with the straight hips and protruding belly who benefited from a generous cut where the jacket buttoned, or the young man who needed an extra few centimeters in the shoulders when buying his first suit before his body had finished growing. These shops today had lost the art of the handsewn hem and the perfectly positioned buttonhole. The suits were cheap and tawdry mass-produced copies of each other unworthy of a tailor's son. He waved the price tag aside.

And yet.

The starshina was not so blind with prejudice that he could not see the state he was in. To make a good impression, it wouldn't hurt to have the air of the successful man around him. If these modern goods were the equivalent of what passed for luxury these days, he might need to adjust his standards. At least temporarily. Later, when the girl was his, he'd hire ten tailors from home to make him the finest suits money could buy. In the meantime, since he was changing clothes anyway, there was nothing to prevent him from getting a little bloody.

"I could shave ten percent off the price, if you're interested." The shopkeeper clasped his hands behind his back and smiled, hoping his dangled bait had snagged the fish.

He caught the wolf instead.

CHAPTER TWENTY-TWO

Petra understood her position perfectly. If the vlkodlak had followed them over hundreds of kilometers, killing along the way, it had to be greed motivating him. Or revenge, but she didn't like to think about that. So Bako was right. She, alone, had to be the one to draw him in.

"You don't understand," Josef argued again. "A vlkodlak's speed and strength are no match for a mortal or a witch. Remember our first training session? You couldn't knock me over with your spell. Not if I knew it was coming. That's why it should be me. He knows me. He'll show himself, if only to try and rip my head off, and then the rest of you can kill him."

"If you're not dead first," Petra said. "Which is why you aren't putting yourself at risk. If it's me he wants, then he wants me alive."

"She's right," Yanis said, intervening. "That hesitation he shows her will buy us the time we need to complete the mission, which is what we were tasked to do."

Any further argument disintegrated in Josef's mouth, because he knew they were both right. He was letting his emotions influence his opinion rather than remain objective and see the truth for what it was. Petra understood she was their best shot at getting the maniac to show himself before he had time to hurt someone in the city.

At last Josef set aside his complaints. "All right, we do it your way, but we plan everything down to the last detail."

"Good," Bako said. "Now, if we're done with this martyring business, may I suggest we look at a map of the city and explore our options." He pointed to a shelf containing several leather-sided tubes.

Yanis sorted through the outside labels until he found one that would work. He removed the end cap, gently slid the rolled-up paper from the tube, and spread the map open on the table. It proved to be a moderately detailed depiction of the Old Town, commissioned by the emperor nearly a decade earlier.

"This will do," Petra said. She and Josef leaned over the map, shoulders touching, as they pointed to familiar landmarks—the castle, the bridge, the old city gate. "This is the storeroom, and this is where we are now," she said, dragging her finger the short distance from one spot to the other.

"We need to find someplace secluded," Bako said. "A park might make sense."

Josef objected. "Open land will only favor his unique abilities. He could run, and we'd be no match for his speed."

"A courtyard, then," Yanis suggested. "Something on the outskirts of the city where there are fewer people and more walls." The sorcerer indicated a place next to the river. "What if we trap him here?" he asked, but not knowing the city, he didn't realize he'd pointed to the old castle grounds to the south. Not a very accessible place to catch a vlkodlak.

As Petra took another look at their location, her eye snagged on something interesting just a few streets south of where they were. An intersection where five roads converged at a small public square. Her body reacted with a shiver that radiated out from her chest to her extremities. "This is the place to do it. This is where we'll trap him."

The three men leaned in for a closer look. "Here?" Bako asked. "It's too centralized. There will be too many people on the street. We can't risk innocent victims."

Josef said nothing, but Petra could tell he agreed with Bako's assessment by the way he crossed his arms. But Yanis slowly nodded, and then the light came into his eyes after seeing what she'd seen.

"She's right." Yanis borrowed one of the magnifying glasses and used it to study the five roads leading to the small square. "This could work."

"How is drawing a vlkodlak into the heart of the Old Town a good idea?" Josef asked. "My family lives only a few streets from there."

"Because of the crossroads," Petra said. She knew he didn't understand the significance, but a crossroads with five roads was a place of enormous power. "Five roads converging create their own boost of energy. Do you see the star shape? Whatever spell we devise to slow or restrain him will be magnified by the powerful convergence of five roads on that one spot."

Yanis had them look through the magnifying glass to see the pattern for themselves. "He won't know what hit him."

The hussar played devil's advocate. "But if we lure him here, won't he have five escape routes?"

Petra shook her head. "I'll seal the roads off with a spell wall once he's inside the perimeter of the public square. It will be an illusion of normalcy to the outside public, but the boosted energy will hold him inside. He'll be trapped."

"Like what you used to hide the upíri from the soldiers in camp," Josef said, understanding.

"Exactly. I can hold him there long enough for you all to do whatever it is you need to do to destroy a vlkodlak."

"If he doesn't attack you first." Josef scratched at his stubble, thinking. "How will we see past the spell wall if we're on the outside?"

Petra smiled. "Yanis or Viktor can latch on to the spell and create an opening with a blessed knife for you to walk through, but our vlkodlak won't be able to cross out of the spell wall once he's inside. Not until he's dead."

"So how do we make sure he comes to this spot when we want him to?" Bako asked.

Josef exhaled. "If it's Petra he's after, he'll sniff her out and track her to the intersection. That won't be a problem. We'll do it at midnight, when most people are off the streets."

Yanis agreed. "Now all we have to do is figure out if our vlkodlak has arrived yet."

"Oh, he's here," Franz said, interrupting their planning session. He threw down a special edition newspaper on the table that was so fresh off the printer it still smelled of wet ink. The headline running across the top read: MAN MAULED BY WILD ANIMAL IN THE HEART OF THE CITY! A series of gruesome details followed with a reference to a blood-soaked floor and footprints leading away in the shape of a bear or wolf, yet one that no one saw. "The man was discovered a little over an hour ago."

Petra's intestines slumped inside her at the thought of the killer being so near. This vlkodlak had only just arrived and already he'd killed an innocent bystander within the city. He was up there now, snuffling in the streets looking for her; or wandering over the old king's bridge, hunting for his next victim; or curled up in someone's private courtyard, picking his teeth and complaining of a bloated stomach. A vision of the man she'd seen in the attic flashed in her mind, but with fangs bared and bloody. It wasn't a normal emotion for a witch to feel like prey, but all it took was one vicious predator on the hunt to make her sympathize with the rabbit under a hawk's eye. But this rabbit had claws of her own, she told herself, eyeing the axe on the table.

Josef picked up the paper and scanned the article. "According to this report the perpetrator ran off with some expensive clothing too. As bears often do." He threw the paper down and stared at Petra. His breath came heavy as his nostrils flared. "A murderer *and* a dandy."

"The authorities at the highest levels will already know the truth," Yanis said. "Hugo will have informed them of our situation, but they won't alert the public. It would create a scenario of pure panic."

"He'll be sleeping it off now, if his past behavior is any indication," Bako said. "But once he recovers in a few hours, he'll be on the prowl again. There is no room for error tonight. We have to get him on the first try or more people are going to die."

Yanis took the arrows out of his sleeve. "Our job is to make sure that doesn't happen." He turned to Franz and asked, "Would you by any chance have a supply of *strychnos toxifera* on hand for a curare?"

"Right this way," the researcher said. "Haven't mixed up a decent arrow neurotoxin in an age. Are we killing or merely stunning?"

"Oh, definitely killing," Yanis said, while Petra internalized the conviction in his voice.

CHAPTER
TWENTY-THREE

Josef couldn't pick up the man's scent from where they were below-ground. Not yet. Leastwise, not as a man. If he could change form, he was certain his nose would find the trail like a bright ribbon fluttering in the air, but his human physiology had limitations. He held the partial bottle of elixir in his hand and gave it a small shake. He didn't even know if the solution inside was still viable. The smell was right, but how old was the potion? Could something like that go bad? What if half a bottle wasn't enough to help him recover if he changed?

If only they had more time.

He pocketed the bottle and glanced over at Yanis, who stood boiling bark over an open flame to make poison for his arrows. Franz helped him, sprinkling in crushed herbs when instructed. There was a gleam in the sorcerer's eye that suggested a part of him relished the preparation for confrontation with the vlkodlak. Bako wore the same look. The hussar pulled the pair of pearl-handled revolvers from his heirloom case and polished the barrels until the metal glinted in the light. Strange business, he thought, being recruited to work for the Order. It was one part enforcing a universal system of justice and one part letting mercenaries do their worst against the evils in the world.

Needing something less toxic to focus on, Josef walked down the hall and found Petra tucked away in a corner of the library studying her father's journal. The Society's copy, judging by the empty spot on the shelf. Her magic required no potions, no boiling bark or crushing of herbs in iron mortars, so she'd slipped away to read on her own.

He still couldn't believe he'd found her. Petra had been in hiding for ten years. After she vanished as a child, everyone assumed she was dead, including the authorities. But Hana knew. She'd found her by tossing the bones and looking through the veil into the world beyond. He wondered if one of the ghosts Petra had photographed had given her up that day. Or had Hana just made a lucky guess she was in the city and his nose had done the rest? Either way, it no longer mattered. Because that one thing he'd been wishing for when he found Petra alone in that tiny courtyard long past midnight had still managed to come true. What he'd thought she could do for him with her magic, she'd done instead with looks like the one she gave him now.

"I was just thinking about you," Petra said.

"Good thoughts, I hope." Josef sat down beside her at the table.

"I wanted to take a closer look at the sun and moon illustration. The original," she whispered. "Look here." She tilted the book and offered him a magnifying glass. "Do you see the added details in their eyes?"

Josef looked through the glass at the page and saw what looked like little sparks radiating from the eyes of the sun and moon lovers her father had drawn. He blinked, self-conscious about the similarity to the glint in his own eyes. "What does it mean?"

"I'm not sure, but sitting here in this place, with the obvious connection to the alchemists who built these tunnels, I can't help but wonder if my father had stumbled onto something, I don't know, dangerous. Something that maybe got him into trouble."

"What exactly is a grimoire?" he asked, leaning forward on his elbows. "Is that like the notes we've been reading that belonged to Ava König?"

"Similar," Petra said. "But the journals they have here don't contain her spells. Only her lecture notes and hints at some of the ideas she was developing." She thumbed through her father's book and pointed to another illustration of a plant with small leaves growing alongside a center stem and small red berries. Beside it were step-by-step instructions in the various ways he used rowan leaf, including as an aid to a stomach ailment. "A grimoire is more like a recipe book. Witches write down their spells, thoughts, and experiences for later reference."

"Do you have one of these?"

She shook her head. "My magic is almost all touch," she said, opening her hand and staring at her fingers as if they were foreign to her. "I remember a few incantations from Hana and my father, but I never got the chance to write any of them down in my own book when I was younger. Later, I didn't want anyone to know who or what I was, so I didn't bother."

In some ways, Josef could relate. Everyone in his family was a baker. Or a cook. It was always assumed he'd work in the bakery and eventually take over for his father, using those same recipes handed down from one generation to the next. He'd always expected that future for himself, too, until he'd joined the army and a random attack on a night patrol had left him bleeding from a bite that nearly took his arm off.

"Your husband was a mortal, yet he never knew about any of this?"

"There were a lot of things my husband never bothered to learn about me." Her gaze drifted off briefly before she brought her attention back to the book. "There's something really odd about the missing pages."

"Maybe your father made a mistake and took out the parts he got wrong."

"Your knowledge builds as you get older," Petra said, unconvinced. "So you always leave a little room at the bottom of the page to add new information or corrections. But I remember my father accompanied his notes with a drawing first, like this one of the rowan." She turned to another page and pointed to a sketch of linden leaves. "And this one too. He taught me how to use a bundle of the leaves as a protection amulet."

The memory of the citrusy scent of the linden leaves registered in Josef's nose, reminding him again of the first night he'd seen her in the snow. He cleared his throat to help him concentrate on the book again. "So, according to his habit, there should be a spell to go with the sun and moon your father drew with room to add on more later." Josef flipped through the pages to the back again. "Whatever was removed had to be at least, what, ten pages long, judging by the torn fragments along the spine? None of the other spells or notes left that much space for later epiphanies."

"Ten pages exactly, if you count front and back. I checked. And if you look at the date of the next spell in the book, whatever he'd written down was during the time Martina said he was working here. Which makes me think it was something to do with his final days as a researcher. I think this spell is what got him into trouble." She looked up to see if there was anyone near the door. "Listen, Max, the junior researcher, told me yesterday, when we were putting on our coats to leave, that he heard my father was forced out because Augustus and Martina were angry he wouldn't share his research findings. That's why he was accused of stealing gold, but they conveniently never pressed charges."

"If he was swallowing it, they wouldn't have exactly been able to prove he had the gold on him."

"My father wasn't a thief," Petra said. "He never once asked me to change something worthless into something valuable for his own benefit. Even when money was tight and we had to eat thin potato soup for a month." She gazed at their medieval surroundings, pursing her lips. "Gold and silver. Didn't Viktor say there was an elixir of life that contained gold? The old alchemists believed gold was a potent element that could impart immortality in the drinker. Maybe my father was working on a spell that would do just that when something happened."

"You think he figured out immortality?" The part he didn't say out loud was that her father had died fairly young, which didn't say a lot for any immortality spell.

Petra's shoulders slumped slightly. "I guess it sounds ridiculous. But I still think whatever experiments he was conducting with gold had something to do with these missing pages. Either he didn't want anyone else to see his work and he destroyed the spell knowing his grimoire might someday be confiscated, or someone else got to it before he died."

"Except if someone stole it, why leave the illustration behind? Doesn't that belong with the spell? If there was an illustration to go with a recipe I was following, I'd want the picture for a reference to make sure the dish turned out how it was supposed to. Unless, of course, your father tore the pages out and left the drawing behind on purpose."

"Why?"

Josef reexamined the dancing sun and moon. "Maybe he wanted someone familiar with his habit of creating an illustration for each spell to know there was more. That it wasn't a mistake. That it hadn't been stolen."

Petra's eyes widened slightly at the idea. "He wanted me to know there was a written spell for whatever he'd been working on." She leaned in closer and whispered, "Only he was trying to protect it from getting into the wrong hands. But what could it be? And where are those pages? Did he leave the drawing as a torment or a clue?"

Petra traced a finger gently over the drawing, almost as if she were reaching out to touch whatever residual energy remained of her father within the ink. "As a child, I always had the sense my father was hiding something. That *something* had changed when we left the city. I just assumed it was me. That he was being overprotective and secretive because my magic was so different. But maybe that was my child's mind thinking that." She paused, pressing her fingers to her lips as her memories seemed to overtake her thoughts. "He made a discovery. Here in this place. Something to do with the gold, I just know it. Ava König said he was brilliant. Brilliant enough for them to work together." She nodded slowly. "He hid those pages somewhere safe, I'm almost certain of it. He would never have destroyed them."

"Knock, knock." Martina tapped lightly on the cavern wall and smiled. "Sorry to interrupt, but I wonder if Petra wouldn't mind joining me in the lab. We have those blood results back. I'd like to go over them with you. I think you'll find them fascinating."

"I'd better go," Petra said. "After the hair samples, I can't wait to see what surprises are swimming in my blood."

The back of her hand brushed against Josef's fingers as she slid the grimoire toward him, sending a quickening pulse coursing through his body. If not for the chance to sit with Petra a little bit longer, he would have left already. The elixir was gone, all but the half bottle Bako had held back. In his heart, he knew it wouldn't be enough. The altered curse demanded his body voluntarily transform into the crafty wolf between every lunar cycle or else succumb to the howling madness of the vlkodlak under the full moon. That was the temporary reprieve Hana had given him with her potion, but his time had run out. Life as he knew it had run out.

Josef held the half-empty bottle of elixir up to the lamplight and stared at its contents. He had one last opportunity to transform into the wolf with his human wits still intact. He'd already decided it was the only way. The others didn't understand what they were up against. He and Dimitri . . . their cursed instincts were too strong, too sharp, to fall for traps. Only another wolf could corner and kill the vlkodlak. One that still possessed the mind of a man.

But he had to wait just a little longer. With the group's plans in place, he had no choice but to let Petra go stand in the square with her crossroads magic and wall of illusion. It was the only way to keep her and the others safe. Meanwhile, he would lure the beast to the river. And may the sharpest claw win.

CHAPTER
TWENTY-FOUR

The starshina caught a whiff of familiar sweat through the window, pungent with the muskiness of the wolf. So, the soldier in the fur hat was nearby. He adjusted the puff tie at his throat, a red silk beauty in a paisley design. The rhinestone pin just below the knot gave him the air of an aristocrat. And why not? Was he not the pinnacle of creatures? An apex predator? He smiled at himself in the mirror and shrugged on the jacket.

The suit fit better than he expected, for being machine sewn. Perhaps he should not have been so hasty with the man in the shop. It was a new world in the west, after all. A world he intended to crack open like a raw egg to suck the yolk and drain all the nourishment he could from it. But first he must take the young woman. The witch.

She was no Baba Yaga, not like the old woman in the stories who lived in a house that stood on chicken legs and had given him nightmares as a child. He remembered the young woman having a calm voice. Empathy. But there was also deception. Lies wrapped around her words like fishing nets that trapped the truth inside. He must remember she was the slippery eel who must be gently lured in to set the hook.

The starshina combed his hair back using the pomade he'd found in his host's bathroom cabinet. His sideburns needed trimming, but there was little time to search for a pair of scissors. He'd already slept half the day away. Such ferocious appetites he experienced! Only to end up flopped on the sofa afterward like a stuffed rag doll, with his stomach bloated and the dried blood making his mustache itch. But he was recovered now and already feeling peckish.

The man in the front room moaned to life again. In the starshina's post-feeding frenzy, he'd merely bitten the man's shoulder to overpower him and gain access to his apartment, but he hadn't forgotten the staggering toll it took on his own body when he'd first been attacked by the vlkodlak in the mountains. The veins filled with fire first as the curse spread. The infection—for what else could it be?—made his body reel as though it had been drained of all its natural fluids. Flaccid, useless, spent. His body had lain unconscious for a full day while his mind ran wild in dreams of old-growth forests full of ferns, fog, and moss-covered trees. But then a sort of electrical charge, like too much caffeine, steeped into his bones, both exhilarating and exhausting him at the same time. His mind cleared and his muscles spasmed with a need to run, and then just when he thought he would break free of the man he used to be, an old woman poured a bottle of elixir down his throat and the soldier tightened his restraints, chaining him to the wall like an animal in a circus. All that frenzied energy, waiting to break free, disintegrated into feckless mush, and he slept until the moon sank beneath the horizon.

"Do not worry, my friend," he called to the man. "You will have your strength back in no time. Lucky for you, I have not restrained you in a straitjacket and chained you to a wall, only to force a nasty concoction down your throat." Yes, he'd had to gag the man's mouth and tie his hands and feet while he bled on the floor, but it was purely out of a need to be practical in the situation. The one scream had been plenty.

"How do I look?" the starshina asked, stepping into the front room fully attired in his new suit and stiff white shirt. "I must make a good impression, after all."

The man moaned and vomited against the gag in his mouth.

The starshina took a step back, checking his trousers to make certain they were still as pristine as when he'd stolen them off the shop display. He couldn't afford to look anything less than perfect. Not tonight, when he must win over his prize. His strategy was to use all the charm he could muster to beguile the little witch. To make her see their brilliant future together through his eyes. But if she resisted, he felt no compunction against using the necessary force to coerce her to do his bidding. Not when violence had readily given him everything he ever wanted so far.

CHAPTER
TWENTY-FIVE

Petra stared at the slide of her blood under the microscope. Tiny, shimmering specks swam in the sample as though they were alive. Having nothing to compare it to, she lifted her head, slightly confused by the bright-eyed excitement displayed on Martina's face. The woman nearly drooled out of the corner of her mouth from her fermented expectation while waiting for Petra to say something.

"Is there something unusual about the sample I should know about?" Petra couldn't decipher what she was looking at.

Augustus had been called away to a seminar in the Empire's capital city, so it was just Martina there to explain. The witch seemed put out with Petra, as though she'd said something impertinent. Her weight shifted, and she put her hand on her hip. "Do you have any understanding of what those flecks in your blood are?" Martina came around the table and looked through the lens on the microscope again, as if she couldn't believe her own eyes. "We've never seen it before. The results are likely the key to your very rare condition."

"My condition?"

Martina clasped her hand over Petra's. A brief tingle, like the radiating energy produced from a cycling spell, sent a small jolt of electricity buzzing under her skin. The prickling sensation felt strangely like the energy swirling beneath the illusion spell she kept in place over her scar so no one would see it.

"Do you not see the resemblance to the samples of your hair? The tiny flecks you see in your blood are definitely not typical," Martina said.

"What does that mean?"

"You have gold dust in your blood." Martina reached for a type-written report on the table, holding it up like an exhibit of evidence in a trial. "And the hair sample we thought was shimmering under the microscope because of a dual-witch parentage?" She shook her head. "On second inspection that proved to be traces of gold clinging to the shaft. Uncanny how similar it appeared to pure witch hair."

Petra peered through the microscope again. Now that she knew what she was looking at, she could see the slight shimmer to the particles. They moved constantly, as though energized. "Are you sure my sample didn't get mixed up with something in the lab? Some chemical or mineral?" She knew her father had been accused of swallowing gold, but she'd never put any in her body. Ever. "What would that even do to a person? To me?"

"We drew two blood samples, and both appeared identical," Martina said. "Your blood is saturated with microscopic particles of gold. However, it doesn't appear to be causing you any harm." Martina touched Petra's shoulder in a reassuring manner. "There's little cause for concern. In fact, I'd venture to say you've derived some benefit from the element in your veins."

"How did it get there?" Petra was tiring of this endless obsession with gold.

"Given your father's history here at the laboratory . . ." Martina paused as though searching for the right words. "We did notice a sizable amount go missing while he worked here. Did he ever inject you with any shots? Or spoon-feed you any elixir of life?"

"No, never."

Martina gazed at her without blinking. "Did he ever discuss with you how your unusual magical gift came to be? Did he mention a spell? Or any procedure he might have used to influence your unique ability?"

Petra thought back to when she was a little girl. Her father had always been so pleased when she was able to turn a spoon, or shoe, or rock into whatever object he asked for. There were hugs and sweets and conspiratorial smiles that they shared this secret magic together. But there had never been a spell recited or an offering of herbs placed in a fire. And there'd been no gold involved. Not asked for by him, and not provided by her.

"No, it wasn't like that," she said. "My magic was born with me. If I couldn't reach a toy on a shelf, I made one out of a shoe or a comb or napkin. He and my mother had to watch me closely until I understood what I was doing."

Martina frowned. "No. You must be mistaken. It's common for children to adjust their memories to fit the stories they've been told as they got older. Try thinking back to what you remember of your own experiences when you were younger. You must recall something out of the ordinary occurring. A spell your father used? Something you've never quite been able to explain."

"No, I don't think so."

"Your father stole gold from this facility, that's indisputable," Martina said. "I've come to believe he used it to enhance a spell he used on you." She lowered her chin and crossed her arms as she continued. "Gold is a very powerful element. It can both absorb and transmit spell energy. The proof is in your blood and your ability. I only seek to uncover how he did it, so your cooperation would be useful here."

"He didn't do anything to me. He was just my father."

The witch made a tsk sound with her tongue. "We've all experimented on ourselves, including your father," she said, slipping off her gloves to reveal bare hands that were mottled red and white by scars resembling burns. "A spell here. A spell there. They take their toll," she said, turning her hands over. "But imagine using your own child as a test subject." She attempted to push a strand of hair back from Petra's face with her scarred finger, but Petra recoiled. "What kind of father would do that to his own offspring?" Martina continued, undeterred.

"And for what? Glory? Money? Only to end up with nothing for himself in the end but an early death."

Petra was beginning to believe Max hadn't merely been gossiping when he said her father was asked to leave out of jealousy and resentment rather than for stealing gold. "My father was a good man who taught me everything I know," she said. "Now, if you'll excuse me, I need to check on my friends' progress. We have a vlkodlak to confront tonight."

Martina called after Petra as she fled down the tunnel. "We need to figure out the incantation your father used to create your magic, Petra. There's a balance due for what he took."

CHAPTER TWENTY-SIX

Josef watched as Yanis carefully dipped a thin glass vial into his concoction of boiled bark using a pair of specialized tongs. He let the oily brown liquid seep inside the tube, then capped the glass with a dab of warm wax to seal it. The sorcerer passed the tube over a candle flame that had been centered inside a circle drawn with foreign-looking symbols. Yanis called them sigils and said each was imbued with powerful energy that would call up the magic needed to take down their prey. Josef observed the entire spectacle half-impressed, half-nauseated. The poison was meant for Dimitri, but the spell that went with it was for the vlkodlak—any vlkodlak.

Josef's precarious position between working on behalf of a clandestine league of supernatural adjudicators and being a fingertip's grip away from becoming the thing they were commissioned to destroy had about done his head in. He'd been walking in two worlds for months, and he was exhausted. By the time Bako passed him the flask of brandy, he gladly accepted and drank deeply.

"So how do we lure Dimitri into the intersection at the moment we want?" Bako asked. "How long will it take before he knows Petra is there?"

"He'll know exactly when she's there," Josef said. "He probably knows already what her general location is. Mine too." He took another drink before Bako snatched the flask away. "People's scents, they get in the nose," he said with a wave of his hand toward his face. "They get filed away as memories and images. Emotions sometimes. Later, when scents you're already familiar with suddenly get stronger, or more saturated, it's like the card catalog in your brain tosses out the directions on exactly where to find the source of the increased smell. Over the bridge, two streets north, one to the left, room on the top floor in the corner," he said, remembering how he had found Petra's apartment the first night after he'd picked up the scent of her hair and the linden leaves in her pocket.

"Can you find him?"

"I'm not picking up much of anything from down here yet," Josef said, wary of letting on too much of what his nose had already detected on their walk from the storeroom. "But he's here. This side of the river. Once I get aboveground again, I'll know exactly when he's about to enter the intersection, even if we can't see him."

What Josef didn't say out loud was how he could smell the fresh kill when Dimitri had attacked. He could trace the scent to the exact street. Knew the shop where it happened. He'd met the shopkeeper there when he'd gone to the store with his father at age fourteen for his first suit. His stomach contents rose into his throat at the thought of what had happened to the man who'd treated him like a respected adult that day as he cultivated a future customer.

"He'll know we're there, too, unless we use the wolfsbane," Bako said. "I better prepare enough for all of us to rub on. I'll ask Franz if they have more in storage."

Soon after Bako walked away, Viktor showed up in a leather apron, red-faced and sweating from his furnace. He beamed from ear to ear. "I think I did it," he said. The witch carried a bundle wrapped in a cloth. As he did with the sacred glass vessel he took everywhere he went, he gently unveiled his latest creation, cradling the object in his arms like a newborn for presentation. "Go ahead, pick it up," he said to Josef.

The smell of charred wood and burnished glass had invaded Josef's nostrils all afternoon, and here was the source. It resembled a round lantern the way it was shaped. The outer glass panels were tinted and held together by copper on the top, sides, and bottom. But it had a second cylinder on the inside that rotated with a knob. "How does it work?" he asked.

"It's made to be adjustable." Viktor took the lantern back and showed him how the handle on top moved the cylinder on the inside. "Two layers of glass. One lightly tinted like sunglasses, and one that's tinted in gradient shades from midnight blue to clear. That way we can control how much light escapes. If you build up enough tolerance, we can remove the outer layer." He'd already filled the inside with a soft beam of moonlight, and rotated the piece to demonstrate how it worked like the phases of the moon by shining it at the wall. "We can work our way up to full moonlight a little at a time," he said.

Josef hadn't put too much faith in the idea of the lantern when he'd first heard about it, but he couldn't deny the way the pure moonlight had made him react. Could such a simple contraption work? Could he be weaned off the moon's tidal pull on his cursed blood? Be rid of his need for more elixir? It seemed impossible. "Thank you, Viktor. It's a marvel."

"We'll try it as soon as this business is over with. When the moon turns her face toward us again. It will work, you'll see."

Josef wished he had a tenth of Viktor's faith. His mortal side had stubbornly held on to its skeptical attitude toward the unexplainable. He knew better, after all he'd been through from his contact with the supernatural, yet he couldn't shake the need for proof. "When this is all over," he said and patted Viktor on the back. "Until then, let's make sure we're ready to defend Petra when Dimitri walks into our trap."

Viktor set his moon lantern aside and helped Yanis and Franz load the poison ampules into the arrows for the crossbow. Across the room, Bako set out the supply of wolfsbane, divvying it up so the rest of them could hide their scent from the vlkodlak. While the others were busy, Josef slipped Petra's scarf off the back of her coat and held it to his nose. Before anyone could notice, he rolled it up and stashed it under his ushanka, then contemplated how to leave the tunnels without anyone noticing.

CHAPTER
TWENTY-SEVEN

The starshina stood on the street corner and inhaled. She was close. And yet the scent trail crisscrossed all over the city. The smell of her perspiration was in the main square, a small churchyard, side streets that wound back on each other, and on the footpath leading over the saint-lined bridge. He hadn't counted on her being from the city. Or the other one either. The halfling wolf.

He shook his head to clear it of the overload of information. There were too many people and too much contamination. A miasma of filth, rot, and commerce all rolled up into a ball of useless information. But he knew she was near. He kept getting whiffs of the oils in her hair or the damp wool in the armpits of her jacket. He'd been on the hunt long enough that the odor made his mouth salivate at the prospect of finding her soon. He flicked his tongue in the air and inhaled again.

A little to the north and a short jaunt to the west.

The starshina tugged the points of his waistcoat down and strolled through the Old Town Square as the astronomical clock chimed the hour. He stopped to observe the carved apostles as they paraded on their mechanical orbit with their keys and cups and weapons, threatening damnation with one hand and offering salvation with the other. Then the skeleton rattled its bones and rang its bell. "But for whom does the bell toll?" he asked under his breath and chuckled. He found a beer garden not far from the clock's apostles and death-peddling skeleton and sat down to experience his rare good mood and budding future.

The starshina nibbled on a pickled sausage, then sipped his beer. He'd not given much thought to the improved state of his life since his glorious rebirth. Parts of his previous existence had already faded from his memory like tattered cloth shot through with bullet holes. He was a tailor's son; he remembered that well enough. But some of the details between him and his father had grown fuzzy. He had an odd recollection of holding a stolen pocket watch, gloating over the price it would fetch, and soon after being dragged before the authorities to face a reckoning for theft.

Had that been his father's doing? Did he recall correctly that he had been given the choice between reporting to a work camp in the north or being conscripted into the army, only to be shipped off to the coldest corner of hell and left to die anyway? He should have chosen the work camp. At least then he would have known to expect one torturous day followed by another.

But had he not made the choice he did, he would not have been given this grand second chance. A life impervious to the degradation of poverty and indifference. No one could ignore him now. He was on the verge of becoming everything he'd ever dreamed of. His was the fist that rattled the table now.

The starshina drank heavily from his glass and wanted another. Best not to be too keen with the witch. He did not wish to frighten her. He intended to steal her away, of course, but he didn't want to endure any screaming this time. Being near a woman when her voice hit that high screech of panic stabbed like a saber through the brain. He shook his head, not wanting to go through that again, so he ordered another beer to temper his excitement, another sausage to whet his appetite, and sat with something to look forward to for the first time in a long while.

By the time he finished his second sausage, the clock had struck the hour again. The stars shone above the tower in a kaleidoscope of natural beauty, while that hag of a moon prowled the sky like a sliver of hangnail he couldn't be rid of. To glance upon her now made his eyes ache as though he'd had sand rubbed in them. He turned away and thought about who he would kill first, the sorcerer or the soldier, then he swallowed the last of his beer and waited for a ribbon of the witch's scent to lure him to her.

CHAPTER
TWENTY-EIGHT

Petra hid in the botanical room where they hung the herbs from the ceiling to dry. The scent of lavender and chamomile calmed her down, and she sank to the floor to sit with her legs crossed and her back against the wall. First her hair and now her blood? Both tainted with gold? It made no sense. They'd made a mistake. Maybe Martina and Augustus really were charlatans hiding in their underground tunnels. Maybe Viktor really was touched in the head. Maybe they all were.

A basket of dried hops sat near the toe of Petra's boot. The earthy-smelling flower heads were a gentle reminder of the sane side of magic. Long before there were alchemists and bloody kings, it was the bierhexen who first added the gentle-tasting flower heads to their brews to turn the bitter piss-water into mellow beer. Petra ran her fingers through the dried flower heads. More recently, she'd heard a new generation of bierhexen had found a way to boost the flavor in the blooms to make the smooth pilsner that Marek had said sipped like a gift from the gods. When the witches had perfected the flavored blooms, they'd enchanted the plants in their care to replicate the same flower every time, passing on the identical traits from one generation of plants to the next to ensure they always got the best results.

The notion of gene inheritance pricked Petra's intuition like the prickles on a rose stem. Her hand froze in the bowl of flower heads, and her eyes lifted to the mural of the sun and moon lovers painted on the wall. As she gazed at it, her mind spun out all the interconnections her intuition had already identified. Sun and moon. Gold and silver. Swallowed gold. Gold in her blood. Gold in her hair. A mortal mother and witch father. Alchemists and witches.

Martina's damaged hands.

Petra dropped the flowers and got to her feet.

Martina had said the alchemists routinely did experiments on themselves to test ideas. Was that what her father had done? Had he swallowed the gold to test a theory? To work out a spell on himself, only to pass some version of it on to her? She studied the mural again. Sun and moon, gold and silver. Gold in her blood; silver in Josef's eyes. It couldn't be a coincidence. Not when her father and Ava König had worked side by side in these tunnels. Not when the designer of the vlkodlak curse constantly praised her father for his innovative ideas.

There was a spell. An incantation. A potion. Something written down in those missing pages in his grimoire. Something to do with the gold in her blood. Josef was right. He'd left that illustration behind to let her know there was more. An explanation. A confession. An apology. But why hide it? And where? How would she ever find it if nothing of her old life existed anymore?

Petra ran to the workroom where the others were preparing to confront Dimitri in the crossroads. Viktor, Bako, and Yanis were all there, but Josef wasn't.

Yanis looked up from loading arrows into a short leather quiver. "Is something wrong?" he asked, after seeing Petra out of breath.

"Where's Josef?"

The sorcerer looked around as if expecting to see the team leader still sitting behind him. "He must have stepped out to stretch his legs."

Petra's enthusiasm dimmed only a little, but she had to share what she'd stumbled upon or burst. "The illustration in my father's grimoire. It means something." She reached for the stack of Ava König's notebooks. "König and my father were working together. They were trying to figure out how to use gold and silver in their spells."

Viktor stopped playing with the lantern in his hands and came over to look in the books with her. "There is some mention of it in a few of König's notes. Let me help you."

Petra slid the books to Viktor. "Martina said people here experiment on themselves."

"Sure, sometimes," Viktor said, looking for the right notebook. "When it's sensitive research and they don't want news leaving the confines of the tunnels. Or they just have a hunch about something and want an answer right away."

"The researchers said my father was experimenting with the gold they claim he stole by swallowing it. I think König was experimenting with silver at the same time. It's how it became a component of her wolf curse."

"Wait, I don't understand," Yanis said. "What experiments?"

Petra dug out her copy of her father's grimoire from her coat while Viktor flipped through König's notes. It only mildly registered with her that her scarf wasn't hung over her coat anymore, but it wasn't important. She opened the grimoire to the illustration of the sun and moon. "The missing pages. There's a spell that goes with the drawing. A spell that has to do with the gold he was swallowing. About the gold in my blood."

Bako stopped polishing the pearl handles on his revolvers. "You have gold in your blood?"

Petra nodded. "Martina just showed me under the microscope. It's in my hair, my blood, and probably in my brain and bones too."

"How?"

Petra didn't know, not yet, but she knew whatever incantation her father had written in the missing pages would have told her exactly how it got in her bloodstream. "Somehow the gold passed from him to me through his spellwork. More urgently, I think König did something similar. They were both experimenting with precious metals together.

I have a hunch if we looked at Josef's blood under the microscope, it would have silver dust in it. I think the silver in his eyes is the key to his curse and maybe reversing it."

"I've never heard of using gold or silver that way," Yanis said. "That doesn't mean it isn't possible. Gold has the rare quality of being almost indestructible. When they make it into wire, it can be drawn out thinner than a human hair and not lose any of its malleability or strength."

"Could it be stretched small enough to enter into someone's bloodstream?" Bako asked.

Yanis gave a reluctant shrug. "If aided by magic, anything is possible."

"Gold and silver are also reliable conductors of electricity," Viktor said, stabbing König's book in triumph. "I knew I'd seen mentions of it in König's notes." He set the book down in front of Petra and pointed to an entry that mentioned her first ideas on using electricity in spellcasting. "We'd seen a lecture note about the possibility of using blood as a carrier for a transformation spell earlier. But later she added her thoughts in her journal on using electricity as a way to charge the spell to make it last longer."

January 10, 1889. Imperial University lecture. Professor Schuster.

~ The professors here all seem to think that blood is the only conduit to transformation. Their thinking is so medieval. The world is changing constantly. Even mortals are coming up with extraordinary discoveries. Honza and I both think the electric light bulb is the greatest invention of the century. Not just for the convenience it will bring to a dark world, but for all the other possibilities that will ride in on its electric coattails. Telephones, telegraphs, phonographs. The application to magic, too, cannot be denied. If a flow of current can make a copper wire come alive and transmit information from one place to another, what might it do to an incantation? Why couldn't magic be transported from one place to another the same as a voice over a wire?

Viktor looked up from the notes. "What if they brought their ideas on electricity here after university and figured out a way to use precious metals inside the body to keep a spell in perpetual motion?" He was thinking out loud, but his confidence in his idea grew the more he spoke. "What if they figured out how to attach electricity to a spell inside the body using gold and silver?" he asked. "What would that do?"

"Inside a body?" Yanis blew air out of his mouth as though he were out of his depth.

Viktor doubled down. "What if they were able to create some kind of living pathway inside the body. What if they figured out how to use gold as a capacitor that keeps the spell your father created in perpetual motion in here," he said to Petra, indicating her heart.

Petra felt a little queasy at the thought of a spell constantly cycling through her body, but she couldn't deny the tingle she often felt thrumming under her skin after transforming an object, particularly in her wrists.

"I'm no expert, but doesn't electricity need to run on some kind of circuit to work?" Yanis asked, stuffing his remaining poisonous ampules into the quiver.

"They wouldn't have to figure that part out." Bako took a sip from his flask. "A perfectly good circuit already exists in the body."

Viktor snapped his fingers. "The pathway of blood."

"They don't call it the circulatory system for nothing," Bako said.

Petra's mouth fell open. The idea was simple yet astonishing, if true.

"Just add charged particles of gold or silver enchanted with an incantation." Yanis rubbed the sweat from his forehead with the sleeve from his robe. "But would something like that really be possible? Even the jinn do not use magic like this."

"It's long been understood that witches tap into their own source of energy," Viktor said. "Augustus claims our magic is already electrical in nature. They could have used an outside source to charge the particles, then relied on the energy inherent in a witch's body to keep it going."

"They must have figured out a way," Petra said, pointing to the illustration in her father's book. "My father used gold and she used silver. See how the figures are dancing, holding hands as they go around in a circle like a flowing current. It's them. Their magic. They did it together. He created the ultimate alchemist's dream, and she devised a curse that she could control like a light, on or off."

"Because if the magic runs on a circuit, that means there's a way to break it," Yanis said. "A switch of some kind." He took out a piece of paper and began sketching out ideas.

Petra looked again at the gap of missing pages, knowing the answer had to be in them. If only she knew where to look. But she knew in her heart they were on the right track. They'd just have to experiment to find the right solution.

"Where's Josef?" Petra asked again. "He needs to know this."

Bako checked his watch. "He should be back. We're set to rendez-vous at our positions in thirty minutes."

Petra hadn't realized it was so late. If they were going to attract Dimitri to the square at midnight, they had less than an hour to pre-pare. And they had to go through with their plan tonight or risk letting someone else be murdered. She closed her copy of her father's grimoire and secured it inside her coat. "I'm going to go look for him."

"Who's that?" Franz stood by the door, putting on his jacket to leave.

"Josef. You haven't seen him, have you?"

Franz adjusted his glasses when they slid down his nose. "Yes, he left about fifteen minutes ago. I had to let him out." He did up his buttons and adjusted his scarf. "I was just about to lock up. Are you really going out there tonight? To call a vlkodlak to you?" He pursed his lips and looked down the hallway toward the exit as though having second thoughts about leaving. "Perhaps I ought to stay and work on some experiments in case you need anything."

"Did Josef say where he was going?" Petra asked, dread creeping in to displace her excitement.

Franz appeared as though he'd never been asked such a detailed question before. "Well, no. He just left. Took off at a run as soon as he got outside."

"Which way?"

"Toward the river, I think."

"He's up to something." Petra's intuition flared and she checked her coat again. "My scarf is missing. He's taken my scarf!"

"Maybe he was just cold?" Franz offered.

"He doesn't feel the cold like we do. Besides, he took *my* scarf with *my* scent on it."

"Vial of elixir is gone too," Bako said. "And someone's helped themselves to the wolfsbane."

"What's he planning to do?" Viktor closed the witch's journal. "Meet wolf to wolf?"

The four of them exchanged worried glances. "That fool!" Petra frantically threw on her coat. "He can't take on a vlkodlak by himself."

"He doesn't have to." Yanis grabbed his crossbow and arrows. Bako followed, stuffing both revolvers into the holsters he wore strapped to his chest. Viktor picked up his lantern loaded with moonlight and the short-handled pike and followed the others out the door to hunt for a killer, while Petra fashioned a belt and holster for her axe. One way or another, they were dragging a vlkodlak to his death tonight.

CHAPTER
TWENTY-NINE

Josef stared through the bars of the old cemetery gate with the six-sided star above the lock. He knew it was a desecration, but he couldn't think of anywhere else to go. This was the only place in the city that would be truly empty of people at this time of night. Leastwise, anyone alive.

He jumped over the wall and walked carefully among the ancient headstones. Some were so old as to not even resemble memorials for the dead anymore. They were slick with green moss or half-eaten by trees that had swallowed the granite slabs with their bark as they'd grown around them, reclaiming not only the dead but the marking of their passing. For those still standing, small stones had been placed on top as a sign of remembrance and respect. Josef said a quick apology to the dead and crossed to the far side.

A diminished moon peeked out from behind a passing cloud. Her hold on Josef's blood had receded slightly with the waning phase. He could look her in the eye again without feeling the fuzz form on the underside of his tongue. He'd not told the others about that, too worried it made him out to be less human than he'd have them believe. This curse, this madness his body was forced to contend with, was a war wound like no other. He'd seen his share of combat disfigurement. Friends who'd gone home missing limbs, noses, eyes. Skin that looked like it had been baked in a bread oven from the bromine gas released in the air. Others who didn't survive at all, because who can live with their intestines on the outside of their body or only half a face? At the lowest moments of his transition, he'd wished he'd been one of the dead. And now?

A breeze stirred the branches overhead, bringing with it a scent that made Josef's heart leap with fear and anticipation. He unbuttoned his shirt, slipped off his boots, and stripped down to his bare skin. He draped Petra's scarf over a headstone and waited in the dark for his cursed brethren. Come what may, he was done straddling a life in the in-between.

CHAPTER THIRTY

The ribbon of scent shifted direction slightly. The young woman was on the move. The starshina set his beer glass down and walked across the square. His blood pumped at the prospect of a chase. He knew the witch would be out at night. None of them could resist the call of the moon. At least that's what his grandmother always said when she told stories by the fire on a midwinter's eve. His grandmother told stories about wolves too. "What big hands you have!" she'd say and raise her bent fingers in the air. "All the better to embrace you with," she'd add, and then she'd lunge.

The memory made him smile as his hands tingled with the urge to transform. But not yet! *Let her see me as a man first. The rest will come.*

But damn the convoluted medieval streets. He'd let his mind wander, and now he'd turned down a narrow lane that veered northeast, taking him in the wrong direction. A mistake, and yet her scent was just as strong as it had been when he was back at the square. Curious, he put his nose in the air and closed his eyes. The smell of her sweat left the most unusual metallic taste on his palate. It made the hairs underneath his tongue bristle, confirming how special she was. But he was getting mixed signals. Her scent came from the north *and* the west.

The starshina took stock of his surroundings and found himself standing at the center of a crossroads where five streets met.

He spun around, confused. Something wasn't right.

The unnerving energy in the air grazed against his skin. It pulsed beneath his feet and in his veins. The hairs on his neck ruffled in warning. The convergence of so many roads was a bad omen. But then he understood. The city's strange magic was trying to fool him into believing his prize was ahead when her true scent was to the west as he'd first detected. Grateful to his senses for helping him escape the troubling energy seeping out at the crossroads, he slunk back the way he'd come, retracing his steps.

A car honked its horn as the starshina stepped off the curb to return to the main square. He slapped his hand against the hood and growled at the driver until he moved on. He did not want to run—he'd spent too much attention on his sartorial appearance to have it ruined by rushing—but he would not lose her to these befuddling streets. Taking more care this time to watch *and* smell where he was going, he crept along a northerly road. The cauldron of city smells conspired to keep him from her—the old potatoes gone green with rot in the pantry, the unwashed bodies rolling beneath the unwashed sheets, the chamber pots full to the brim that would wait until morning to be emptied—all blending like a stew to throw him off. It was a miracle he detected the slight correction he'd needed to make to the west to stay on her trail.

Soon the starshina came to a high wall, where the scent of her was strong enough he ought to be able to see her. The hairs under his tongue stood erect, prickling the skin behind his teeth, but still he could not find her. He'd been led to an enclosure of some kind. The wrought-iron gate was locked, so he peered through the bars and inhaled. There, in the corner. Under the tree. He couldn't make out her shape, yet his nose filled with her musk. And only hers. She was alone. But what illicit magic was she up to in a graveyard at this time of night? He wondered if it could be related to her visit days before to the bone church, with its dangling femurs and skulls. He smiled at the prospect, thinking of all the graves they could dig up together.

Climbing high enough to put a foot on the gate's decorative six-pointed star, he launched himself over the bars, landing in a crouch on the ground. He stood and straightened his jacket. He ran his tongue over his teeth and walked toward the tree, but something was wrong. She should be standing two meters before him, but all he saw was a scarf hanging over a stone monument.

He picked up the scarf and held it to his nose. A sort of delirium overtook him at having come so close to his prize. Some called what happened to him a curse, but he knew it for what it was. To have such power over himself and others was no affliction; it was a gift. He had the strength of a wild animal, the cunning of a thief, and a heart dedicated to sucking every opportunity owed to him out of the miserable world. But where was the young woman hiding?

"I'm not going to hurt you," he called out. "I just wish to say hello, since we were never properly introduced."

Something rustled in the hedge along the wall. *Ah, she is just being shy.* He spun around, eager for them to make their acquaintance, for he wanted to initially win her over without force. That was a must. He didn't wish to frighten her into running. He didn't like to think what that might trigger in him, or what might slip through his fingers.

The starshina took a step closer, peering through the darkness. He reached a hand out to part the hedge, hoping to find the young woman and settle her fears.

What he found instead was a large gray wolf baring its teeth at him.

CHAPTER THIRTY-ONE

Up ahead, Petra spotted a figure in a top hat standing in the crossroads where the five roads met. The man did a slow pirouette in the courtyard, as though confused. On the quarter turn, with his profile backlit by the lamplight, she recognized his silhouette. It was him. Dimitri. The man from the attic. Her breath caught in her chest. Without a word to the others, she took off running.

Yanis called after her in a harsh whisper. "Petra, wait!"

A tram shuttled by in front of Petra, missing her by an arm's length as she stopped just in time. The others caught up, and Bako pulled her away from the tracks by her collar. By the time she looked up again, there was no one standing in the crossroads.

Bako gave her collar a yank. "That was a damn fool thing to do!"

"I saw him," she said, tugging herself free. "Dimitri. He was just there."

"Where?"

"At the place we planned to trap him." She pointed to the next lane over. "The intersection. He was there."

"All right, let's go." Yanis double-checked the quiver of poison arrows strapped to his chest. "But be careful this time."

Petra got to the crossroads, her breath coming fast as she spun around, still pumped on adrenaline. She glanced in all five directions.

A few people passed her on the street, but Dimitri was gone. "Which way did he go?"

Bako held one of his revolvers at his side as he craned his neck to see the road across the public square. "If we're right about his motive for being here, he ought to be standing on top of us."

Yanis paused as though taking note of all his senses. "He's been drawn off by another scent. Josef must have used the scarf to lure him away, just as Petra said."

"Where would Josef go?" Viktor asked, gripping the pike handle so hard that his knuckles showed white in the dark.

"Somewhere quiet where he can kill him without a lot of witnesses would be my guess." Bako spun around, studying their options. "Didn't Franz say he was heading for the river?"

"That way," Petra said and pointed to a narrow residential lane. Halfway along the route, she stopped walking. They were in a section of town that held a hidden sanctuary behind its walls, one where only the dead would be disturbed in the middle of the night. "He's in the graveyard," she said with sudden certainty.

"Graveyard?" Bako looked around but apparently saw nothing to suggest they were near a cemetery.

Viktor nudged his chin toward the long wall ahead on their right. "If you were looking for a quiet place, that would be it."

Yanis eyed the enclosure as they approached. "How do we get in?"

Before they could even try the gate, a growl from the other side of the wall, deep and primal, made gooseflesh of Petra's skin. It was answered by one of equal ferocity.

CHAPTER
THIRTY-TWO

How easily he slipped into his wolf skin. Josef let his blood rise until his fangs grew sharp, his claws elongated, and the muscles in his shoulders and legs engorged. Once Dimitri took the bait, he stepped out of the bushes, teeth bared, and growled for blood.

He'd caught Dimitri off guard. The man stood like a fool in his pin-striped suit and puffed-up tie, gawping at him while holding Petra's scarf to his nose. Josef lunged with such force he nearly lost control, but he caught the man by his shoulder and knocked them both to the ground. He bared his teeth, ready to plunge them into the man's neck and snap it in half, when he was thrown off by a vicious blow to both his ears.

Dimitri jumped to his feet and grinned. "Ah, the tutor thinks he has come to teach me more lessons," he said and ripped his fine jacket and shirt off in one swift motion. Before Josef could shake off the blow, the man transformed—muscle rippling under fur, a snout that grew thick and wide to accommodate a full row of flesh-ripping teeth, and claws too large to belong to any natural animal of this world.

Josef had seen the man transform before in the attic, mesmerized by witnessing the process of what he had only ever felt from the inside. Back then the man had been in restraints enchanted to hold him under Hana's careful observation. But this was different. Dimitri had given himself over to the power of the curse. His body, covered in shaggy gray fur, had nearly doubled in size as he rose to his full height on his hind legs. His eyes glowed silver in the dark as they found Josef. The vlkodlak growled and swiped his enormous claw, missing Josef's throat by the width of a whisker. He'd barely reacted in time. He knew then he'd made a terrible error in judgment.

Knowing he couldn't outfight him, Josef clambered over the tops of a dozen moss-covered headstones to get away. He'd had no plan other than to kill Dimitri, knowing there was no cure and no salvation for him. But physically he was no match for his enemy. He'd underestimated the full power of the cursed creature when transformed. He was a wolf, but the vlkodlak was a monster. Josef jumped for the roof of a large sepulcher and clung to the top by his claws. The vlkodlak chased.

"I knew you'd try to stop me," Dimitri said in a voice, deep and guttural. "But the young woman is destined to be mine." The vlkodlak balanced his feet against the tops of two gravestones, dislodging them in the ground by the weight of his enormous body so that they slanted sideways. "I knew it from the moment I heard you both talking about the miraculous things she can do. Changing smoke into dust, falling leaves into rain, rocks into flame. So why not bottle caps into rubles?" He puffed out his chest. "And now look at me. I am as worthy of this wondrous magic as any god in my new body." Dimitri leaped off the stones, landing in a crouch in front of Josef.

Josef's breath came out in quick huffs. He snarled and flattened his ears at the vlkodlak. The beast roared back, readying to pounce. Josef calculated the distance he'd have to jump to reach the top of the wall when a shadow moved in his peripheral view on the street side of the gate. But if he took his eyes off Dimitri now, he was dead.

Worried someone might see the horror of their standoff and become a needless victim, Josef plunged off the back of the crypt, landing awkwardly on his haunches. He took off running as the vlkodlak sailed through the air over the stone-lined tomb.

"Josef!"

Petra!

No, no, no. She isn't supposed to be here.

Josef rounded the back of the graveyard, scrambling over gnarled tree roots and broken stones as his claws tore up the ground. This time the vlkodlak did not follow. Instead, the fiend stood on his hind legs beneath the lone streetlamp and lifted his snout into the air. Saliva oozed from his mouth as he shook out his fur.

"It's her," Dimitri said. "My prize." He lowered onto all fours and disappeared into the shadows.

Josef, in a near panic after losing sight of Dimitri, skulked against the back wall with his teeth bared. He had to get to the gate. He had to stop Petra from coming any closer. An unnatural noise to his left stole his attention as the mincing of bone and muscle played in his fur-lined ear. The vlkodlak was transforming again. He had the briefest of chances.

Josef ran to the gate, but the bars were gone. In their place was a pair of blue velvet curtains suspended on what was left of the gate's frame. Petra already stood inside the graveyard, searching among the headstones. She saw him then and turned to run, but Dimitri got there first. He approached her half-dressed, with his ripped jacket, shredded shirt, and tattered trousers hanging off his body. His hair stood on end as he held his top hat in his hands. His feet were bare and hairy.

"My dear, it's a pleasure to meet you again." Dimitri bowed at the waist, as though they were at a cotillion. "I've been looking so forward to our reunion."

"Stay away from me." Petra took an unsteady step backward and nearly stumbled on the broken, jumbled-together headstones. She found her footing and put a chest-high memorial between her and the beast.

"My dear, let us be friends." Dimitri reached a hand out. "I've thought about you nonstop since I was freed from my shackles," he said like a humble schoolboy. "Do you remember that night you visited me? You came to the attic like a seraph in winter to present me with your gift. I knew as soon as I heard you speak the gift was meant for me. Greatness has become my destiny since getting that little scratch on the battlefield."

Petra crept backward, twisting her body between the gravestones behind her. "You're mad."

Josef stole closer on soft paws. He had to go for the throat and lock his jaw until the neckbone snapped. He would get only the one chance. He lowered his shoulders, readying to pounce. A snarl swelled in his throat as he leaped.

Dimitri turned and caught him with a swipe of his paw. He'd changed so fast, so easy. No effort at all. Half-man, half-wolf, standing on two legs and baring his teeth. Josef flew into the wall and crumpled to the ground.

The last thing he remembered was the scent of a lit cigar.

CHAPTER THIRTY-THREE

He'd scared her. He'd scared his Petra when he hadn't meant to. She'd gotten herself entangled in the maze of headstones, and now she clutched at an axe to protect herself. The starshina put the vlkodlak away again.

"Be careful you don't twist an ankle on the uneven ground, my dear." Yes, that was the thing to say. His remark came across as caring. His words showed concern for her welfare and that he was a man of manners. She could trust him.

"I'm warning you to get away," she said, holding the axe higher.

He nearly laughed. *Or what?*

The starshina decided he ought to be a little more circumspect in his approach with her. He made a half turn to his left to where her . . . what—companion, brother, lover?—was sprawled out on the ground unconscious. His form had reverted from wolf to man as he lay exposed, naked and mostly hairless. A pup.

"Touch him and die," she said.

The starshina lifted a corner of his lip to expose a fang in warning, then inhaled deeply over the man, not finding her scent on him. *Hmm, not a lover, then.* He wondered, though, if he ought to give her a demonstration of what he was capable of. After all, he couldn't have her shouting orders at him. He took a step toward the man on the ground, and she lifted the axe in her hands, transforming it into a spear with a longer reach. An oversize toothpick, to his eyes. He was astonished by the swift grace of her magic, but he'd long ago crossed the threshold of disbelief in such extraordinary things.

He ignored her minor threat and transformed back into the full vlkodlak, roaring from the pit of his stomach.

He was surprised when she held her ground in the face of the man's looming violent death. Brave for a young woman, he thought. She brandished the weapon again, almost as if she were taunting him, daring him to attack her.

"Come on," she shouted. "What are you waiting for?"

Was this some witch's trick? Or had she figured out her worth to him, knowing he wouldn't intentionally harm her? A canny calculation, if so.

The pup on the ground roused awake. Concern flooded the young woman's eyes when the man began to tremble as if he suffered from a fever. Perhaps he was wrong about them. Perhaps they were lovers. Whatever they were, it was over now.

"You and I, we've been empowered with great abilities." The starshina straightened to his full height so she might appreciate his superior physique in comparison to the sickly human convulsing on the ground. "Think for a moment of all the brilliant things we could achieve together," he said to her. "Your talent. My brawn. We'll blaze our way across the continent like a forest fire. The kingdoms will bow at *our* feet when this war is over. You will be a queen."

"You're insane." She ignored his entreaties and turned her attention to the pup. "Josef, where's your elixir?"

The starshina growled. "He's no use to you anymore. You may as well call out to the dead with your pleadings."

"Speak for yourself." She looked over his shoulder as though searching for somebody. "Now, Bako!" she yelled, but whatever she was expecting didn't happen. Her eyes scanned the entrance to the graveyard as she raised the spear in her shaking hands.

He almost felt sorry for her, but if this partnership was going to work to his liking, she needed to learn not to provoke him. He had just raised his paw, ready to rip the head off the man at his feet, when he was suddenly blinded by a sharp silver light. The intensity drove him back until he stumbled into the wall. He tried to cover his eyes with his arms, but the light was too strong. It seeped behind his eyes to stun his brain. It pulled at the blood in his veins until he thought he might float out of his body.

He heard the snap of a trigger just before something sharp pierced his chest. He caught a wisp of sulfur and ammonia, like the butchers on the battle lines used after lopping off the limbs of the broken soldiers. For a brief moment the shot brought him relief as the light blessedly faded from his eyes and he sank to his knees. Blood matted his fur. So much blood, but this time the gore on his hands was his own. And then the poison took a bite out of his heart. "What devilry is this?"

A woman stood before him. *Petra?* He saw white spots dancing around her as the blinding light left halos circling in his eyes. A strangled growl rose out of his throat as he toppled onto his side, and then the world went dark.

CHAPTER THIRTY-FOUR

Concentrated moonlight flashed in Josef's face, stinging his retinas and stunning his senses. He squeezed his eyes tight and tried to roll over to protect himself, but his body wouldn't respond. His head thudded from the pressure of the light in his eyes so soon after transforming. Then his stomach rose into his mouth, and a foreign sound gurgled out of his throat. He realized only after the wave passed he'd tried and failed to scream for help.

Beside him, Petra argued with someone. It burned with the heat of Hell itself, but Josef opened his eyes to mere slits. A woman stood in front of Petra. She wore a scarf on her head and carried a lantern like the one Viktor had made, only larger. For the moment no light radiated out of it.

The woman nudged a heap on the ground hard with her shoe. The vlkodlak. She adjusted the lantern as she spoke to Petra. There was a threat in her tone.

"Leave him," she said. "You're coming with me."

Petra tried to walk away from her. "I need to help him. He needs his elixir."

Thank God. He tried to say the word "help" again, but no sound came out. He wasn't even sure his lips moved.

The woman raised the lantern. "I said leave him."

Petra ignored her and walked toward him. The woman rotated the screen on the lantern until a brilliant light emanated from inside. He squinted to protect himself, but unlike the silver moonlight that had struck him before, this was warm, golden light. The shaft of daylight illuminated Petra in the center of the dark cemetery. The woman raised the lantern higher. Petra's eyes glittered gold in the light. She tried to back up, to cover her face, but she doubled over instead, clutching her head in both hands as she fell to her knees.

Josef forced himself up on his elbow and nearly passed out again. His head dropped to the ground, and all he could do was watch as the woman snapped the lantern shut while Petra writhed on her side. The woman called out to someone on the street. "Hurry, let's get them loaded in the truck. I need to examine them both."

The man and woman picked Petra up and carried her through the curtains where the gate ought to be. A minute later they returned, but instead of grabbing Josef, they dragged Dimitri's body out of the grave-yard and hauled it away. Josef clawed at the ground, pulling himself a few centimeters at a time to get to his clothes by the wall. He had to get the elixir. Whatever examination this woman had in mind, it couldn't be good. He had to stop her.

Josef had crawled only an arm's length when the woman casually walked over and stood in front of him, blocking his way. The reek of sulfur and ammonia clouded the air he breathed.

Martina?

"Looking for this?" she asked, waving the half-empty bottle of elixir between her thumb and forefinger. Before he could beg, she dropped the vial on the ground and stomped on it, crushing the bottle and its contents beneath her heel.

"No." He barely got the word out when she wiped her boot sole on a patch of weeds and walked out of the graveyard, leaving him to join the dead around him.

Josef gulped in the damp night air after she'd gone. His head still reeled and his heart was bruised with shame, but in his wounded state, he'd been able to place where he'd first smelled the combination of sulfur and ammonia. He rolled on his back and stared at the stars. He remembered being in the infirmary after he'd been attacked on patrol. A man on the gurney next to him had lost an arm, and his leg had been punctured by shrapnel. The doctor had treated the wounds with lunar caustic and gauze, but by the fourth day, the infection had already begun attacking the injured tissue, bringing with it the odor of spoiled beef. He had no idea why the sulfur-ammonia scent clung to the woman the way it did, but the catalog of smells formed in his brain since becoming cursed had filed it away as a known threat. If he didn't die atop the grave he lay on, he'd hunt her down and return the favor.

Josef's body shook from cold and fever. He rarely felt the deep chill of winter anymore since the curse had invaded his blood, but he truly feared he'd die of hypothermia alone and naked in the middle of the graveyard. He closed his eyes, summoning the strength to scream out for help one last time, when he heard the step-scrape cadence of a one-legged man.

"It's Josef. He's here, he's still here."

He opened his eyes. Yanis and Bako hurried toward him and propped him up like a child's doll against a headstone, while adrenaline pumped him full of hope he might yet live.

"Where are your clothes?"

Josef pointed to the bushes by the wall. "They took her." His voice scraped over his dry throat. "Martina took Petra."

"She got us too," Bako said, holding his flask of brandy to Josef's lips. "Used some sort of witch's spell powder to knock us out just as we were getting ready to kill Dimitri." The hussar looked over his shoulder. "He's not still on the prowl, is he?"

"I think he's dead." Josef drank from the flask, feeling the fire burn down to his stomach.

"My crossbow is gone." Yanis pivoted to scan the graveyard. "We'll assume the poison in the arrows worked."

"She hauled Dimitri's body away too. Said she had to examine them both."

"Where? What does that mean?"

"I don't know," Josef said. "The woman has a scent on her, though. Like a septic wound. I could find her, if I could stand."

Bako stepped on something that crunched and backed up. "Is this your vial of elixir?" he asked, sorting through the broken glass at his feet.

Josef's head wouldn't move when he wanted to nod. "She crushed it under her heel."

"Let's get him out of here," Yanis said.

"Where to? The storeroom?" Bako asked.

"See if you can find us a taxi," Yanis said. "I have another idea."

Yanis got Josef dressed and marginally warmer while Bako flagged down a ride; then they each got a shoulder under his arms and carried him to the waiting automobile. A few minutes later they crossed the bridge to the Lesser Town district. Josef had no recollection of how he'd gotten from the car to Hugo Reitman's tower apartment, but when he opened his eyes again, he was lying on a curved settee built against the wall of a cramped wooden tower and looking up at a cogwheel universe spinning in motion under an open sky. The seven stars of Ursa Major blinked above.

"While the moon can be a problem for a young man like him, the stars soothe like a healing ointment." Hugo leaned over Josef to inspect his eyes with soft lamplight while he spoke to someone climbing the stairs below. "See, he is already coming to. Now, if you'll just sit up for me, young man, we can get the elixir flowing through your system."

"Elixir?" Josef was confused. The bottle had been shattered. There was no elixir.

Josef felt an arm at his back as he was gently raised to a sitting position. His head spun briefly, but he did feel mildly better. "Where's the roof?"

"We're in the tower observatory above the attic," Yanis said, climbing into the tiny space. "The dome opens with the turn of a crank for the best stargazing. Here, drink this."

Yanis uncorked a small bottle. Josef took a whiff and thought it smelled right. He poured the medicine over his lips and waited, while his eyes cooled from their fevered blur. The fatigue began to recede from his limbs in moments. "It's working. How did you get this?"

"Come downstairs when you're able," Yanis said, then he and Hugo disappeared through the hole in the floor.

A few minutes later, when he thought he could walk again, Josef took the spiral staircase to the main floor, ducking his head at the bottom to avoid hitting a beam. Bako and Viktor sat at the table with Hugo, who was studying his magical armillary and sipping fresh coffee. Behind them, gazing up in the middle of the room at the astrological gadgets like a moon-eyed child, was an elderly woman wearing a flowered shawl.

"What's going on?"

The woman turned full around. "Josef, you're back among the living."

"Hana?" He rushed over to her with his arms open. "But how did you get here?"

"I came as soon as I heard," she said.

Josef embraced the old woman. "But I only just fell ill," he said, confused.

"No, not you," she said, releasing him. "I came when I heard about the killings."

Hugo stirred sugar into his coffee. "Your friend had asked me to search for Hana with my instruments, but she was already on her way to the city by the time I located her."

"The direction this vlkodlak was moving was clear," Hana said, waving a finger. "It had to be Dimitri. He was the only victim of the curse Valentina and I had been treating in the area. I didn't even need to toss the bones to know he was headed for the city."

"And where is Valentina?" Josef asked, looking around. "How did you both get away?"

Hana threw up her hands. "We ran west like everyone else. She's gone home to replenish her supply of herbs." The witch reached in her travel bag and produced four bottles of elixir. "We didn't let him go, by the way. His own people did that. Absolutely careless of their command. Anyway, he won't be needing these anymore." She passed the bottles to Josef, folding her hands over his as though to remind him to keep them safe and sound.

Josef was relieved to see the old woman. Grateful she had her supply of elixir with her. But there were more urgent matters. "Dimitri's dead, but Martina has Petra. We have to find her," he said. "Something's happened to the woman's mind. She's deranged. Dangerous."

"Yes, we got a firsthand lesson in her betrayal," Bako said. He'd been nursing a cut on the side of his temple with a cloth, which he tossed aside. "We were right behind Petra at the graveyard. Martina's oaf knocked us out just as we were getting ready to kill Dimitri ourselves. Besides the crossbow, they stole my guns, and I want them back."

"Still have my lantern," Viktor added, resting his hand atop his invention. Soft wisps of moonlight seeped out of the cracks.

"I got an up-close introduction to a larger lantern earlier, one that exposed me to pure moonlight." Josef had to wipe his eyes just thinking about the intense light that had been aimed at his face.

"That's the one I made for her." Viktor stood. "She knew how to stun you with it?"

"Yes, she did." He paused, thinking about the moment. "And then she used it on Petra. Only it wasn't moonlight then. The rays were more like sunbeams. Petra was surrounded by them. She collapsed the same way I did, as if the light had knocked her out."

"Wait, you're saying she had the sun and moon trapped in the lantern together? And used it on both of you?" Viktor rubbed his forehead as he paced the attic full of astrolabes and mechanical universes. "Everything keeps leading back to the drawing in Honza's grimoire and the missing spell. Martina must have figured something out. But not all of it, or she wouldn't have needed to overpower Petra or Dimitri."

"I don't follow," Yanis said. "What would the light from the lantern do?"

"The silver reacts with the moon," Josef said, pointing to his eyes. "I'm going to assume sunlight does the same to Petra."

"Why would it?"

"Because she has gold in her blood," Viktor said. "It's somehow related to her magic. Something she was born with, but it's got to be connected to Honza's and König's experiments all those years ago. The gold must be in her eyes, too, only they're amber colored, so the flecks don't show."

Hugo cleared his throat. "I don't mean to upset anyone, but do you recall the gray mist I showed you earlier?"

"There was a threat hanging over us because of Dimitri," Josef explained to Hana and Bako when they shook their heads in ignorance.

"Well, that was certainly what we suspected at the time." Hugo beckoned them with his fingers to come closer to the astrolabe. "However, Dimitri is presumably dead, and yet the cloud has only grown in intensity."

"Meaning?" Viktor asked, looking from face to face.

"Meaning, as much of a threat as your vlkodlak appeared to be, it pales in comparison to what Martina Danek might do if she has her way. I believe now it was her malevolent energy hovering over you this whole time."

"We have no idea what she's capable of," Yanis said.

All eyes turned to Viktor. He held up his hands defensively. "Believe me, she's always been completely normal until now. I mean, well, except when she was going through that odd period."

"Odd how?" Josef didn't mean to growl, but he was almost fully recovered.

"About two years ago, she started staying late in the lab doing experiments. Alone. On herself. Scientist witches all do it sometimes to test their hunches, but with her it always seemed like things went too far."

"What kind of experiments?"

Viktor shook his head. "Not sure exactly, but that's when she started having all her injuries. The burned hands. Open wounds and bruises on her arms and legs. She started wearing high-collar dresses and gloves every day." He gazed off to his left as though remembering something. "Come to think of it, that's when she started mentioning König and her research a lot more too. And the rumors about Petra and what she could do. Asking people if they really thought she could still be alive. If they believed she could turn common brass coins into gold like her stepfather had said. Apparently she'd gone to visit Pavel Radek in prison before he died."

Josef pounded the table with his palms. "We have to figure out where she's taken Petra."

"They wouldn't have gone back to the Society lab," Bako said. "Too dangerous."

"And not likely anywhere her colleagues would be aware of," Yanis said. "But how will we ever narrow down a location in time?"

Hana rattled a small pile of sheep knuckles in her palm. "Mind if I give it a try?"

CHAPTER THIRTY-FIVE

Candlelight stung Petra's eyes as she woke. She blinked several times, as though she had an eyelash stuck under her lid that she couldn't flush out. She tried to raise her hand to shield her eyes from the light, but her right arm wouldn't respond. Neither would the other one. She tugged, but her wrists were tied to a table, and there was an odd dulling sensation along her skin. Her voice still worked as she fretted and fought against the restraints, but her tongue was trapped behind a rubber gag. Fear spiked her blood with adrenaline when she realized her head, too, was attached to some kind of contraption.

Where was she and how had she gotten there? Why couldn't she remember?

"It will do you no good to pull against the leather straps, so I suggest you calm down." Martina stood at Petra's feet wearing a white lab coat. "We use these buckles for our most challenging subjects. Many more formidable than you, I might add."

The last thing she remembered was being blinded by a bright yellow light just before something poked her in the neck. A sedative of some kind? She had no recollection of anything after that, but her intuition was already forming a likely scenario, one based on the feeling there'd always been something about Martina that nagged at her memory. She, out of all those at the Society, had been the only one to come to their house in the country village to visit Petra's father. But why? Why had she visited her father in a show of support when he'd been accused, presumably by her, of stealing gold from the Libuše Society? If Petra could have freed her legs, she would have kicked herself for having trusted this woman enough to let her take samples of her hair and blood.

Whatever the reason for Martina pretending to be a family friend in the past, Petra didn't intend to wait around and find out what the woman's current motives were. Forming an image of delicate spiderwebs encircling her wrists and ankles instead of sturdy leather straps, she pressed her skin against the restraints and tugged.

Nothing happened.

"Did you just attempt to use your magic?" Martina checked a machine hooked up to a battery by a thick wire. "Interesting. There was a slight jump in the reading," she said, writing the observation down in her notebook.

Petra screamed in frustration through her gag.

"I've attached wire sensors to your temples so I can monitor the electrical impulses between your thoughts and the application of your magic. There's a clamp affixed to your skull, which might feel quite heavy, so I wouldn't advise moving too much." Martina lifted her green-tinted glasses from her nose and rested them atop her head. "And if you're wondering why your magic isn't working right now, it's because I've blocked the electrical impulse flowing through your skin from making contact with objects. You're wearing a pair of thick rubber gloves up to your elbows. They work as an insulator. The gurney is covered in a rubber sheet as well. My apologies, but I can't have you undoing all my research while we're in the midst of finding a few final answers."

Even Petra's tongue was no use against the rubber gag in her mouth when she tried to turn it into a sugar cube so she could scream threats of violence at the woman.

Martina leaned forward, eager to confide. "I figured out the electrical impulse facet of the spell about two years ago. It was when we had the lighting installed in the tunnels. Seeing the copper wiring carry

211

all that electrical energy made for an enlightening breakthrough, you might say." She tugged a pair of cotton gloves onto her scarred hands. "Honza and Ava were the first to ever incorporate an outside electrical pulse into a spell. For that I give them full credit."

Petra struggled against her restraints on the table, thrashing like a child having their worst tantrum. She tossed her head back and forth, despite the clamp and wires, until her eyes caught sight of the hairy body on the table next to her. The vlkodlak—Dimitri. Was he unconscious? No, Martina had shot him with the crossbow. She remembered that part. He was dead, but she still had him strapped to the table. How did she get Yanis's crossbow? Where was Bako? Viktor?

And Josef?

She blew her breath out slowly, remembering. He'd been hit with the lantern light like her. He'd collapsed on the ground. Petra twisted her neck to her other side. But instead of finding Josef on an adjacent table, all she saw was a wooden sideboard filled with mortars, half-filled bottles with peeling labels, dried herbs tied up in bundles, and three ceramic jars labeled COPPER, GOLD, and SILVER.

An obvious witch's lair. But where? The place was tiny. A hovel. A single room half the size of the apartment she'd shared with Marek. The ceiling was so low at one end, Martina's head nearly touched the overhead beams when she stood up straight. At first she thought they were in the tunnel, but there was moonlight coming through the cracks in the wooden door, so they were aboveground somewhere. But they could be anywhere in the city. A place where no one might find her.

"You woke earlier than I anticipated." Martina lowered the pair of colored glasses over her eyes again, then picked up a syringe. "You'll need to be patient a little longer while I finish up with the vlkodlak."

Petra wanted to scream again. How could she get free if she couldn't use her magic? She struggled to lift her head high enough to see her arms. Just as Martina said, the strange sensation she'd felt on her arms was some kind of rubber glove that had been slipped over her skin up to her elbows. She fought in her mind to change the rubber into ash, water, or even smoke, but she couldn't get a reaction.

Taking a deep breath, she let her head tilt slightly to her left. Martina stood over Dimitri, whose body had oddly remained in vlko-dlak form after he'd died. His lips were pulled back in a slightly dehy-drated grimace, and his tongue hung limp over his teeth. His dead eyes reminded her of the upíri, whose lifeless reanimated irises showed up as eyeshine on the photos she'd taken.

Martina plunged the syringe into Dimitri's thigh, drawing out a vial of his blood. "It's quite sterile," she said. "Useful for all kinds of things. We'll run the usual tests for precious metals, too, to see if there's any variation from our expectations. Same as we did for you earlier."

Petra wondered if there was a black market for the cursed wolf's blood. Were there spells that could be conjured with it? Or hexes? Could a curse be weaponized if bottled? Bought and sold? Was Martina doing this for money?

Someone tapped lightly on the door three times before entering. He wore a black trench coat and a fedora tugged low over his face. He hesi-tated outside, then made a long step as though avoiding the threshold.

"I told you it would be fine," Martina said, sparing a brief look in the man's direction. "We still have a little time." She filled six vials of blood before capping them and placing them in a wooden box while the man removed his coat. "The straw and ice will keep the blood protected while we finish up." There was confidence in her voice, as though she did this sort of thing all the time.

"What about the eyes?" the man asked.

Petra strained to lift her head to look beyond her feet, where she saw Franz slip on a white lab coat like Martina's. He had the nerve to offer her a friendly smile when he caught her watching him.

"There's a scalpel on the table behind you." Martina held her hand out, waiting for Franz to respond. "We'll do his first."

First?

Petra banged her head against the table. Franz came over her and patted her cheek. "Don't fret. It will all be over soon," he said and flashed the light from the lantern in her eyes again. "We're so very close to understanding everything."

Petra squeezed her eyes tight as golden halos flashed beneath her eyelids, temporarily paralyzing her body as she lay motionless on the table.

CHAPTER
THIRTY-SIX

The knucklebones scattered across the table. Two of the sheep's bones landed grooved side up. One lay with the flat of the knuckle on top and one with the curved side of the bone exposed. Josef remembered that the position the knuckle landed in was important, but so was the direction it pointed. Hana studied the pattern they'd made, then closed her eyes.

Josef fought the urge to pace the room while he waited to learn which direction Petra had been taken. His blood was pumping fast through his body, and his muscles twitched with the need to run, but he had to appear calm. He wouldn't jeopardize the moment. Hana had found Petra before. She could do it again.

On the other side of the room, Hugo fidgeted with his instruments, trying to achieve the same thing Hana was attempting to do with the bones. Neither method was considered scientific or credible under any normal circumstances, and yet Josef knew without a doubt he'd found Petra in the city square the first time because of the woman's talent with these sheep's dice. And Hugo knew how to keep track of Yanis, so between the two of them, someone ought to be able to point him in the right direction. His nose could do the rest.

"They have not taken her far," Hana said, opening her eyes at last. "I don't know the city as well as you, so this may or may not be useful. But the place she is in is high and low at the same time." She pointed to the pairing of the sheep bones: two alike matched with two opposites. The old woman tilted her head slightly, as though trying to listen to a conversation just out of range. "The place she is in is large to the eye, yet so small as to be claustrophobic."

Yanis rubbed his temples. "The research tunnels? I thought we decided that was too risky for Martina."

"We should be out there looking for them." Bako blew cigar smoke out the window before catching Josef's eye. "We should be sniffing them out."

"No," Hana said. "It's not underground."

"Because it's on a hill," Hugo said, gazing at his astrolabe before writing down his findings. "Two hundred and fifty-eight meters aboveground, to be exact."

"A hill? Which one?" Josef put his ushanka on and went to the door. "Bako's right, we should be out there."

"Wait." Viktor stood from the table. "How many hills have buildings? Or a place that's high and low. And small."

Yanis stood up and double-checked the contents of his satchel. "Does anything come to mind?"

Viktor went to the window and pointed. "I think she could be there," he said, indicating the castle on the hill.

"She's in the castle?" Josef didn't believe it.

"Not the castle. But maybe the row of houses attached to it." Viktor stared up at the palace cathedral, aglow with gaslights. "They're high on the hill near the castle, but the lane is more of a slum than anything. Lowly."

"And the houses are all connected so they look like one, but each room is small enough to be claustrophobic to someone my height." Josef looked at Hana, feeling a shiver of truth travel under his skin. "That's got to be it."

"But would Martina go to such a place in the middle of the night?" Yanis asked.

"Martina would absolutely go there," Viktor said. "The place would have meaning to her."

Bako and Yanis exchanged glances. "Why?"

"Because it's called Goldsmith Lane," the glassmaker said. "And because it was a frequent haunt of the alchemists who served the king three hundred years ago."

Needing no more convincing, Bako and Yanis grabbed their gear. "Let's go."

Josef hugged Hana and kissed the top of Hugo's head. "Thank you," he said, and he and the others took the handful of weapons remaining on Hugo's wall and left to climb the hill to the castle.

Fifteen minutes later they arrived at the bottom of Goldsmith Lane. A single gaslight, flickering weakly, barely lit the row of houses, each joined at the hip to the one next to it, all the way up the narrow road. The only people out were those who scrounged their living after dark. Which, Josef reasoned, was exactly what *they* were up to as well.

"Where do we start looking?" Yanis asked. "It's not like we can go knocking on doors." He carried a curved scimitar with an engraved silver handle that looked like it could gut an elephant.

Josef put his nose in the air. He was looking for the woman's irritating scent, but the lane had a strong odor of its own full of animal smells, body musk, overripe food waste, and buckets of night soil. He tucked his nose into the crook of his arm and breathed in the familiar aroma of his coat. The cook-smoke and wet-wool odors helped cleanse his sinuses after the overdose of foreign smells.

The others waited in the shadow of a long wall while he changed position to try and get upwind. He walked past the first few houses and sniffed again. He still couldn't sort out the woman's odd scent from the cluster of other human smells, but there was no mistaking the musk of the vlkodlak. Once the stream of molecules hit his nose, it overpowered everything else. "This way," he said and removed his pistol from its holster.

The agents of the Order gripped their weapons and followed, prowling along the narrow, dingy lane. They'd come for blood, and this time they weren't leaving until they got it.

CHAPTER
THIRTY-SEVEN

The air in the room had grown stifling warm from so many bodies in such a small space. Petra couldn't breathe. She tried to swallow, but the gag made it difficult. Beside her, Franz held a scalpel poised over the vlkodlak. Were they really going to dissect him in front of her? Was she next?

Her stomach heaved. She couldn't get enough air. Her tongue backed up on her against the gag in her mouth, then the muscles in her abdomen spasmed, making her tug against her restraints.

"I think she might actually be choking," Franz said with mild concern in his voice.

Martina paused her work on Dimitri with an audible sigh. She turned and looked at Petra over the tops of her colored glasses. Her eyebrows tightened. "Very well, take the gag off her," she said to Franz. She held her gloved hands, which were smeared with blood, away from her body so as not to touch anything. "After all, I do still need her alive to complete the rest of my tests."

Franz removed the device tied over Petra's mouth. She gulped in a lungful of air.

"There's no need for dramatics." Martina slipped off her bloody gloves and tossed them on the end of the table. "You really have no idea the sacrifices it takes to make progress in magical research these days, do you? Or even the cost Honza was willing to pay for his breakthrough? Or Ava?"

"Sacrifices?" Petra screamed. "I'm the one strapped to the table."

"Show a little more respect for your father." Martina narrowed her eyes at Petra behind her tinted glasses, staring uncomfortably for what felt like a harsh minute. "Would you like to see what sacrifice looks like for those who truly believe in what they do?"

"Martina, no," Franz said, tugging gently on her arm. "You don't need to do that."

"Oh, but I do. I want her to understand our dedication to deciphering the origins of magic. Especially unexplained magic like hers." Martina took her glasses off and tucked them in her lab coat. "Yes, it's very easy to be born with special abilities. I imagine you even take your talent for granted most days, never giving its unique source a second thought. Haven't you ever wondered how your magic was born inside you?"

"Of course I've wondered about it," Petra said, unable to lift her head fully to argue. The gag was gone, but the cage-like device was still attached to her head, monitoring her mind and magical impulses. She might be able to disintegrate the device into pulp or ashes at the points where it touched her temples, but her hands were still bound, and she worried the attempt would only anger Martina further. "My father always said my ability was a gift. But why me? Why was I so special? My mother wasn't even a witch."

Martina took a step closer. "That's right. Your mother was a mortal, despite what Augustus thought he saw under the microscope. Easier to let him believe he saw the shimmer of witchcraft on those strands of hair than the truth."

"The gold," Petra said. "You know why it's in my blood and my hair."

"Yes." Martina peered at Petra with an almost trancelike scrutiny. "But you don't have any of the scars. And that's the part I can't quite figure out."

"Scars?"

Martina exhaled, and a veil of illusion she'd been keeping in place fell away. Her skin, where it had been wrinkled in all the normal places for a woman of her age, now showed open sores that wept a pinkish fluid. Her right eye was covered with a black patch, and her bottom lip was half-corroded, as if the skin had been eaten away by acid. Her scalp was frizzled at the hairline. It looked like the roots had been burned with candle wax. When Martina grinned, knowing the effect her appearance had on Petra, a gap in her gumline showed where two teeth were missing.

"This is what twenty years of research has done to me. Twenty years of trying to figure out what Honza had been up to all those late nights in the lab. To learn what had put that smug grin on his face when he suddenly stopped ingesting the gold. He and Ava always huddled in the library together. Always on the verge of some breakthrough that would earn them a name in the higher echelons of scientific magical study." Martina looked at her hands, front and back. "I went to the same university. Worked just as hard as they did. I also stayed late working in the lab every night. I read every dusty old grimoire housed in that library. But they got all the accolades, all the opportunities. I could never match their accomplishments, no matter how hard I worked."

"I don't understand," Petra said, still shocked at the woman's condition. "What happened to you?"

"What happened to me?" Martina's lip curled over her remaining canine tooth. "Your father happened to me. His great contribution to magic, the only thing anyone could talk about for years, has been my curse for two decades. Forced to self-cauterize with lunar caustic to keep from falling apart from all the failed attempts to integrate the gold into the skin, the blood, the bone."

Franz put his arm around Martina and pulled her back. "You have to understand. She's been trying to replicate the original spell ever since Honza left the Society. It's taken all that time to get to the point we think we understand how the transfer takes place. But without the written instructions, it's been nothing but trial and error to get here."

Petra took in Martina's scars: the open sores, the missing teeth, the wounded eye. They were all self-inflicted wounds. The results of failed, dangerous experiments done on herself in the pursuit of . . . what? Keeping up with her father's accomplishments? Ava König's? Was that what she wanted? To be one of the brilliant ones hailed by the Empire's society of witches? Willing to mutilate herself for fame?

A knot formed in Petra's stomach. "Which spell are you trying to replicate?"

"Don't be obtuse." Martina snapped her bloody gloves back on. "Your father wouldn't approve of a stupid daughter." She tapped a finger under the eye with the patch. "I earned this after sprinkling both silver and gold dust directly in my eye. I'd tried combining it with a common eyebright spell to see if your father and Ava had outsmarted me by using such a simple and obvious incantation that I might overlook it. But replacing the eyebright with precious metals only burned the cornea so that it melded with all the other gelatinous goo in the eye. Not so bright after all."

Petra thought she'd be ill again. "Why would you do that to yourself?"

The woman held up a finger. "It was painful, yes, but it was an important step in eliminating my hypothesis that the metallic flecks in the eyes were done by physical injection. So the knowledge gained prevented the experiment from being a complete loss." The woman leaned in closer until her tormented face hovered over Petra's. "And now you see what it means to truly sacrifice for your beliefs."

Petra blinked back at the woman, convinced she'd corrupted her own mind with her experiments. Martina had spent more than twenty years trying to figure out her father's spell, the one written on the ripped-out pages. The missing explanation for why gold dust shimmered inside her body. Finally she understood what had prompted him to tear those pages out of the book. He must have known what Martina was capable of.

"Sometimes," Martina said, "you have to play with heat to get comfortable with fire." She gestured to the other visible wounds on her face and hands as though the scars were merely emblems of a deferred success she'd yet to achieve. "Every failed experiment has gotten us one step closer to the truth. And now? We're very nearly there, aren't we, Franz?"

"We're confident now we know how the silver was used in König's vlkodlak curse," he said, taking a second scalpel from the drawer. "We believe we know how the gold allows you to do what you do. We're just not clear on how the gold got into your system or how to replicate it." He inspected the tool in the lamplight. "But we will soon."

"You see, our theory works perfectly well in the lab," Martina said. "The electricity charges the gold particles, and they carry the spell as they were designed to do, but something always goes wrong when we inject the solution into a living body. Same for when either Franz or I ingest it." She pressed her hand to her stomach, suggesting there might be internal injuries to match those on the outside. "Of course, the silver reacts differently. Ava did something to her spell that allows blood to carry the electrified silver from host to host. But for some reason, the same can't be said for the gold. That's where you're unique."

Her father's drawing. The sun and moon dancing. Gold and silver in the blood, hair, and eyes. Josef's curse and her magic were intertwined, just as she'd thought. The same thread of magic had been stitched into both of them, but with very different results. At least Martina seemed to think so.

"And now," Franz said, holding the scalpel over Petra. He quickly sliced off a strand of her hair to demonstrate how sharp the blade was. "I'm only going to say this one time. We're done with guesswork, so tell us where you've hidden the missing pages that hold your father's incantation."

"It was you, wasn't it." Petra imagined the blade slicing open mattresses and sacks of coffee in a frenzied search for something that wasn't there. "You broke into the storeroom. That's what you were looking for. The missing pages from the grimoire."

"Imagine my surprise when you showed up on my doorstep," Martina said. "The one person who might actually hold the code to all the enigmas I've been chasing for so long. A daughter who embodied her father's work, who was trusted to keep the secret." She cocked her head to the side and pursed her lips. Petra knew an ultimatum was coming. "Now, tell us where you've hidden the spell, or we'll be forced to begin the final round of live experiments using our one and only specimen: you."

Whether it was the mad threat in Martina's voice or her palpable envy of what Honza Stamitz and Ava König had achieved at the Society, another mystery cleared for Petra. The nagging doubt that had been hovering at the edge of her memory finally came into focus. Yes, Martina had come to the house in the country to see her father that Easter when she was a small girl, but instead of it being a friendly visit from her father's former colleague, Petra recalled raised voices in her father's study and being shooed away by her mother to go play in the yard. When the woman finally left the house, it was punctuated by the slam of the front door.

"You wanted his research notes all those years ago when you came to the house," Petra said, remembering. "You said the pages belonged to the Society. You were the one who'd forced him to resign. You were jealous of his success. I'll bet you even lied about him stealing gold."

"It was only half a lie," Martina said. "He'd been swallowing more than normal. Enough that he had no ready defense when Augustus confronted him about the missing gold. It was only natural that I should have taken over his research and continue the work after he left. Ava had already gone to the gilded city to seek her fame, and I had delved deep enough into the theories about gold and magic that he should have willingly passed his spell on to me. But he didn't. He wouldn't. He kept it selfishly bound up in that grimoire of his, locked away in a drawer in some sleepy village. So you know what I did?" Martina rested the edge of her bloodied scalpel against Petra's cheek, where the burn scar lay hidden beneath an illusion spell of her own. "I came back a month later, waited for you all to leave the house for one of your silly walks, then I spiked his brandy with a little oleander and foxglove to cause a heart attack. Days later it was only natural for a representative of the Libuše Society to come by, pay their respects, and collect his important work for posterity. Your mortal mother couldn't wait to hand over his books."

Petra's hands were still restrained, so when the tears flooded her eyes, ran out at the corners onto her cheeks, and flooded her ears, there was nothing she could do. No changing the scalpel into a feather, no transforming her restraints into daisy chains to break free. All she could do was look into the dead eye of the woman who'd just admitted she'd killed her father for a spell.

Unable to move her arms, Petra spit at the woman. "But you didn't get it, did you. He knew what you were about. He knew you couldn't be trusted. You didn't inherit the spell and you never will."

Martina slapped Petra's face, then wiped off the spit on her lab coat with the heel of her hand. "You're out of time. Tell us where it is," Martina said. "Or maybe it's all up here?" She tapped on Petra's head with the scalpel. "Shall we open it up and see what's inside that brain of yours? I'm happy to slice off a sliver of your brain tissue to study under the microscope, if that's what it takes."

With a quick flick of her wrist, Martina sliced open a small cut at Petra's hairline to make her point. Franz sighed and grabbed a strip of gauze from the sideboard and a jar of honey from the cupboard. "Let's not accidentally kill her before she tells us what we want to know. Now, I've searched your clothing and your living quarters," he said, dabbing at the blood on Petra's forehead before covering it with the honey and a bandage. "So if it really is in your head, now is the time to divulge the secrets."

Petra couldn't help but laugh. They'd waited more than ten years after her father died to get their hands on that spell. A spell that could give them the touch of gold at their fingertips. Make them the center of attention in a small circle of elite witches. But she didn't have it. She didn't even think it existed anymore. Martina had done endless experiments on herself, mutilated her body in pursuit of this magical unicorn, and for what? A dream that existed only in her imagination.

"There is no spell," Petra said. "Whatever my father did with those pages, they're long gone." She closed her eyes, exhausted with talk of the past. "If you want to be one of the luminous ones, you'll have to do it on your own."

Martina held it together for a brief few seconds before she picked up the nearest tray of surgical instruments and threw them across the room. "Get her under the light," she said to Franz. She picked up a fresh scalpel and put her glasses back on. "Time to take a closer look at those eyes."

CHAPTER THIRTY-EIGHT

The smell was strongest at the far end of the lane, where the glow of the gaslight didn't quite reach. Josef led the others, holding a finger over his mouth to warn them to go quietly. They took only a few steps before he felt a tug at his arm.

"Be careful, there could be spells protecting the place," Viktor whispered. "Jinxes or maybe even hexes."

The warning made Josef pause, but mostly to consider how a man would even recognize such a thing. Were there telltale signs of an impending jolt from a witch's spell? He waved his hand in front of him to test the air for some invisible fluctuation in energy, but all he felt were a few spindly spiderwebs.

Yanis limped forward and sniffed the air. He reached in his satchel and removed a small pouch of a yellowish substance. "It's a specialized mixture of lycopodium powder. If there's any negative spell energy cast around the perimeter, it should react and show us where." He tossed a handful of powder in the air. A small flash ignited below the house's single window like a sprinkling of glitter but fizzled quickly. Yanis raised his brows, seemingly satisfied the threat was minimal.

"Come on," Josef whispered with a nudge of his head.

The men gathered outside the front of the tiny house. The roofline was so low Josef could have pulled himself up on top without using a stepladder. He ducked and put his ear to the door. The pungent odor of the vlkodlak's fur seeped through the cracks. He thrust his chin at the others and raised his weapon.

Bako stepped forward and grabbed the door handle, testing it gently. It gave way and the hussar moved inside. Josef bent his legs to lunge after him, but Bako stood blocking the doorway. He could neither move forward to let the others follow nor retreat.

Bako was simply stuck with his weapon raised.

Inside, a woman in a white coat swung around at the intrusion. It had to be Martina, but her hair and face had been altered. Injured somehow. The face might have been shocking, if not for the men Josef had seen in the aftermath of exploding artillery shells. Franz was there too. He reached for a hammer when he saw them but didn't hold it with much urgency. Why didn't Bako move? Josef gave him a nudge from behind to push him inside, but the man stood as rigid as a locked door.

Martina lost her look of surprise and slipped her hands casually inside her lab coat pockets. "Well, that was quicker than I anticipated. I thought at least Viktor might cast a few counterspells to check for traps first. I did train you better, you know."

Viktor opened his mouth, looked at his fellow fighters, then shut his mouth again.

"Get me out of here," Bako shouted. His arms and legs were stuck in a position of forward motion with his torso vulnerably exposed.

"What'd you do to him?" Josef pulled on his comrade's arms, but his body stayed stubbornly rooted to the floorboards. While he attempted to yank Bako out by the collar, he spotted Petra strapped to a table. She had some sort of contraption attached to her head, and her arms and legs were covered in an odd rubber sheathing. He pushed forward, trying to squeeze his body past Bako's. "Petra!"

"I'm here." Petra barely turned her head. "But I'm unable to *touch* anything."

Martina moved closer, blocking Josef's view of Petra. "Your friend has been caught in a vertical plane of stationary motion. It only activates when someone other than Franz or myself opens the door. As for Petra, we've merely been having a chat about some missing paperwork. No one has been harmed. So far."

"Release him!" Josef shouted.

Martina smiled. "No, I don't think I will."

Yanis and Viktor stood behind Josef. Yanis tapped on his shoulder and quietly whispered, "May I try?"

Josef took a reluctant step backward, not sure what to do next. As soon as he was out of the way, Yanis threw half the bag of yellow lycopodium powder at the doorway. The spell energy holding Bako motionless sizzled in a bright orange flash. The magic released him, and he collapsed to his knees.

"Fire, glassmaker!"

Viktor released a stream of flame that slipped over Bako's head. The flash hit the wall near Franz and burst into several small embers that rained down on the man's lab coat. Franz quickly patted down his charred sleeve, but the vlkodlak on the table beside Petra was not so lucky. A few of the embers had landed on its fur and began smoldering. The pungent odor of singed flesh and hair clouded the room.

Franz retaliated by hurling a stream of fire of his own, while Martina grabbed a surgical blade and held it over Petra.

"Josef!"

The flames flew out the door, barely missing Josef and Viktor as they leaned back. Yanis might have been hit by the fire, if not for kneeling by Bako a second earlier to yank the hussar out of the doorway.

Josef aimed his pistol, eager to shoot, when Martina crouched behind Petra and slid the blade under her ear, dangerously close to the carotid artery. One slice and Petra would bleed out.

Martina and Franz were backed into a literal corner with nowhere to go, but there was little Josef could do for fear the woman might follow through on her threat to harm Petra. He slowly placed his pistol back into its holster.

"We seem to be at an impasse," Martina said. Her disfigured face morphed back into the woman he knew from the laboratory as she straightened. "Now, here is what we're going to do. You're going to toss down your weapons, close the door, and all of you are going to walk down to the bottom of the lane and forget you ever came here."

"And if we don't?" Bako asked, seething with an unbridled desire to lunge at the woman.

Martina tilted her head to the side to see Petra's face. "If you don't, she'll have a lovely red choker to wear in death."

"You'll die first," Josef warned.

"Care to test your hypothesis, wolf man?"

Viktor and Yanis held Josef back while Franz smirked, still patting down stray embers on his burned lab coat. "They won't hurt her," Viktor said. "She's too valuable to them, as long as we don't force them."

The men pulled Josef away from the door. A few neighbors stuck their heads out their windows to see what the commotion was about but ducked back in and secured their shutters when they saw strangers with weapons lurking outside.

The men retreated to the other side of the lane. "There has to be something we can do." Josef paced to burn off the energy building in his body.

"We can devise a spell to flush them out," Yanis suggested, "but it will take time to prepare one that won't be so easily swatted away by a witch as proficient as Martina."

Josef swung his head in disbelief. How had his life brought him to a dark lane to battle witches in the middle of the night with a witch-finder, a sorcerer, and a fire thrower at his side? For the moment, he felt defeated and didn't argue when the others convinced him to step out of sight of the house so they might regroup.

They made it only a few steps down the lane before they heard the first scream.

CHAPTER
THIRTY-NINE

His head pounded and his tongue stuck to the roof of his mouth, but it was the smell of burned fur that had aroused the starshina from his unconscious state. His last recollection was of being hit with something. A dart. And a bright light that had stunned him to his brain's core. He thought he'd died, only to wake and wish he had, once the burning sensation in his shoulder registered.

The starshina opened one eye. He squinted and tried to open the other, but it would not respond. And then it, too, stung with the fire of injury. Angry, he lifted his head. The blurry outline of thick fur came into view. He tried to lift his arm, but he'd been restrained. *Not again!* A snarl rose in his throat, erupting in a howl that made the window glass rattle. A woman screamed, and the blood rushed in his veins to revive him. He snapped the leather restraints and freed his limbs. He got to his feet to confront whoever had thought they could tame the vlkodlak and smiled a wolfish grin to see the woman from the graveyard who had shot him with the dart. The pungent, unmistakable smell of sulfur and ammonia rose from her flesh.

The woman backed herself into a corner, wielding a surgical knife. "Franz, you fool! You made the curare solution too weak. He's awake already. Stop him!"

The man, slight of build and insignificant in the starshina's periphery, made a half-hearted attempt to jab him with a tiny blade that wouldn't even peel a potato properly. The starshina bared his fangs to the gums, wrinkling his nose, and swiped a claw across the man's chest. The razor-sharp nails cut through the coat, tie, and shirt and into flesh until they hit the breastbone. The starshina cracked the skinny ribs and tore open the heart. The man wilted to the floor, a delightful look of surprise in his eyes.

Oh, but the woman was still very much alive and screeching at the top of her lungs for someone to save her. *Why did they always do that?* She fumbled at the restraints of another body strapped to a table. She seemed almost desperate to get the person free.

That's when the scent in the room changed. The starshina's nose filled with an echo of desire. Of designs and schemes. A bright future filled with gold and silver coins raining down. A prize.

The starshina huffed. "What have you done to her?" The roar of his words threw spittle in the woman's hair.

"I . . ." The woman backed up, flattening her body against the wall as though she might disappear like wallpaper. "Nothing. I haven't done anything to her. She's fine."

The starshina delicately plucked at the wires attached to Petra's temples with his claw, but the wooden contraption was more complicated. Very unnatural. "Take it off," he ordered and had to shout his command again when the infernal woman didn't move quick enough.

Once Petra was released from the box, he ordered her hands be freed from their restraints. This time the woman didn't hesitate, fumbling with the buckles on the leather straps as quickly as she could. When she'd finished, she attempted to free Petra's feet, too, but he snarled at her, preferring to leave the young woman partially confined for the moment.

Petra sat up slowly, keeping her eyes on him. "It's all right, Dimitri. I know what you want."

Dimitri? Had that been his name? It seemed like an age since anyone had called him that.

Petra peeled the rubber gloves off her hands and reached for her leg restraints. His breath came in huffs as her leather straps withered away to brittle straw. She slid her feet to the floor, keeping the table between them.

The shrieking woman cowered behind his Petra, prodding her. "Do something."

The starshina wished to change back to his human form to appeal to Petra, but what had happened to his clothes? How had he awoken in this tiny room? Why could he not see out of one eye? Who was this woman who would not shut up? Nothing made sense but that he just wanted some peace! He banged his arms against the table, then sent the head end crashing into the wall. Both women hunkered down in the corner, and the brief silence that followed was bliss. But this was not how he intended to steal his prize away. Why had his plans gone so topsy-turvy? It wasn't too late, though. They could start again. They just had to be free of this room and this screeching woman.

"Come, my dear, we must be on our way," he said to Petra, extending his enormous paw. "And no more of your tricks."

Petra didn't move. He swore to himself he wouldn't hurt the young woman, but if she didn't stand up this second, he'd pick her up by her hair and drag her to the street until she submitted. He nearly lunged to prove to himself he meant it when the door burst open. The soldier pup stood outside, glaring like a disgruntled customer wanting his money back. He was backed up by at least one other familiar face from the attic and another who bore the memorable scent of the traveler's cigar smoke.

"How convenient of you to come together and save me the trouble of hunting you down one by one," the starshina said through his bared fangs.

A blade was raised, a pistol pointed, and at least one ball of fire crackled in a bearded man's hands.

"Oh, thank heavens," the disfigured woman shouted. "Shoot him. Kill him."

Enough of this woman's shouting! The starshina thrust his arm across the table and grabbed the woman by the neck. He yanked her forward, squeezed her annoying voice box until it squished like a ripe plum in his grip, then threw her body across the room, where she hit the opposite wall, knocking a crossbow to the floor and shattering several small bottles of fluid.

Behind him, Petra had quickly fashioned an axe out of a doctor's stethoscope. So beguiling what she could do with her dainty hands. But such a shame she wouldn't do as she was told. He roared until the window rattled and the medical instruments clattered off their tray from the vibration.

"Petra, get out of the way," the pup called to her.

The young woman moved to her right, still wielding the axe as though she might actually use it on him. And yet he knew the real threat was outside, where the men pointed their weapons. But why hadn't they shot already? What were they waiting for? Was he that intimidating that they doubted even the pistol's effectiveness against him?

He bared his teeth and charged at the door.

CHAPTER FORTY

The vlkodlak hit the plane of the door and growled, but whatever spell had been in place there before had no effect on him. The beast crept outside on all fours, eyes shining, his teeth exposed.

"What happened?" Josef yelled to his comrades as they scrambled for cover. They'd meant to lure him onto the threshold, get him frozen in place like Bako had been, and then gut him with a knife. *Damn these witches and their misbegotten spells.*

"Martina must be dead," Yanis called. "Her spell with it."

Josef swore the creature grinned just before he lunged. Quick as lightning, Viktor threw a ball of fire from behind a water trough, but the vlkodlak batted it away, his fur barely scorched. The fire hit the cobblestones and flamed out. Josef took a quick shot with his pistol while Yanis swung the long curved sword at the beast. If either of them had struck their target, Dimitri showed no sign of it as he lunged at the sorcerer.

Bako rushed out of the shadows, swinging a spiked ball on a chain. He caught the beast in the leg, making the vlkodlak stumble midcharge. But only for a second. Dimitri reared up on his hind legs and swiped a claw at the hussar, catching the morning star by its chain and flinging it onto the rooftop. The beast huffed, looking from man to man, as though deciding which one to kill first. He turned his head to Yanis and growled.

"Dimitri, stop!" Petra stood in the lane. She tossed the axe down on the pavement. "It's me you came for. Leave them be."

"Petra, no." Josef scrambled to his feet. "He can't be reasoned with. Go! Get inside!"

The beast turned from the sorcerer, cocking an ear toward Petra. He took a step toward her, sniffing the air in loud grunts. Josef's hand shook as he raised his weapon. He pointed it at the beast's head.

"Do it!" Bako cried. "Now."

Josef pulled the trigger, but instead of a bullet lodging itself in Dimitri's brain, the gun jammed.

The vlkodlak spun around and laughed. "Pup."

Yanis thrust his scimitar at Dimitri, while Viktor attempted to open his lantern and blind the beast. The vlkodlak knocked both men away as if they were sheaves of wheat, sending the lantern skidding sideways on the cobblestones. Bako rushed in with his knife drawn. The beast stopped him, holding him at arm's length by the neck. He lifted the hussar into the air, gripping the man by the throat, until his tall boots no longer touched the earth and his knife skittered on the pavement.

Petra picked up Bako's knife and dug it into Dimitri's thigh. She jabbed and jabbed until the vlkodlak released his grip. He roared in Petra's face and swiped at her with the back of his paw as blood oozed out of his thigh. She hit the wall and crumpled to the ground. Then the beast turned on Josef, whose heart beat steady with the truth of what he must do.

He had to kill Dimitri. But to do that, he had to let his human side recede behind the wolf's eyes. He'd never gone all the way there. He'd always clung to the stability of his lucid mind. His human heart. But now he must call up the vlkodlak to save his friends.

Josef dived for Viktor's lantern. He turned the cylinder until pure moonlight radiated in his face. He lowered his shoulders and begged the moon's light to transform him into the monster he'd always feared becoming.

The wolf's eyes colored over his own, and he let go. A snarl started deep in his throat. His muscles roiled beneath his skin, splitting his clothes, his boots, the belt strapped around his waist. Claws stretched out, teeth elongated, fur covered his body. Senses came alive—sight, sounds, smells amplified. He saw the glint of silver in his enemy's eyes.

The taste for blood flooded his mouth, and he leaped into the fight eager to rip and kill.

CHAPTER
FORTY-ONE

Petra gasped for air. The blow had knocked the wind out of her. She was forced to lie on her side against the wall until her diaphragm stopped spasming. Across the lane, barely lit by the stars and waning moon, two savage beasts stood on their hind legs, locked in struggle. Teeth flashed and claws swiped. Their growls were thunderous enough to make the roof tiles rattle above her. She pushed herself onto her elbow and forced herself to take a slow breath. It had to be Josef. He'd given in. He'd become the vlkodlak to stop Dimitri.

Petra got to her feet. Bako was on all fours coughing and wincing. Yanis and Viktor were halfway down the lane, bloodied from head to elbow. They limped forward until they understood the battle that was underway. They pressed their backs to the wall, unwilling to get caught in the middle, yet seemingly mesmerized by the ferocity on display.

The vlkodlaci continued their macabre dance, going round and round, while fangs and claws attempted to rip and shred the other. Dimitri was already hurt from Martina's scalpel and Petra's knife. One eye was swollen and bloody, and his fur was singed black on his chest. Josef, in comparison, was lean and agile. His fur was dark and sleek and his teeth terrifyingly long when he pulled his lips back. She thought he had the advantage, but then Dimitri bit into his shoulder, making him roar in pain. Josef's eyes flashed silver. He pounced at Dimitri with full force, knocking them both to the ground. They rolled until they smashed into the wall where Petra had only just managed to flee in time.

Petra careened into Bako. Together they clambered to their feet, pulling each other out of the way as the two vlkodlaci wrestled on the ground, each slashing at the other and drawing blood.

"We need weapons," Bako yelled. "Fire. Guns. Something."

"The crossbow is inside." Petra eyed the path to the doorway, but she'd never make it. Josef had Dimitri pinned to the pavement only a meter away. They could break free at any moment and crush her from the weight of their flailing bodies.

Viktor crept closer, the glow of fire growing in his hands. Josef raised his head and snarled at the glassmaker. Petra thought it was a warning to stay back, but she wasn't sure the others would see the threat that way. Especially Yanis. There'd be no more protection for Josef. He'd crossed the line. Become the vlkodlak. He was beyond the help of elixirs and witches' spells. He'd be in the Order's sights now.

Dimitri took advantage of the distraction. He pushed Josef off with the force of his hind legs, sending him sailing over the lane. Josef crashed on top of the lantern, shattering it and letting the moonlight escape. The beam glinted off Josef's discarded pistol and knife briefly before dissipating into the night. Momentarily disentangled, the vlkodlak leaped onto the roof of the one-story house. There, he flexed and drooled, taunting Josef to chase him.

Josef bared his teeth and eagerly accepted the challenge. In a display of incredible strength, he jumped from his spot on the cobblestones to the roof in a single vault.

Petra backed up to see the pair face off as clay tiles smashed to the ground and someone in a nearby house screamed in terror. She had to do something before Josef got himself killed. She searched the ground and spotted the knife again. It could work, she thought.

Scrambling across the narrow lane, she picked up the knife and gripped it firmly. Channeling an image of the black walking stick with the crystal fixed on top, she transformed the knife into Ava König's wand. She tapped it on the ground as she'd seen Ava do, and a white light shot out of it in a vertical beam. The stick vibrated in her hand, so she used both palms to grip the wand tightly, aiming it at the vlkodlaci.

Josef, perhaps recognizing some shadow of his human self and his memories, shielded his face and turned away, scaling the taller roof of the adjoining house. Petra envisioned her body flowing with electrical current, then directed the energy through the center of the wand. A stream of white-hot light shot out of the crystal, catching Dimitri in the chest. His body jerked and spasmed as his fur smoldered from the electric heat. Petra called back the energy, and it retreated into the crystal as the vlkodlak swayed and toppled.

A splatter of coughed-up blood hit the pavement. The beast sputtered a cry of disbelief before rolling off the roof and landing at her feet in a pile of singed fur. The breath went out of the beast, and Dimitri's body shrank into the broken form of a man.

"You got him."

Bako's strangled voice broke the trance of staring at the corpse. She looked up to see Viktor and Yanis limping over, gazing from the wand to the rooftop to the dead body.

"Did anyone see where Josef went?" she asked, keeping her hand poised on the walking stick.

"Fair to say he's gone," Yanis answered. And she knew by the tone in his voice he hadn't only meant Josef's rooftop escape.

Petra waited and listened a few minutes longer, watching the skyline, but the longer she searched the dark for Josef, the tighter her heart constricted, knowing what he'd sacrificed. For them.

She picked up Josef's things and cradled them in her arms while Yanis and the others carried the body inside the tiny house. The sorcerer made a series of marks on the door with chalk, magic sigils he claimed would keep the curious away until the Order could send someone over to assess the mess and reconfigure any witnesses' memories into nothing more than bad dreams they'd had in the night. He assured everyone there was a team of people who routinely cleaned up after supernatural mayhem, such as what they'd left behind in the room. "Hugo will sort it out," he said. "But first we have to let him know."

The moon peeked out from behind a cloud as the group made the walk back to the tower on the hill in Lesser Town. Hugo had left the lights on in the courtyard to let them know to come up when they returned. The envoy greeted them at the door and offered coffee while he worked on putting something together to eat. He hadn't looked up to notice Josef wasn't with them.

"I take it since you're all still in one piece, our vlkodlak is dead?" he finally asked.

Yanis laid his satchel and scimitar on the table. "He and the two witches from the Libuše Society are dead. We were only responsible for killing the beast," he said with a nod toward Petra. "The rest was Dimitri's doing. Your team will require a large handcart and several buckets to clean up the mess when they arrive."

"No worries," Hugo said, setting out a plate of pastries. "I have a pair of jinn I rely on for such matters."

"There's one more thing," Yanis said. "Josef didn't come back with us."

"Dead?"

"Changed."

"Full vlkodlak?" Hugo looked over his shoulder to check the position of one of the spinning devices and made a face. "That's the problem with the curse. There are no true half measures. Not for long."

Petra leaned the walking stick against the table. "He saved our lives tonight."

Hugo studied the wand with the crystal with mild curiosity and said nothing to counter Petra's remark. She was on the verge of tears when a figure on the sofa roused from sleep, startling her.

"Have they returned?" A woman emerged from the blankets with a flowered shawl wrapped around her shoulders. She smoothed a few loose gray hairs back in place as her eyes adjusted to waking up.

"Hana?" Petra had to look twice to make sure she wasn't hallucinating from whatever drugs Martina had injected her with.

"You're back." The woman stood. "That took longer than I expected, but then I don't know the city as well as the rest of you."

"She and Hugo told us where to look for you," Yanis said to Petra.

"But where is Josef?" Hana asked.

They explained what had happened after the men found Petra, yet Hana did not appear surprised to hear about Josef, saying she knew him well enough to understand the path he'd taken and why. "I wouldn't fret about him," she said, patting Petra's hand. "He's a survivor."

Petra didn't know what to make of the old woman's remark. She could already see the change in demeanor in Yanis and Hugo. Josef was the enemy now. Orders would be issued in the morning to kill him on sight. Photos of him would go out to the Order's bounty hunters across the region, like the couple they'd fought in the courtyard. Kill first and worry about the fallout later.

Exhausted and in shock, yet still too awake with adrenaline to do anything but sit at the table and sip coffee while staring into the distance, Petra tried to think where Josef might go—Home? The storeroom? A park?—until Hana interrupted her train of thought.

"What do you think Martina hoped to achieve by kidnapping you and Dimitri?"

Petra pulled out her father's grimoire and showed Hana the drawing of the sun and moon holding hands. "Martina was trying to replicate the spell that went with this drawing. She believed it was the source of my magic." Petra appreciated again the attention to detail in the drawing made by a man whose eye saw beyond the obvious. "I think a large part of her wanted to outshine both my father's and Ava König's work. Ava had gone public with her research and became famous for it, which is probably why she was tapped to be the emperor's witch. But my father never did share his findings. I suspect she wanted to re-create the spell and claim it as her own." She closed the book. "Anyway, whatever spell had been entered in the book seems to have been lost to time. It breaks my heart, because my father may only ever be remembered professionally for stealing gold from the Libuše Society, but Franz and

Martina knew the truth. He discovered a source of magic that allows me to change the structure of objects with a finger's touch. He did that. He did what the old alchemists had set out to do."

Hana took in a steady breath. "I won't ask if there's any breach of trust in this room," she said. "I already know your hearts are sewn together as one tapestry."

Petra caught Yanis's eye, wondering if the old woman had shown signs of getting senile before, but he merely gave her a raised brow and a small shake of his head as though he didn't know what she meant either.

Hana undid the top two buttons on her collar to reveal a silver-link chain worn around her neck. She pulled it free from her blouse to reveal a small tool like the kind used to rip out stitches on a piece of cloth. The old woman freed the tool from the chain, lifted the hem of her skirt, then began ripping out the threads of a pocket that had been sewn into the cotton petticoat beneath. "You mustn't be so shocked to see an old woman's ankles," she said to Viktor and laughed softly to herself as she finished cutting the stitches near the hem.

The men politely averted their eyes, pretending to study the mechanical whirligigs spinning at the perimeter of the room, but Petra watched in fascination to see what Hana was up to. The hedge witch, whom she'd known from their country village before greed and murder forced Petra to run away, pulled a thin packet wrapped in sheep's skin free from its hiding place. Hana unwrapped the protective outer layer to reveal a small stack of worn pages whose torn edges matched the stubble inside Honza's book of spells. She gently laid them on the table in front of Petra.

"The missing spell." Petra spread the pages apart in disbelief, immediately recognizing her father's handwriting and the odd quirk he had of adding a fanciful flair to his *F*s and *W*s. "But this is impossible. How did you get these?"

The others turned from their intense interest in celestial gadgets, eager to know as well.

Hana dropped her skirt back over her petticoat. "Before you and your father moved to the village, I was the only witch living there.

People knew me for my stomach potions and herb plasters. It didn't take long for Honza and I to discover each other. It's inevitable in such a small town for like to be drawn to like."

"My father used to send me to your house on Walpurgisnacht," Petra said, remembering.

Hana nodded thoughtfully. "He'd arrived from the city with an unusual daughter and a mortal wife. But anyone who met your father knew instantly he was not your ordinary country witch who dabbled in beer making or wart creams. He had a knowledge of magic that went deeper than reciting incantations."

Bako carefully picked up the first page. "It's titled *The Transmutation of Metals*."

"Transmutation was always the main goal of the old alchemists," Viktor said.

"It's been the goal of men everywhere since the world began." Yanis gave the page a brief glance before asking Hana, "But how did you get this? Why was the spell torn from the book?"

"I was asked to hide it," Hana said. "I never knew from whom exactly until tonight, but Honza made me promise to keep it safe. In case anything should happen to him."

"But something did happen to him," Petra said. "Martina murdered him. She admitted she poisoned him to get the book and this spell."

Hana took Petra's hands in hers, letting the energy of their shared heritage pass between them. "I think he must have suspected what she was capable of. But this spell he entrusted me with, Petra . . . this spell is yours, and yours alone. That's partly why Honza asked me to take you in on each Walpurgisnacht. To watch over you and teach you about your birthright as a witch. So you'd have someone to go to just in case. He wanted me to hold on to the spell until you were old enough to understand all that it entails for yourself." The old woman leaned back in her chair. "But then that weasel Pavel Radek showed up."

"And I ran away."

Hana nodded. "I've kept it safe for over ten years now. Sometimes in my petticoat, sometimes in the lining of my coat, sometimes in the bottom of a small chest at the foot of the bed, if I'm lucky enough to be at home for a long stretch. I've kept on the move in large part because of what's contained in those pages. I fretted for a long while that you really had died, but then I cast the bones one more time for Josef," she said, with a sideways glance at Hugo. "It was he who found you. He'll tell you it was his nose that let him find you, but I believe in stronger stuff than that. What's meant to be is meant to be." The old woman dropped Petra's hands and slid the stack of handwritten notes in front of her. "Read the pages and then we'll talk more."

The paper was creased, and her father's handwriting was faded and smudged in places, but the pages were still legible. Petra began reading, then passed the writing on to the others.

May 17th, 1897, The Transmutation of Metals

To properly explain how it became possible to transmute one metal into another, one must first wholeheartedly embrace the notion of happy accidents in an otherwise controlled environment.

While conducting research on precious metals at the Libuše Society with Fräu Ava König (née Sigwart), we discovered a way to maintain an electrical charge in freestanding copper, gold, and silver by infusing the particles with a common binding spell that adhered the energy to them. While at university, we'd both been impressed with the human invention of harnessing electricity via the use of copper wires and wished to incorporate the same sort of design in our magical applications. Earlier research had already revealed the electrical current present—and indeed necessary—in the human body to function properly, but it had not been known prior to our research that the voltage in witches is higher than it is in mortals. Supremely higher in the witch, in fact, when in the midst of calling up magic for the purpose of casting a spell.

* As an aside, Fräu König had already taken the initiative years earlier while at university to have a charged crystal affixed to the top of her walking stick, which doubled as a wand for channeling concentrated spell energy. It was this which we subsequently used to amplify the voltage of our spells.

Our first success came in the manipulation of matter. While charged, the particles of gold and silver proved eager to morph into whatever shape we demanded. A golden cup or a silver chalice could be made to change into a dish or bell or candlestick, but the transformation remained little more than a parlor trick, as it was merely the gold or silver particles rearranging themselves into various crude forms. We soon grew bored with the result, but from there our individual interests, talents, and curiosities led us to new avenues of research. I focused on the gold, believing we were very close to discovering how to break the bonds of ordinary elements to rearrange them into those of the long-desired precious metal. Meanwhile, Fräulein Sigwart's imagination was drawn in by the natural alliance between silver and the moon and the effect of both on the human body and mind.

Since my research focus was taking me down the path of the alchemists, I adopted some of the old-fashioned practices they'd sworn by as a way to honor their prior contributions. I began ingesting gold in the form of the elixir of life, which consisted mainly of brandy, a few sprigs of rosemary and fennel, and a quarter teaspoon of gold dust stirred in, which I'd charged with the electrical current via our bonding spell. My new mortal wife, wishing to be supportive of our unusual union, also partook of the elixir. Knowing it would cause no harm, yet curious to know what, if any, differences in reactions might occur between witch and mortal blood, we consistently drank the solution for months. While I felt little changed, my wife insisted the formula delivered on its promise. She consistently displayed a delightful spritely attitude toward life, though it was soon revealed she was with child, which may or may not have contributed to her happy disposition at that time.

Petra looked up from her reading. "It says he fed the gold to my mother too. A month later she was with child." She dabbed at the sweat forming on her upper lip. "She took small doses of the elixir continually until I was born, hoping to pass the life-giving effects of the gold on to me, even though my father had doubts. That's how it got in my blood and my hair."

She passed more pages to the others and kept reading.

There was little reason to believe the gold had any real effect on my mortal wife. And yet tests revealed the gold had not left her system. It remained, circulating through her body. The final proof was in my newborn daughter, whose amber eyes sparkled with a hint of gold. Her blood, too, revealed the presence of the gold under the microscope. To my amazement, the electrical charge from the spell remained. It had been transfused from mother to child through the umbilical cord. But nothing prepared me for what consequences that small indiscretion of giving sips of the elixir of life to my pregnant wife brought to bear later.

While the charged gold particles appeared to have little effect on myself or my mortal wife, the passing of the gold dust to my daughter had gone through an altogether different transformation. One seemingly made possible by her conception. By the age of three, Petra showed signs of an advanced form of magic that had the ability to change not only the shape of objects, as the gold had done for us in the lab, but the very molecules that made up those objects, rearranging them at will into anything she wished them to be. Wooden cups turned into tin horses. Leather belts became silk ribbons at her touch. The revelation was both astonishing and terrifying.

During that same period, Fräulein Ava Sigwart had taken a leave of absence to travel to the eastern and northern ends of the continent to research the origins of a transformation curse she'd begun working on. She returned several months later from visiting the tsar's palace . . . changed. Different somehow. Sad almost, as though she'd suffered some loss of confidence. Yet she was determined to continue her research, which dovetailed perfectly with my own study and discovery. But rather than the molecules of inanimate objects changing shape, she was dedicated to altering the human form. A dangerous study, but one that has its place in the history of magic. For this reason, her vlkodlak curse was an obvious choice for her experiments with the charged silver particles, with the idea that any positive results might be adapted for future applications, such as regrowing teeth or transplanting damaged organs. If successful, her research could prove invaluable in times of pestilence or war.

The curse she eventually perfected was blood-borne, not unlike how my daughter's ability had developed in the womb. Now, however, after the successful outcomes of our initial hypotheses, we have each come to the conclusion that both strains of our discoveries could become weaponized in the wrong hands. But while I struggle with the morality of what I've done to my daughter, Ava (now Frau König after her recent marriage to a member of the Empire's ministerial council on magic) holds only one reservation going forward: That we must find a way to reverse the effects in the human body before we share our findings with the world. We must discover a cure.

CHAPTER
FORTY-TWO

Josef stood in the shadow of a bronze saint, huddling beneath a stolen blanket. He stared at the dark water flowing under the bridge, imagining himself immersed beneath the surface—his body carried away downstream, his lungs constricting from the hypothermia. Would the curse die with him, or would his blood be tainted and infect the birds and fish?

He'd had no choice, but it didn't make the pain of the decision any easier to face in the aftermath. He'd crossed over the point of no return. He was a vlkodlak now, which meant he'd be hunted without mercy, and rightfully so. How long until the bloodlust overtook him? How long before his mind was lost to the curse and someone died? Even if he could hold out, there were only a few short weeks left until the next full moon. No amount of elixir could save him from that. No cure to keep him back from the steep decline into madness.

He put his hand on the foot of the drowned saint immortalized in bronze, then climbed onto the railing.

CHAPTER FORTY-THREE

Petra could feel Yanis standing behind her shoulder, reading ahead when they got to the page on Ava König's curse. "My father claims König wouldn't allow the curse to be used by any entity, private or royal, until she sorted out the cure," she said, running her finger along the page. She looked up at the others gathered around the table, still catching up as their eyes scanned the handwritten lines of the previous notes. "It says they found a way to rid the body of the precious metals."

The glassmaker leaned against the windowsill, watching the sky. "So there really is a cure?"

Yanis relayed the next part. "They took inspiration from gold and silver miners who used chemicals to leach the precious metals from the less desirable quartz. Unbelievable."

Major Bako pushed his coffee away and accepted another torn-out page from the grimoire from Yanis. "Don't they use cyanide to do that?" he asked, grimacing at the idea.

"Cyanide?" Petra scanned the notes in front of her until she came to the very word Bako had mentioned. "You're right. That's what it says. Cyanide, laced with a spell, is ingested to leach the metal from the body." The bright rush of hope Petra had felt only a moment earlier, knowing they'd found the cure, had turned to pale doubt. "But isn't cyanide deadly?"

"I don't think death is the cure anyone is looking for," Hugo said and took a bite of a fruit-filled *koláč*.

Hana cleared her throat. "That's where it got thorny for me," the witch said. She explained it was only a few months into the start of the war when she heard the first rumors of men being afflicted with the vlkodlak curse. "At that time the different empires were gathering up younger witches left and right to fight on either side, but others like myself were left to tend to the wounded. Mostly those suffering from spell-borne injuries, regardless of who they fought for. We straddled the front lines, looking for casualties of curses and hexes."

Hana clarified that Josef hadn't been her first vlkodlak case. She'd had one other young man brought to her a month earlier who'd had his arm bitten off. "Naturally, I'd already read the pages from Honza's grimoire, so I was not surprised when I saw the curse for myself."

"Did you attempt to cure him using Honza's spell?" Yanis asked.

"I'm quite knowledgeable about poisons and their properties," Hana said without being boastful. "But I was not prepared to attempt a cure that relied on reaching the upper threshold of a poison tolerance on my own." She rummaged through her medicinal bag and produced a handful of horse chestnuts. "The officers in the tsar's army shot the man when they'd seen what he'd become under the full moon, but I wouldn't let it happen to the next man, if I could prevent it."

Petra's stomach recoiled remembering the torment Dimitri had been in during those first few hours in the attic after he'd been bitten.

"Since I wasn't prepared to dole out cyanide in the hope it might work on a man's tainted blood, I set my mind to work on a different solution." She pushed the hard seeds around with her finger. "Soon after, I was scrubbing the copper pot I use to boil potions in when I'd remembered something my mother taught me about silverware. She'd told me acetone is a good cleaner for getting coffee stains off china cups, but it will dull your silver if you aren't careful. I knew silver dust was the kicker in the curse, so then I thought, well, if I can't draw the silver out with cyanide, maybe I could at least dull it inside the body and slow the curse down. The conkers themselves were poisonous, but I knew I could distill acetone from a handful of them, so I gave it a try."

"From horse chestnuts?" Yanis's mouth fell open as he picked up the handful Hana had set on the table.

"That's the missing ingredient in the elixir?" Petra asked, seeing what they'd missed. "That's how you stopped Josef from turning into the full vlkodlak?"

"The elixir needed time to work to dilute the effect of the silver," Hana admitted. "It caused terrible stomach problems, so I refined it some, adding a little bit of this, a little bit of that for flavor and energy. We were lucky it worked, so long as we could keep the patient restrained until the harshest phase passed. After that, it was best if the young men could transform at the weakest phase of the moon to release the pressure of the need to change."

"But there is a more permanent cure," Petra said, stabbing her finger on the page she'd just read. "The steps are all documented in the grimoire. Ava was adamant it would work when we saw her."

"Which is why your father implored me to keep those pages for you until you were older," Hana said. "He worried something might happen to him before he had a chance to explain. He wrote those entries when you were only four years old."

"Just before we moved to the country."

Hana nodded. "He wanted you to know there was a cure for you, too, if you wanted it. But it will take a more practiced witch than me to concoct a potion using cyanide."

The room grew eerily quiet at the witch's implied warning until the overriding sound was the ticking of the mechanical universes turning on their axes. Petra had never considered her magic something she'd need a cure for, but she understood why her father might have thought he owed her the option of being free of it. When she was younger she hadn't even realized she was that different, except on the rare occasion she caught the astonishment on her parents' faces after she'd transformed something with the touch of her finger. The magic was just a part of who she was. It was only later, when others learned what she could do, that the trouble started. Greed had been her only curse, not magic.

"Where does one even find cyanide?" Viktor asked, breaking the silence.

Hugo grunted and brushed the pastry flakes off his fingers. "That, my friend, is not the difficult part." He picked up one of the remaining koláče and gestured to the fruit filling. "It's the pits, you see. You get acetone from horse chestnuts," he said, pointing to the nuts on the table. "But cherry pits will give you cyanide. Peaches, too, if you're lucky enough to afford them in wartime."

"That's what the notes say." Petra held the page up, but with less enthusiasm than she had before, knowing the danger it presented. "Ground cherry stones are required for the spell. They keep jars of them in the botanical room of the Society. I saw them on the shelf."

Yanis and Hugo huddled together over the page with the instructions for the spell. "The process is intricate but not overly complicated. The difficult part is having a reliable body weight measurement to gauge the amount of cyanide to use so it doesn't become deadly."

Petra stood and put on her coat. "We have to find Josef."

"It's past three in the morning," Yanis said, checking one of the multiple clocks hanging on the walls.

Bako and Viktor each shoved a koláče in their mouth and grabbed their coats. "We're coming with you." The hussar tucked his recovered revolvers in their holsters. "Just in case."

"He won't be far," Hana speculated, dipping into her second sight. "If he's not already lost."

Petra picked up the walking stick and headed out the door. Outside, the humid air seeped under her collar, reminding her of the late nights she'd sneaked out to photograph the city's ghosts.

But where to start? Her strongest instinct said he'd go back to the storeroom, so they headed toward the bridge to return to the Old Town district. She'd lived in the city only a few short years, but she'd come to know the bridge intimately, crossing it nearly daily, morning and night. The statues sat on pedestals along the railings and were spaced at fairly even intervals, which made the sight of two figures, one large and one small, so closely aligned stand out to her. It was only when they got close enough to see a cloud of breath escape the mouth of the one nearest to them that she understood what she was seeing.

"Josef." Petra took off at a run across the bridge with Viktor and Bako close behind.

He stood on the wall. His bare feet were dangerously near the edge facing the water. Petra slowed down as they approached. She did not wish to startle him, as part of her did not know which Josef she might find.

His head turned, alerted to their presence by his superior senses. "Have you come to kill me?" he called, pulling a blanket tighter around his shoulders.

"Josef, come down," Petra said.

"I won't live with the curse any longer, but I've been standing here for twenty minutes and can't quite muster the courage to jump," he said, looking down at the water. "I think if you put a bullet in the back of my head, I'd fall neatly into the river."

"Nobody's going to shoot you." Bako pushed his coat back to reveal his revolvers. "We've come to save you, you dumb bastard." He took the guns out of their holsters and laid them on the ground.

"It's true, Josef." Petra risked a few steps closer. "We found the spell. Hana had the missing pages this whole time; she just didn't know how to do it. We have the cure, if you'll please come down."

Josef took a sharp inhale of breath. His body shook and he began to sway, as though the possibility of relief from his affliction were too heavy to bear after contemplating the end. Viktor, seeing the danger, ran up and hugged Josef's legs, pulling him back just as he might have toppled over in the wrong direction. Bako helped get him to the ground, where Viktor infused the blanket he was wrapped in with a gently simmering fire spell to warm his body. Petra cradled Josef's head in her lap, and when he opened his eyes, reflecting the starlight above, she thought they might be the most beautiful eyes she'd ever seen.

CHAPTER
FORTY-FOUR

Josef had always had a fatalistic view of his circumstances—pleased to have enjoyed the temporary stay the elixir had provided him these several months, but ultimately still a cursed man with a doomed future. And then he'd crossed over the last barrier to become the vlkodlak, letting the curse have him, body and soul.

But now.

At first, the choice for him was an easy one. After Viktor had returned to the tower with the cherry stones and Bako had calculated his weight to the nearest kilogram, Hugo and Yanis began stirring their witch's brew. It smelled like bitterness and regret, but he'd take whatever potion they gave him, cyanide or not, if it meant the chance at a cure and a normal life. And if it brought death? He could abide that for himself too. He'd already stared the possibility down that night. With no more temporary fixes, without a cure, his future was cast: live as a murderer or die at the hands of bounty hunters for the abomination he'd become.

"We'll have you sit on the sofa, I think." Hugo tossed aside the extra blankets and propped up a pillow.

Josef had to hold up the trousers Hugo had loaned him with one hand so they didn't slide down over his hips. He leaned back against the pillow and stretched his legs out on the cushions. Viktor lit several candles in the room, and then he and Bako stood behind the sofa while Petra sat on an ottoman near Josef's head. Hana squeezed in on the cushion beside his feet, resting her hand on his legs like a mother comforting a sick child.

He'd written a letter to his parents while Yanis had ground the cherry pits to dust. The same sort of letter all young men write when they're called to war and suffer that first night of terror when the shelling won't stop and death feels imminent. He handed it to Petra and asked her to deliver it, should anything go wrong.

Yanis carried over a measuring cup filled precisely halfway with the potion. Hugo double-checked the instructions in the torn-out pages and nodded they'd done everything correctly. "Now it is up to fate and fortitude," the envoy said, crossing his arms.

Dawn slipped in through a crack in the curtains as Josef held the cup to his lips. He hesitated only a second before he poured the drink into his mouth and swallowed.

Almost immediately the liquid swelled his tongue. It felt like fingernails scraping the inside of his esophagus as the potion traveled through his body, only to curl up in his stomach and spit flame.

Josef coughed and sputtered. Petra put her hand on his back to soothe him, reminding him to breathe. Hana produced a bucket, should he need to empty his stomach. And he thought he might, until the liquid began to swirl inside him. Heat radiated out from beneath his ribs, finding his heart. The muscle clenched, and he feared he'd made a terrible mistake, but then the heat seeped into his veins, racing from his chest to his feet, to his arm, to his head, and back again. He blinked, feeling sweat bead on his forehead. A catch in his throat made him cough again, only this time a shimmering puff of air escaped his mouth.

"I think it's working," Yanis said, checking the papers again for what to expect.

Josef gave in to an urge to open his mouth wider. A silvery mist rose out of him as he exhaled. His eyes, too, had clouded over, almost as though a form of transpiration were drawing out the curse through his membranes.

"Yes, keep breathing," Hugo said as a thin trail of sparkling mist floated over their heads. "The chemical reaction is drawing out the precious metal, little by little."

Another round of heat burned through his veins, but after a few more minutes, Josef felt his blood cool. The overpowering scents in the attic room receded, the creaking wood beams ceased their cacophony in his ears, and he could no longer pinpoint the tiny yet somehow monstrous vermin he'd spotted crawling along the far wall. He sat up, tasting a metallic residue on his tongue.

Was he cured? That test had yet to face the full moon's pull on his newly cleansed blood.

CHAPTER
FORTY-FIVE

Due to Viktor's ingenuity, the group didn't have to wait for the next full moon to put the cure to the test. The glassmaker, with his hot shop and tubes of glass located deep within the alchemists' tunnels, had created a pumpkin-size vessel, as fat and round as the moon herself. One that would hold enough of the moon's silvery glow to make a vlkodlak mad for blood.

Once the newly blown glass had cooled, Viktor and Petra remained in his workshop to take advantage of the small street-level window to call down his *bella luna*. The others, meanwhile, walked ahead, escorting Josef deep inside the tunnels. Viktor went through his ritual of asking the moon for her grace, and soon the orb filled with a trickle of light. The moonbeam swam inside the clear glass like liquid silver, mesmerizing Petra, until the glassmaker covered the vase with a black cloth and said he was ready.

Petra straightened with her hand on the walking stick and blinked nervously several times, her whole heart banking on the moonlight inside the globe being enough. Viktor cradled his creation in both hands as Bako returned to lead them to the end of the alchemists' tunnels where she'd once sensed a gaping darkness exhaling in the beyond. Two candles flickered ahead. Hugo, Yanis, and Augustus stood before a metal cage. Inside, Josef sat on the edge of a wooden bench with his body leaning forward and his head hung low. She didn't have to wonder at the heavy thoughts weighing him down.

Josef stood when he saw her approach. He put his hands on the bars and smiled weakly. "Any trouble?" he asked Viktor.

"I think she favors you," the glassmaker said. "She offered up a pure silver moonbeam." Viktor set the vase on a wooden stand that once held the globe in the library, making sure to keep the orb covered.

"Are we sure these will hold?" Yanis gave the bars a tug. "Just in case?"

Hugo discounted the sorcerer's concern with a wave. "They used to keep the golem down here centuries ago. The cell is reinforced with a spell that could hold a herd of elephants. The bars will hold."

"But let us hope there is no need to test them," Augustus said, trying to remain positive. The researcher had done everything in his power to restore faith in the Society when he'd learned what Martina and Franz had done, including providing a safe holding cell for Josef while his recovery was tested. He'd even offered Petra the original copy of her father's grimoire, allowing her to reclaim her camera.

"In that case, I suggest we proceed," Yanis said. He gave the cell a final inspection before stepping out of the way.

Josef stared through the bars at Petra. "If anything goes wrong, you know what to do," he said. "Maybe you should all wait outside. Leave me in here alone with the globe."

Petra approached the cell, slipping a hand through the bars to cradle his cheek. "We'll see you on the other side," she said.

"Thank you for this." He quickly kissed her palm before she stepped back.

Petra centered herself before the bars, the walking stick held tightly in her grip as she channeled a low-frequency energy. She prayed she wouldn't have to use the deadly power, but she'd made a promise to Josef, and she would fulfill it, if worse came to worst.

Bako wished his friend luck, then doused the candles when Viktor said he was ready. The room sank into an eerie obscurity. Petra had known darkness, but this stole all sense of time and place. She steadied her feet and waited.

Viktor lifted the cloth off the glowing vase. Silver moonlight displaced the darkness, all but the shadowy dark-blue hues that clung to the corners. Josef stood with his eyes shut, the light gleaming across his face as Viktor drew nearer with the glowing orb. His knuckles turned white as he gripped the bars. He exhaled and opened his eyes to stare down the moonlight.

Petra readied the wand, prepared to send a jolt of electricity into Josef's chest should his eyes reflect the silver light and his body morph in response to the call of the moon. But she needn't have bothered. The light merely washed over Josef until he blinked and laughed nervously, relaxing his grip on the bars. "I don't feel anything." He checked his hands, chest, feet, and under his tongue. "I'm not cursed anymore." Overcome with relief, he covered his eyes with both hands and collapsed to his knees.

Hugo insisted later that day that for the Order to officially sign off on the cure one hundred percent, they would still need to monitor Josef through the passing of the natural full moon, preferably outside the city limits. "Spells and enchantments are all well and good," he said, referring to Viktor's orb filled with moonlight, "but we will let nature have the final say." There were mild protests, but when the envoy conceded they could have a week of leisure time in the city before being dispatched to the front again on their next assignment, their demeanor changed.

In the meantime, Hugo advised Josef to continue his exposure to starlight to make sure the healing process was complete. It was in the stargazing tower above the attic that Petra found him sitting on the velvet settee studying a leaflet. He'd cranked the domed roof all the way open to take advantage of the starlight unencumbered. The room was chilly but full of pinpoints of light.

"There goes the wagon," she said, pointing to Ursa Major.

Josef made room for her to sit beside him. "I asked Yanis once why the organization is called the Order of the Seven Stars. He said it was because of Ursa Major. Because everything beneath the constellation's path fell under their purview. They have people stationed all across the Northern Hemisphere investigating supernatural incidents."

"That's a lot of territory," she said, leaning her head back to gaze at the stars beside him. "I'd like to see some of it."

"So you're going to stay on with the team?" he asked.

"You know this war isn't nearly over. There's still a lot of work to be done. More curses that will be flung into battle. More undead, more beasts, more spells. And if this empire loses the war, then there's a strong chance our people will fight for their independence."

He nodded along. "Imagine having a country of our own with no more faraway kings dictating our everyday lives."

"There's so much still hanging in the balance, and I want to be there for all of it," she said.

"As do I," he said, though his words were tainted with uncharacteristic ennui. What he'd left hanging in the air was the question of whether he'd be allowed to remain with the Order now that he was no longer under the influence of the supernatural.

"Major Bako is a mortal," she said, sitting up again. "You have the same skills but with an even deeper understanding of those who are cursed. The job will still be yours."

His eyes steamed up at the prospect. "You know I came here looking for you that night in the square because I had hoped your magic might cure me."

Petra shifted on the narrow settee to face him. "You know I would have, if it had been possible."

"But that's just it. You did. If not for you, I'd still be limping from one bottle of elixir to the next. You gave me my life back."

"And if not for you insisting that I come on this journey, I'd have been left shrinking under the glare of paní Kurková, passing my days trying to learn to embroider. So maybe we saved each other."

They leaned back again to watch the stars, while the smell of Hugo's coffee wafted up from the floor below. After a few quiet moments, Petra was curious to know what the leaflet was about.

"This?" Josef leaned closer, holding the paper up so they could read it together. "There's a concert at the Municipal House tomorrow night. They're introducing a new clarinetist. I doubt he can compare to Benjamin Laska, but I wondered if you'd like to go, since we have the time off?"

"Is this your attempt to court me?"

He lowered the leaflet and looked at her, slightly taken aback, as though it had only just occurred to him that's what he was doing. "Uh . . . yes, I suppose it is."

"In that case, I'd love to go," she said, leaning her head against his shoulder as a shooting star flickered across the sky.

The next night, as they sat holding hands and listening as the carefree notes of the clarinet filled the music hall with its sonata, inspiring the heart to restless optimism, Petra wondered if there hadn't been another reason the group had needed to return to the city. They'd come seeking a cure for Josef, but after witnessing the cruelty of war and battling the undead, that wasn't the only healing they'd needed. To finish the work that lay ahead, to see the war through to the end, perhaps the heart needed to be reassured that cures could be found, that people's independence was still possible, and that the moon was made of more than mere rock.

ACKNOWLEDGMENTS

The Wolf's Eye is my seventh book with 47North. It's been a privilege to work with the same team of people throughout my publishing experience thus far. While I write the stories, it's because of the brilliant detailed efforts of the editors, proofreaders, typesetters, designers, and narrators that my novels make it into book form for people to read or listen to. As always, enormous thanks go to Marlene Stringer, Adrienne Procaccini, Clarence Haynes, Jon, Kellie, Lauren, Gayle Shalen, Kimberly Glyder, and the rest of the crew at 47North. Thank you for always encouraging me to work toward the best version of the story. And finally, a special shout-out to the beautiful city of Prague for its magical inspiration!

ABOUT THE AUTHOR

Photo © 2018 Bob Carmichael

Luanne G. Smith is the Amazon Charts and *Washington Post* bestselling author of *The Witch's Lens*, *The Raven Spell*, *The Raven Song*, *The Vine Witch*, *The Glamourist*, and *The Conjurer*. She lives in Colorado at the base of the beautiful Rocky Mountains, where she enjoys hiking, gardening, and a glass of wine at the end of the day. For more information, visit www.luannegsmith.com.